He took his hand held one out to her. "Dance with me."

She shouldn't, she really shouldn't, but she made the mistake of looking into Mike's green-flecked eyes. They were so hot, they practically scorched her. Oh boy was she a goner. She put her champagne down, put her hand into his, and followed him onto the dance floor.

He put his hands on her hips and pulled her in close to him. She wrapped her arms around his neck and melted against him while the band played Duke Ellington's *Prelude to a Kiss.*

Mike moved with all the elegance and grace of a natural athlete. The band's alto sax lovingly crooned a hot melody that seemed made just for them. Andi sighed and lost herself in the moment.

It shouldn't feel so good to be held by this man, but it did. He felt warm and solid and safe. Only traces of his aftershave lingered, so her nose caught elusive wisps of wood and spice. His thumbs rubbed up and down on her hips, which made her shiver. He didn't know the song, but hummed along anyway, off-key. She couldn't remember when she last had heard more beautiful music.

The music ended. For a long moment, they remained locked against each other, unaware of the applause that replaced the music. She looked up at him, then away. She didn't want him to see more than she was ready to show.

# Mike's Best Bet

## At The End Zone, Book I

by

Doreen Alsen

**Mike's Best Bet: At The End Zone, Book I**

Copyright © 2009 by Doreen Kelly Alsen

Contact Information:
info@thewildrosepress.com

Cover art by *Angela Anderson*

The Wild Rose Press
PO Box 708
Adams Basin, NY 14410-0706
Visit us at www.thewildrosepress.com

Publishing History
First Champagne Rose Edition, 2010
Print ISBN 1-60154-640-8

Published in the United States of America

## Dedication

To Eberhard, Emilia and Louisa,
who never ever gave up on me! I love you so much!
And to Uncle Mike,
who encouraged a little girl's compulsion to read
everything she could lay her hands on. I miss you!

# CHAPTER ONE

"Ineligible? What do you mean, you're ineligible?"

Coach Mike Kelly sat back in his chair, his feet crossed at the ankles and propped up on his desk. When the two boys in front of his desk wouldn't look at him, he dropped his feet to the floor, sat up in the chair, and cocked a brow at them. His stomach dropped to the floor along with his feet. If they were really on the ineligible list, he was screwed. "Well? Care to enlighten me?"

The two football players standing in front of him exchanged looks of furtive misery. Tim Baldwin swallowed hard, raised his chin, and looked at some point over Mike's head. "We, uh, we... aw, man! You're gonna hate this, Coach." Tim was one of Mike's star players, a wide receiver with fast feet and sure hands. "It's totally *whack*."

"Why don't you tell me, and let me decide what's *whack* and what's not?" Mike kept his voice cool, making himself the poster child for patience.

"It's the new chorus teacher. I mean she acts real strict and all, if you know what I mean, but we thought she'd cut us some slack, 'cause we've never been in chorus before." Jeff Myers was Mike's other star player, an extremely smart and accurate quarterback.

"Chorus?" Mike didn't like the sound of this. "Maybe you could be a little clearer."

Jeff and Tim exchanged worried glances. After a few seconds of strained silence, Jeff bit the bullet. "We're ineligible to play in Friday's game because we

1

flunked chorus."

Mike skewered the two with an intense glare. Jeff looked down at the floor, and Tim focused on the diplomas hung on the wall behind Mike. The bell for the late busses rang, and the boys flinched.

Mike laughed. "This is a joke, right? Who put you up to it?" Man, the person who came up with this gag was due for some serious payback.

Of course, it was a joke. It had to be.

Jeff and Tim looked at each other then back at Mike. "It's not a joke, Coach," Jeff said. "The new chorus teacher flunked us. We can't play on Friday."

"Naw, c'mon. Give it up. I bet Mason put you up to this, right?"

"Sorry, Coach. Mr. Mason didn't put us up to this. It's not a joke." Tim scuffed his feet against the floor.

"Believe me, we wish it was." Jeff looked down at the floor, obviously ashamed, and then again up at Mike.

Mike got that queasy feeling in his stomach again. "Well, how can you flunk chorus? You open your mouth, you make some noise, you pass the course. No problem." His eyes narrowed as he looked at the pair. "How did you end up in *chorus* anyway? I've never known you guys to be big music fans."

"We needed a fine arts credit to graduate. By the time we got around to registering, art class was filled." Tim shifted his weight from one foot to the other. "We don't play any instruments, so we got stuck in chorus."

Mike picked up a pencil and started drumming on his desk blotter. "Well, you two not playing this weekend isn't an option." Mike's desperate brain raced to find some course of action. Those two boys *had* to play. "I'll go up and talk to the teacher about cutting you guys some slack. What's her name again?"

2

"Ms. Nelson."

Mike pushed up from his desk and got to his feet. "Ms. Nelson, huh? She must be new if she doesn't realize the importance of this game on Friday." He slid into his patented, works-every-time, confident grin. "Not to worry, guys." Mike was going to worry enough for the three of them. "You go on down to the locker room while I go talk to Ms. Nelson."

He motioned to the boys to leave, then followed them out the door, whistling a jaunty little tune as he left. It never hurt to look confident, especially when your life was going to hell in a hand basket.

****

Andi Nelson was well on her way to a headache. It started as a dull throb right after her second period Music Theory class, and it continued to threaten her during her confrontation with Jeff Myers and Tim Baldwin, the two jocks in her seventh period chorus.

God knew how hard she had tried to work with them, but the situation had become intolerable. The two boys were rude and disruptive. They were making her rehearsal time a living hell. Flunking the pair had been her last resort.

She looked down at the music she was sorting into piles on the auditorium's piano. She hated sorting and filing music. It wasn't doing wonders for either her headache or her disposition.

Jeff and Tim had been indignant, but she had expected that. If they truly thought that because they were the star players of the football team she would change her mind about flunking them, they could think again.

Ha! Fat chance.

She would have sighed, but it hurt too much. Instead, she stuffed some music scores into a file folder for her student accompanist.

The door to the auditorium flew open with a bang. Andi winced and then squinted at the perpetrator of the noise. A very large man, wearing an Addington Minutemen warm-up suit, walked down the center aisle. A whistle hung around his neck, bumping against his chest with each determined step. When he got within hailing distance, he extended a hand and flashed the most stunning smile she had ever seen.

"Hi. I'm Mike Kelly, the head football coach here at Addington High. You must be Ms. Nelson. You'll have to forgive me for not dropping in sooner to welcome you."

Still blinded by his amazing smile, Andi goggled at him, unable for a moment to come up with a reply. Coach Mike Kelly grabbed her hand and pumped away with an enthusiastic handshake. That damn grin never wavered in its brilliance. He had outrageous dimples bracketing his mouth. His eyes were green, but shot through with amber and gray flecks. His hair was dark blond and cut short. He was tall, 6' 4" if she had to guess. His chest was wide and muscular, his hips slim.

She invoked whatever deity was listening to make Coach Mike turn around because, headache notwithstanding, she wanted in the worst way to check out his butt.

Realizing he had stopped talking, she looked at his expression, which was expectant. "I'm sorry. I didn't catch what you said."

The tiniest bit of annoyance crept into his gaze, and his smile stiffened. She guessed he wasn't used to people zoning out on him.

"I'd like to talk to you about this situation." His voice held a hint of asperity.

"Situation?"

Mike sighed. "It's been brought to my attention that my two best players can't play on Friday because you flunked them." He snorted. "Now surely you can see this is wrong. They're just not used to being in a singing group. They didn't understand what you expected of them. They promise that they'll try harder if you'll give them a second chance and not flunk them." Mike beamed. "You do me this favor, and you have my personal guarantee they'll be model chorus members."

Andi's head nearly exploded. He was here to lobby for Jeff Myers and Tim Baldwin? Too bad. There was no way she was letting those kids off the hook, especially for a football game. "No."

The smile froze on Mike's face. "What did you say?"

"No."

Mike shook his head as if he needed to clear his ears. His smile faded. "Excuse me, I must have heard you wrong. Did you say *no*?"

It was Andi's turn to smile. "Not bad, Coach. It only took you twice to understand *no*." She straightened the sheet music she held. "Give the man a cigar."

"But..." Mike's eyes went hard and flinty. "You have to let these kids maintain their eligibility. I need them to play on Friday."

"I need order in my chorus. They have been rude and disruptive, and I'm not putting up with it anymore. I don't care what you need."

"Then think about the good of the team, the good of the school. We need to win this game."

"Why? What's at stake? A cure for cancer? World peace?" Andi dropped the stack of music onto the piano then leaned against the stage and crossed her arms under her breasts.

"A win this weekend is important for our school's pride. Surely you have some pride and loyalty to this institution."

"I have plenty of pride and loyalty to this

institution. I've got no use for football." If she looked real close, she thought she could see smoke coming out of his ears.

"Look, can't you cut these guys some slack? They're good guys, and I..."

"No, *you* look." Andi took a step forward and stabbed an index finger at his chest. "These *good guys* have done nothing but disrupt my chorus since day one. They make disgusting noises, they make inappropriate comments, and they mock the kids who want to be here. You know what? I'm not going to put up with it."

"Then send them to detention. That's what it's for."

"I did. Sending them to detention didn't make one bit of difference in their behavior. They have to learn there are serious consequences for their actions. They have to lose something they really want." She shrugged. "Maybe sitting out a few football games is the only thing that will make a point with them."

"But you're not just punishing them. You're punishing the whole team."

"I'm not punishing the team, Mr. Kelly. Your players are. I've got a team to think of too." She gestured to the empty seats in the auditorium. "The chorus is getting ready for a big choral competition. It's important to us, and it's important to the school. Just as important as your football game."

She watched him study her. His eyes were hostile as well as assessing. "Looks like we're at an impasse then."

"Guess so."

****

Mike gave a curt nod, pinning her with his most hostile glare. Without a doubt, Ms. Andi Nelson was one of those uptight cultural snobs, the kind of woman who never failed to make him feel clumsy

6

and stupid. Blond, blue-eyed, and decked out with nary a wrinkle on her fashion model outfit, she looked like she needed to eat a sandwich. Or ten! She'd all but called him stupid with that crack about needing two tries to understand no. Well, he was not going to give her the pleasure of seeing him grovel and beg. He'd go talk to Dave Mason, the school's vice-principal, and see what he could finagle.

He turned to leave.

"On the other hand, since you're obviously the sporting type, maybe we could make a little wager."

He stopped in his tracks. What the hell was this about? He turned to assess her. "A wager? A bet, you mean. Why would you make a bet?"

The dragon lady shrugged and smiled the kind of smile he'd expect an angel might. He didn't trust it. She pursed her lips, then took a deep breath. "There might be a way to solve our dilemma, even Steven."

Okay. Against his better judgment, he'd bite. "What would we bet? What would be the terms?"

"How about if you win, I give the boys their fine arts credit without having to come to class, *and* they'll stay eligible."

Mike whistled long and low. "What happens if you win?"

She smiled. "I win, the boys have to come to chorus and be model choristers. And you have to join my church choir."

"Church choir? What the hell is this about?"

"Put something of yourself on the line, because if you win, it will really and truly hurt me to give those boys a get out of jail free card."

"How long would I have to stay in the choir?"

"Through Christmas sounds fair."

Mike tried to read her face, but she wasn't giving anything away. This was, without a doubt, one of the weirdest things he'd ever considered doing. "What will we bet on?"

"Oh, I don't know. What do people usually bet on?"

Oh, baby. "Horse races, card games. Sporting events."

"Like football games?"

He gave her his most innocent look. "Like football games."

She tapped an index finger against the top of the piano while she digested that information. "That seems appropriate enough." She smiled. "Is there a game tonight we could bet on?"

"Are you sure you want to bet on a football game? I mean, do you know enough to make a good bet?"

"What's to know? Guys in lots of equipment try to knock each other down." She blinked. "So, is there a game tonight?"

"It's Monday." He had to stop himself from rubbing his hands together in evil glee at her blank look.

"What does that have to do with our bet?"

"There's always a game on Monday night. You know, Monday Night Football?"

"So there is a game tonight. Who's playing?"

"The Toledo T-Rexes against the New Rochester Rangers. We could bet on that." The New Rochester team was one of the worst teams in the NFL. It would take a miracle for them to win against the T-Rexes. If he could get her to take them, it would be a sure thing his boys would get their free ride.

"And this would be a good game to bet on?" Andi's smile was self-deprecating. "I really don't follow football."

"It would be the perfect game to bet on."

She bit her lower lip while she thought about it. "Well, then. Let's do it. Who do you think will win?"

"You should choose first."

Again, she considered that. "What color uniforms do they wear?"

Yesssss! The girl question. "The T-Rexes wear orange and black. New Rochester wears green."

"Dark green or light green?"

Like taking candy from a baby. He should feel really bad about this, but there was too much at stake. "I don't know. Kind of dark green."

"Dark green. Is it forest green or more of a hunter green?"

"What's the difference?"

"I like hunter green better than forest green."

"It's hunter green."

Andi took a moment to think about her choices. "I'll take New Rochester, if it's okay with you. Hunter green is one of my favorite colors."

"That's fine, great. I'll take Toledo, if you're sure."

She held out her hand. "We've got a deal?"

He grinned and took her hand. "We've got a deal."

****

Hours later, Mike was whistling the *Theme from Rocky* while on his way to his car. Though it was mid-October, the night was mild. He scooped his keys from his pocket, tossed them high in the air, and after executing a jaunty step, caught them behind his back with the same hand before unlocking his car. Life was good. Practice went well, even though Jeff and Tim weren't able to participate. He smiled, secure in the knowledge that he had worked out a foolproof deal to get the boys reinstated.

Okay, he did feel a bit guilty about manipulating that Nelson woman into a sucker bet, but he was desperate. The Minutemen needed to win this weekend. For that, they needed Tim and Jeff.

Besides, she should have known better than to

choose a football team by the color of their uniforms. He chuckled as he replayed the conversation in his mind.

As annoyances went, Ms. Andi Nelson was an attractive one. Damn, he might as well be honest with himself. She was beyond attractive. She was flat-out, movie star beautiful. She had pale blond hair, big blue eyes and a trim little body. True, she didn't have too much in the way of breasts, but she more than made up for that in the leg department. Hers were long and slim with shapely calves. He'd just bet that her thighs were just as shapely as those awesome calves. Once she realized he'd played her for a sucker, she'd never speak to him again, let alone give him a glimpse of her thighs.

He pulled into the parking lot of The End Zone, his favorite sports bar, more than ready for a hot burger and a cold beer. The game was underway, and he could savor his victory in the company of friends.

The place was packed. Mike made his way through the boisterous crowd to the table where his good buddy Dave Mason sat with Laura, his most recent girlfriend. A loud cry came from the guys at the bar, who were paying close attention to the game on the big screen TV. Mike swerved to avoid being doused by an enthusiastic beer drinker and landed safely at Dave's table. "Hey!"

Dave smiled and leaned back in his chair, draping an arm around the shoulders of a pouting Laura. "We wondered when you were gonna get here. What took you so long?"

"I worked out, caught up on some paperwork, and then got sucked in watching the video from last weekend's game. I wanted to get another look at that late touchdown play Jeff and Tim pulled off." He rolled his shoulders, looking around with anticipation. "Is Gina here? I thought she was working tonight."

"She's here." Dave picked up his beer and took a long slug. "Why did you need to see Jeff and Tim at work again? Gonna try to teach it to Brad and Erik?"

Mike grinned. "Nope. I'm gonna make Jeff and Tim do it again this Friday." He caught a glimpse of Gina and motioned for her to bring him a beer.

Dave frowned. "Jeff and Tim can't play this Friday. They're ineligible."

Uh oh. Dave was going into Vice-Principal mode. Mike could hear the change in his voice. Dave was a good V-P, but he was definitely a by-the-book, play-by-the-rules guy. "Just got a feeling."

"That so?"

"Yep! Hey, gorgeous." He looked up at Gina when she put his beer down in front of him.

"Hey, Mikey." She bent down to kiss his cheek. "You hungry?"

"Yeah. How about a burger with everything and an order of fries?"

"Coming right up." She reached out and smoothed a hand over his hair before going to place Mike's order.

Mike took a drink from his beer as he watched her walk away. Gina Francisco was about as opposite from Andi Nelson as you could get. She was short, with curly auburn hair, big brown eyes, and a ripe, lush figure that would make a centerfold jealous. She was uncomplicated and fun to be with. She never made him feel stupid.

"I don't see how those boys are going to get eligible in just a couple of days."

Mike should have figured Dave wasn't going to give this up. "Don't worry about it."

Dave cursed. "It's not anything to compromise the program, is it?"

"No way."

"I'm still not liking the sound of this."

Mike glowered at him. "Just leave it alone, okay? It's not a big deal." Time to change the subject. "How far ahead are the T-Rexes? I have a little bet going on tonight's game."

"Dave, I want to go home now," Laura wheedled from her corner of the table.

"Not right now, honey. I need to talk to Mike." Dave was smiling. "You have money on tonight's game?"

Laura glared at Mike. If looks could kill, Mike would have been six feet under. He looked back at Laura. Better make that twelve feet under. "Yeah. Just a little wager between colleagues." Okay, it was a lot more than that, and probably a little bit shady, but Andi had suggested it. Nobody was going to get hurt. No harm done... except to Andi Nelson's pride. He refused to feel bad about that.

"Who'd you bet?"

Mike exhaled, sounding like a rusty door hinge. "First off, it was her idea, not mine." He really didn't want to cop to tricking Andi.

"Who'd you bet?"

"Jeez, can't you say anything else?"

"How about tell me about the bet before I reach across the table and choke all the life out of you?'"

Mike grinned. "Anyone ever tell you, you're cute when you're mad?"

"Dave, I really want to go home."

"Not yet." He took his arm from around Laura's shoulders and patted her leg. He continued to glare at Mike. "Anyone ever tell you, you're a jerk?"

"Constantly. I never let praise go to my head." Mike laughed when Dave sputtered and decided to cut him a break. "Okay, here's the deal. We've got a bet going on tonight's game with Andi Nelson. When Toledo wins, she'll change their grades, and they'll be eligible again." He shrugged. "She insisted. What else could I do?"

Dave relaxed and leaned back in his chair. "I should bring you up on charges, you know that, right? But I'm not. Guess why."

Okay, he'd bite. "Why?"

"You bet on Toledo tonight?"

"Since I'm not brain dead, I did indeed take Toledo." He took another sip of beer. "I gave her first choice. She took New Rochester because she likes dark green."

"Oh, she took New Rochester all right, and you can bet it wasn't on account of their uniform colors." Dave grinned at Mike. "Have you been following the game?"

"No. I told you I was working. Toledo is a sure thing, anyway. I'm not worried."

"Maybe you'd better check out the TV."

Mike got an uneasy feeling in his gut. He turned in his chair to look at the TV. When he saw the score posted at the bottom of the screen, his jaw dropped. He turned back to Dave, who was still grinning like an idiot. "That can't be the right score."

"Sorry to tell you, but it is."

Mike looked at the screen just in time to see a dark green quarterback fade back and whip the ball into the air. It arced like a ballistic missile into the waiting hands of a green receiver who leapt up to catch it. The receiver sprinted down the field, dodging every Toledo player who tried to stop him, straight into the end zone for a picture perfect touchdown. The folks at the bar went wild.

Stunned, Mike turned back to look at Dave. "What just happened?"

"Well, it turns out that the Rangers have worked out a secret deal to sign the Terrible Twins."

"No way." Mike shook his head. The Terrible Twins were the sons of Deke Nelson, one of the winningest coaches in football history. The man was a living legend. His twin sons, Buck and Brock, were magic on the football field, especially if they played on the same team. "I thought no pro team was ever going to be able to sign both of them together."

"Well, apparently the Ranger management put together a real sweet deal. Deke may even come out of retirement to coach them." Dave smiled. "At least, that's the rumor."

Mike was dumbfounded. "How come nobody knew about this?"

"I guess secrecy was part of the deal."

Mike turned his attention back to the game and watched as the twins controlled the field. At some point, his burger and fries arrived, and he barely even noticed. The game ended, and he slumped in his chair, awash in abject misery. Dave regarded him evenly while Laura smiled for the first time that night.

"What did you lose?" Dave wanted to know.

Oh, man. "We bet that if Toledo won, she'd pass the boys."

"And if New Rochester won?"

He cleared his throat. Dave would never let him live this down. "The boys stay in chorus, and I..." He brought his beer to his mouth, mumbling into it, "Have to join her church choir."

"What was that last part again? I didn't quite catch it."

Mike scowled at him. "I have to join her church choir."

There was a moment of silence before Dave burst out laughing. He laughed so hard, his eyes teared. He almost had himself under control but looked at Mike and cracked up all over again.

"This isn't that funny," Mike grumbled.

"Yes, it is. This is the funniest damn thing I've heard in a long time."

"It was just her dumb luck, that's all."

Dave settled down and subjected Mike to a

know-it-all grin. "You think so?"

"How else could she have known?"

"Take a look at the screen. Tell me what you see."

The images of the twins flickered on the screen as the sportscaster interviewed them after the game. They looked like a pair of victorious Vikings, home from a successful day of looting and pillaging unsuspecting villages.

He squinted at the screen.

They looked familiar.

Then, the face of the legendary Deke Nelson filled the screen as the interviewer turned to get his take on the game. Mike felt cold when he realized he had seen Deke Nelson's bright blue eyes before.

He'd seen them smack dab in the middle of the new chorus teacher's face. He looked back at Dave. "Were you ever going to tell me Andi Nelson is Deke Nelson's daughter?"

"Oh, eventually. She doesn't necessarily want people to know about it."

It took a minute for Mike to take it all in. His heart pounded like an army of kettle-drums. He could barely hear over the sound of it. "She played me for a fool."

"Probably."

"She knew all along about her brothers."

"Most likely."

"That whole routine about the uniform colors was just a smoke screen so she could get me to make a sucker bet."

"Looks that way."

****

Mike sat at his favorite table in The End Zone staring at his beer going flat. Dave and Laura had left long ago. Actually, most everyone else had left. He was, for all intents and purposes, alone and brooding. How could he have been so stupid?

15

It made him furious that Andi Nelson had played him for a sucker. Never mind that he had tried to do the same thing to her.

Devious female. She was probably home laughing at him. Well, she'd better enjoy her victory while she could. He was hell bent on revenge.

And what was he going to do about Friday's game? He didn't want to admit it, but if the team lost any more games, his job might be in jeopardy.

He couldn't lose his job. He loved it too damn much.

"Hey, Mike." Gina smiled at him, a cleaning rag in one hand, a spray bottle in the other. "You need to drink up. Bobby wants to close."

He pushed the glass away. "It's okay. I'm done." Opening his wallet, he pulled out a twenty and put it in Gina's apron pocket.

"Thanks." She cocked her head to one side and studied him. "You okay?"

"Yeah." He stood up and grabbed his jacket from the back of his chair. After he put it on, he patted his pockets for his keys.

"You got a headache or something?" She bit her lip. "Did I do something to make you mad?"

Mike shook his head. "I'm sorry. It's not you. I've got stuff on my mind."

"Okay." She put her cleaning paraphernalia down on the table and walked him to the front door. "You gonna stop in tomorrow?"

"I don't know. I've got some things to work out."

"Anything I can help with?"

Didn't he wish. "No, I'll figure it out." He looked back at her as he opened the front door. "Good night."

"'Night, Mike."

Mike watched her close the door behind him, listened to the lock click shut, then headed for his car.

The whole damn day had been a disaster from start to finish, but he knew what he had to do.

He had to find a way to get Jeff and Tim eligible fast, and at the same time get even with one smart-ass music teacher.

## CHAPTER TWO

"So, what you guys gotta do is go to chorus and stay out of trouble." Mike fought to keep his voice firm and impartial. Jeff and Tim glared in sullen silence. He could tell from the looks on their faces that they weren't buying it. He could hardly believe it himself. Some days it didn't pay to get out of bed. "Got that?"

Jeff bolted to his feet. "What I *got*, Coach," he said through gritted teeth. "Is you sold us out."

He figured Jeff had a right to be angry, but he wasn't going to let the boy get away with talking back to him. "Sit down and shut up, Jeff."

The kid obviously didn't want to, but only the truly foolish ignored Mike Kelly when he used that tone of voice. Jeff threw himself back in the chair and folded his arms across his chest. He didn't look at Mike.

"Contrary to popular opinion, I did not sell you out. It's not like I made that bet thinking I would lose. And I wasn't the one who made Ms. Nelson mad in the first place. You two did that on your own." He strained to hear what Tim muttered under his breath. He didn't like what he heard. "You clean up your mouth when you talk about Ms. Nelson. You don't say, you don't even *think,* those words about her. I know your mother taught you better than that."

Jeff slid a glance to Tim, but Tim was studying the floor.

"You look at me when I'm talking to you." Mike came around the desk to stand in front of the boys. A long silence filled the room as Jeff, then Tim, who took his time, looked back at Mike.

Mike sat on the edge of the desk. "Now, here is what you boys are gonna do. You're going to go to chorus. You're going to do your best in the class, whether you want to or not. By the time you're done, Ms. Nelson is going to love you, you got that?"

Jeff cleared his throat. "We got it, Coach."

Tim clenched his jaw shut and remained silent.

Mike cleared his throat. "Tim? Do you understand what you have to do?"

"Whatever."

Mike had had it with Tim's attitude. After all, the kid wasn't the only one with a noose around his neck. "There's no *whatever* about it. You will do exactly what you're told, and you won't do anything more to wreck your eligibility." Temper still simmering, he straightened up and went back to his chair. Sitting down, he leaned forward, resting his forearms on the desk. "Now, get out of here and remember what I said. Behave."

The two couldn't leave the room fast enough. They practically fell over each other's feet in their haste to make their getaway.

Mike closed his eyes and pinched the bridge of his nose to alleviate the pressure that was growing behind his temples. Tim wasn't a kid who usually copped an attitude, so why the problem now, when they couldn't afford it? If he didn't get his act together and play the game by Andi Nelson's rules, then he'd have no chance to get his eligibility status back.

Mike got up to pace around his office. Jeff had as much to lose as Mike did. The kid's only chance at going to college was getting an athletic scholarship. If he couldn't play, he certainly couldn't impress any college scouts. Maybe if Mike explained that to Andi...

No. He needed to face reality. Andi was not going to give an inch. Jeff and Tim needed to play by the rules.

And Mike, God help him, had to go to choir practice.

****

Andi groaned and pushed wet hair out of her eyes as she checked out the clock on her bedside table. No help for it, she was going to be late for work. She didn't have a class until third period, but she had to go to the music store and fix some problems with her order. She'd have to rearrange her schedule and go after school.

Stubbing her toe on her bureau, she winced, swore, then high-tailed it back to her bathroom to finish doing her hair. As days went, this one was turning out to be a doozy. She'd fallen asleep right before her alarm went off, so she slept right through it, and the timer on her coffeepot hadn't gone off, so she had to wait for her coffee.

Never mind that she hadn't gotten a wink of sleep because she felt guilty about duping poor Coach Mike.

Ha! Guilt was the last thing she should feel. Mike wouldn't have lost a minute's sleep if the roles had been reversed. Besides, it wasn't her fault he didn't know she was Deke Nelson's daughter.

She sighed, and it felt ragged and edgy in her throat.

Forget about Mike Kelly. She had to focus on her career and build something so great, so undeniably dazzling, that her father would have to sit up and notice. She wasn't going to let anyone or anything stop her, especially not a couple of unruly football players and their coach.

It really hadn't been nice of her to trick good ol' Coach Mike like that, but it was done, and that was that. She not only had a point to make, she had a program to protect.

She had such big plans. Once she established the main choir, she would branch out into specialty choirs, like a Jazz choir, a madrigal choir and both a boys' and a girls' A-cappella doo-wop group.

Her student accompanist, Beth Pritchard, was a huge part of her plans. The girl was possibly the most gifted musician Andi had ever met. It was both frightening and exhilarating to be her mentor.

Hair done, make-up applied, she looked in her closet, thanking God she'd had the time to go to the dry cleaner's yesterday. She pulled out her favorite suit and girded for battle.

Finally dressed and ready, Andi shook her head as she made her way to her kitchen, following the nutty aroma of fresh brewed salvation as it filled her apartment. Taking her favorite mug from the dish drainer, she poured herself a cup, inhaled deeply and enjoyed the smell. There was no way she was getting through the day without a generous dose of caffeine.

Thoughts of Mike Kelly boogied into her brain again. Okay, so she was attracted to him. He was a handsome man with mischievous eyes and a killer grin. And she *did* have a weakness for broad shoulders and a tight butt. She supposed she owed him an apology; he *was* a colleague. She had taken advantage of the fact that he couldn't have known who her father was. She'd take care of it the minute she got to school.

No way was it an excuse to see him or his cute butt.

Really.

**\*\*\*\***

Mike regarded the grade book on the desk in front of him with a sour look. Very few things were more frustrating than trying to put the right numbers in the right boxes. He wasn't stupid. He was dyslexic. He had strategies to decipher what he was seeing.

He grabbed for his Styrofoam cup of take-out coffee, but missed, and spilled the coffee not only on his hand, but also all over the grade book. He stood up and swore, looking around for something to sop up the coffee with.

Someone knocked on his door.

"Come in, dammit!"

The door swung open, revealing heaven and hell in high heels. Andi Nelson looked good enough to eat. Her raspberry sherbet-colored suit showcased legs that went on forever. Her blond hair glowed like an angel's halo.

Except she wasn't an angel. She was a sneaky, ruthless, football hating, sucker betting she-devil.

He didn't trust her. In that moment, he hated her.

"Hi," said the she-devil. "May I come in?"

Mike stood, opening his arms in welcome. "*Mi casa es su casa.*"

He watched as she bit back a giggle. A giggle? No way. He never would have taken her for the giggling type.

"I can come back if this isn't a good time." She eyed the coffee lake pooling on his grade book.

"Now's as good as any." He grabbed a sweatshirt hanging on the back of his chair and plopped it down on the coffee-soaked desktop. He swabbed away at the mess with it. Then he made a vague motion with his head. "Want to sit down?"

"Thanks, but no. It looks like you're busy." She stood up even straighter, if that were possible. "I've come to apologize."

"Oh, really? And do you have something to apologize for?" Now this was something he hadn't expected. Coming in to gloat? Definitely! But lowering herself to apologize? Never! This woman was just one surprise after another.

"You know I do."

"Okay, fine. You're Deke Nelson's daughter. You had inside information. You're sorry." He scowled. "Bye."

She nodded, turned to leave, then stopped. "You should apologize also."

Yeah, right, when donkeys flew. He snorted. "What for?"

"Come on. You know what for. You tried to sucker bet me."

"Isn't that the pot calling the kettle black?" He tossed the coffee stained sweatshirt behind him.

"And I've apologized for that. But it doesn't change the fact that you tried to pull the wool over my eyes too." Was that her foot tapping?

"I did not." Wild horses would not pull an apology out of his mouth.

"You did too. You were only too ready to believe I was so gullible I'd make a choice based on uniform colors."

He had to smile. "What? You don't like hunter green?"

"I like hunter green just fine. It's being manipulated I don't like." She looked at him, as if she were trying to memorize him. "I've apologized for my part in all this. I'll do right by those boys. I won't be unfair."

Mike hoped so. God, he hoped so. "Yeah, well. I'm counting on that."

She smiled, the curl of lips so sweet, he would have sighed if he were that kind of guy. Damn, she was pretty.

"I think they know what's at stake. For them, at least." She looked at his coffee soaked desk. "And I think I need to let you get back to your work." Her mouth rounded into an impish grin. "See you tonight at rehearsal."

"Uh, about that." Mike stopped mopping up his desk. "I've never, *ever*, been in a choir before. I'm probably not going to be an asset to your group."

Andi laughed right out loud. "That's not a problem."

"Don't I, um, need to read music?" He had enough trouble reading words; he couldn't imagine trying to read music especially in front of total strangers.

"That's always a plus, but don't worry about it. There are some others in the choir who don't read music. A lot of them learn by ear. Most of them, in fact."

"Yeah, but..." He shook his head slightly, "I don't get it. Why is it so important that I be in this choir?"

"Are you trying to get out of the terms of our bet?"

"No. I honor my promises. I just want to know what's in it for you." Man, that foot of hers was tapping double-time now.

"You belittle my work. You..." She shook her head when he made a move to interrupt her. "You do. You never would have come to me, asking me to let Tim and Jeff off the hook if you didn't. You'll never know differently unless you experience being in a choir."

"And that's important to you?" Wow, he must have hit a nerve. She was getting way too agitated. He scratched his head.

"Well, yes." Her chin lifted. "It is. Just like it's important to you that I take football seriously. Even though we both know it's just a game."

"Just a game?" He couldn't believe his ears. How could she, of all people, say that? "I'd think you, daughter of the greatest football coach of all time, would know just how important football is."

Her eyes went cold. "I suppose I do." Her tone was brisk and businesslike. "I'll see you tonight.

Don't be late."

He watched her leave, then sat down in his office chair. He stared at the door for a while, trying not to wonder why her good opinion was important to him.

****

Jeff Myers stuffed the last of his pizza calzone in his mouth as a group of freshman girls parked their trays at his table. There was nothing he hated worse than freshman girls.

Nothing worse, except for being on the ineligible list and not being able to play football.

"I'm gonna go shoot some hoops. Wanna come?" Tim Baldwin asked Jeff as they carried their lunch trays to the dish area.

Jeff shook his head. "Not today. I want to go talk to Ms. Nelson."

Tim looked at him as if he'd said, *Not today. I've got to go perform brain surgery.*

"Why?" Tim grunted. "Stupid bitch. Man, I hate her."

Jeff agreed, but he was desperate to play ball. "I want to know what we can do to get eligible faster. I don't want to sit out any more games."

"You can try. I don't think it'll help." Tim repeated his opinion of Ms. Nelson as he aimed an empty milk carton at a trash bin and sent it flying through the air. He grinned when he made the shot. "Man, I'm good."

"Wanna come with me?"

"No way." Tim slapped him on the back before heading off to the gym. "Later."

Jeff made his way to the auditorium on feet made of lead. He hesitated for the span of a heartbeat, then pulled the door open. Music, beautiful in its intensity, floated through the air. Stunned, he didn't immediately see the slender girl seated at the shiny black piano.

He knew who she was, of course. Beth Pritchard. Even though they didn't hang with the same crowd of friends, he had noticed her. She was cute.

He knew she played the piano, but he didn't know she could make that kind of magic. It drew him into the auditorium and down to the stage where she played. He got there just as she sounded the final chord. The air was absolutely still for one beat, then two. When he spoke, his voice was barely a whisper. "That was awesome."

Beth shrieked as she leapt from the piano bench.

Jeff stepped back. "Oops! Sorry! I didn't mean to scare you."

She slapped her right hand with a *thwap* onto her chest. "You took a year off my life." She sat back down and stared at the keyboard.

"I, um, heard you playing. It was beautiful. What was it?"

"Brahms." Her voice was still a little breathless. "The *Intermezzo in A Major*." She slid him a glance and blushed bright red. "*Opus 118*."

He swung his head around, checking to see if they were alone in the room. Funny that he hadn't worried about that while Beth was playing. "I'm looking for Ms. Nelson. She around?"

"No." Beth stood up. "It's her lunch period. She lets me come in here and practice."

"Oh." Jeff shifted his weight from one foot to the other, then back again.

"Is it something I can help you with?" Beth bit her lip.

Jeff focused his gaze onto the foot of the stage. "I don't know. I guess I just wanted to see if there's anything I can do to get eligible again." He smiled at her. "I really miss playing."

"Oh. Do you want me to ask her for you when I

see her?"

"Would you?" Relief burst through his body. If Beth asked Ms. Nelson, how could she say no? "But only if you don't mind."

"I don't mind."

"Thanks a lot. I really appreciate it. I'm not good at this singing stuff. Most of the time, I can barely find my part."

"Would you like me to go over your parts with you?" He saw her blush redden even before she ducked her head to look at the floor.

"No! I mean, it would be way too embarrassing for me to have you hear how bad I am."

"Oh." She brought up her head again. "I could make you an mp3 of your parts, and you could work with them when no one could hear you."

"You'd do that for me?"

"Sure. It's no big deal." She wiped her hands on her jeans.

"It is to me. Thanks." He grinned at her. It was the first time he'd felt like smiling in days.

They stood there, the silence awkward. The bell to change classes rang as Beth pulled the cover over the keys of the piano and put the lock in place. Jeff started to leave, then turned back to her. "There's a party after the game on Friday. Do you want to go with me?" It was his turn to blush. "That is, if you're not already busy."

"I'm not busy." She smiled, and it seemed shy and sweet to him. "I'd love to go."

He grinned, feeling unexpectedly relieved. When was the last time he had worried about a girl saying no? "Great. How about I meet you at the field after the game?" His grin grew when she nodded. "Cool. I'll catch up with you there."

Beth nodded and smiled again.

*Man she's pretty when she smiles*, he thought. He turned to leave. He got to the door and pushed it open. Looking back at Beth, he waved then was swallowed up in the rivers of kids streaming into the hallway on their way to class.

Beth floated to her next class. Jeff Myers, who was totally hot, had asked her out. Omigod! None of her friends would believe her. They were going to be so jealous.

She couldn't wait to tell them.

An awful thought struck her. Her dad was never going to let her go to a party with Jeff. He didn't want her going out with any boy.

As much as she hated lying to her father, she was going to have to come up with a cover story for Friday night. She'd get Katie to help her.

There was no way she was missing that game or that party.

Jeff Myers.

Omigod!

CHAPTER THREE

"I must be out of my freakin' mind. What am I doing here?" Mike turned off his headlights and windshield wipers then killed the engine. He peered morosely through the rain-streaked glass. St. Benedict's Church loomed ahead of him, looking more like Dracula's castle than a house of God. "I hate this, I hate this, I hate this," he chanted under his breath.

Honor won. He forced himself to get out of his car and go into the church. He had to walk around the building, in the rain, to find the right door. If it hadn't been raining, he wouldn't have been so quick to open the door and meet his fate.

Man, he hated getting wet. He stepped inside and paused.

No amount of cleanser could mask the odor of basement. The hallway was dark, save for a lit doorway off to the left. Noise spilled out into the hallway.

He checked his watch to see how much longer he could stall. Its face lit up to tell him it was time to face the music, in more ways than one. Sighing, he steeled himself to join the choir.

He *so* didn't want to do this.

The brightly lit, cheerfully decorated room was a startling contrast to the dark hallway. There were posters with Bible verses on the wall, as well as one wall of shelves holding books and videos. Children's artwork decorated another wall. People sat in metal folding chairs, all talking at once. One group of women sat off to the side, on tables, using chairs as footrests. Andi stood next to the piano, talking with a girl who was sitting on the bench behind it. She looked up and smiled at him. "Mike! Hi! Glad you made it!"

All the heads in the room snapped around to look at him. He felt himself start to blush and cursed. "Did you think I wouldn't?"

"I did wonder."

"Well, you shouldn't have. I promised I'd be here, and I'm here." He was offended that she might think otherwise.

"Why don't you come on in and meet the gang?" Andi asked. "What part do you sing?" She picked an envelope up off the piano and handed it to him.

"I don't have the slightest idea."

"Right." She pursed her lips. "Judging from your speaking voice, I'd guess you're a bass. They sit in the back row there."

He looked at the designated row. Two guys were already sitting there, one dressed in a Hawaiian shirt and chinos, the other, smaller, dressed in work pants and a flannel shirt. They shifted to make room for Mike.

"Wally Devereaux," said the flannel shirt guy. "Glad to have you aboard." He gave Mike's hand a good, hard shake.

The mountain of a man in the Hawaiian shirt reached out a hand. "Heinrich Schumacher." Heinrich had a very heavy German accent. "Velcome."

"Mike Kelly."

Wally and Heinrich sat down, leaving Mike the seat between them. A man in the row in front of Mike turned around in his seat to offer his hand. "Jack Canard."

Mike took his hand, and the two men shook.

Jack Canard smiled a friendly smile. "And what made you decide to join us in all this craziness?"

30

Craziness was an appropriate term, Mike thought. He was certifiably nuts to be going through with this. "Andi talked me into it." No way was he going to admit to this group that she had played him for a sucker.

"Andi can be pretty persuasive." Jack chuckled. "Remind me to tell you about the time she talked me into singing a solo at Easter." He shuddered. "I still get nightmares."

Before Jack could say any more, the kid at the piano played something loud, and the room gradually quieted. Andi perched on a stool in the front of the room, a music stand in front of her.

"Okay, gang. Back to work." She waved her hands, and the piano rang out with a flurry of sound.

They launched into what was, for them, a familiar pattern. Mike was lost. He zigged when he should have zagged. He went up when he should have gone down. It didn't help that Wally was singing one set of notes and Heinrich was singing another. They did more exercises, hummy things he had no hope of ever singing.

Mike didn't think he could take it anymore. The girl stopped playing, and Andi directed the group to take out some piece in a foreign language.

Mike opened up the envelope that Andi had given him and rifled through the contents, but he didn't have a clue. He emptied the envelope into his lap and was fanning through the music when Wally reached over and extracted a folded paper from the pile.

He handed it to Mike with a sympathetic smile. "It's kinda confusing at first, but you'll get the hang of it."

Mike sincerely doubted he'd ever get the hang of it, but he was grateful for Wally's guidance. He opened up the sheet music.

His heart sank.

Mike had a hard enough time deciphering words, but these dots running all over the page were impossible. A very old, very awful feeling flooded him. All of a sudden, Mike was six years old again, and looking at an unsolvable mystery, one everyone but he understood.

Andi spoke to the sopranos, directing them to sing something. The sopranos were the group of women perched on the tables. They dutifully went through their part, once, twice, finally three times. Next, Andi turned her attention to the altos. There was a smart-aleck junior high kid who gave Andi some grief, but Andi only laughed and told her to get over it. The kid, along with the rest of the section, sang, and it sounded good. Impressive.

Andi announced it was the tenors turn to sing. Beth played the part for them. They tried it, but it was rough going.

Some guy in another row of chairs spoke up. "Perhaps the part is just a tad too high? Maybe you could transpose it? I bet it would sound fantastic down a minor third."

Andi laughed. "Dream on, Walt. C'mon tenors, do it again."

Jack said, "Oh, boy," in a great imitation of Donald Duck.

The tenors needed a few more tries, but eventually Andi let them off the hook. Mike got a sinking feeling. There was only one section left for Andi to torture. And Mike was now a card-carrying member of the basses.

Oh, joy.

The kid played a starting note, and Andi smiled at them expectantly. She gave a wave of her hands, and they took off.

At least, Wally and Heinrich took off—in totally different directions. Heinrich sang everything a whole lot lower than Wally did. Mike thought Wally

32

might be right, but Heinrich sang with so much conviction, he couldn't be sure.

She gave them a second shot, but it was no help. Mike had no clue. He didn't even know what row of black dots to follow. He would have left without a backwards glance, but his honor was at stake.

Mike Kelly did not welsh on a bet.

Wally and Heinrich went over the bass part a couple more times before Andi deemed it time to put all four parts together.

It was a train wreck.

No matter how good the parts had sounded alone, together they all fell apart. It was beyond awful, beyond terrible.

"Good first try! Let's go over it again. Beth, give them their notes, please." And the torture began anew.

How it could have gotten worse Mike didn't know, but it did. Andi made them go over it again and again, always with a positive attitude. Her smile never wavered.

Eventually, she took pity on the poor and tuneless, and declared a break. The gang started talking all at once, and to Mike's chagrin, the subject of last Friday's football game came up.

It was obvious they didn't know who he was. Their choice words about his lack of judgment, lack of intelligence and dubious parentage, had him biting his tongue to keep silent.

He did feel he needed to correct the group on one salient point. "The coach didn't put Jeff and Tim in the game because they're on the ineligible list."

Wally scratched his head. "Who was the rocket scientist who did that? Everybody knows without those two the team's got no chance."

Mike grinned at Andi. "Care to enlighten 'em, Ms. Nelson?"

Andi lifted her chin, meeting Mike's challenge.

She raised her voice. "The rocket scientist would be me. The boys flunked chorus. And, just so you know, before you embarrass yourselves even further-" She motioned to Mike. "The no-good, idiot, son-of-a-bitch coach in charge of losing Friday's game is sitting right in the bass section."

****

A moment of silence passed. Andi had never heard her group not make one little peep. It was not nice of her to embarrass the gang like that, but maybe now they'd learn to be quiet in between songs.

Yeah, and the moon was made of green cheese.

Well, she also felt bad for Mike. The crew was really running him down, and she was embarrassed on everybody's behalf. She was glad, actually, that he spoke up when he did.

Then Wally said to Mike, "You still shoulda run that play the boys do with a couple of other kids."

Jack nodded his head. "It couldn't have hurt."

Then everyone else felt free to offer him advice for the next game. She sighed. Time to get the rehearsal back under control. "'Kay, gang, let's go. Take out the *Ave Verum*."

Wally reached over and showed Mike which piece of music to look at. Mike was so clearly out of his element. He hated being there; she could see it all over his face. It made her feel like an ogre.

She didn't think he had sung a note all night. He'd looked at the music with furrowed brow. He'd moved his lips to the warm-ups. It was obvious he was miserable. But at least he had come. He hadn't tried to get out of it.

She could only admire that. Still, she had a rehearsal to run. "We'll start with the sopranos."

Beth hit the sopranos' starting note, and Andi beat a measure to bring them in. With control established once more, she let her mind focus on the music. It was a familiar piece for the choir; they liked it and sang it well.

She noticed that every now and then, Wally would reach over and point at places in Mike's sheet music in a friendly effort to show him where they were. Mike continued to be stoic, his posture stiff, facial expression rigid and closed. Misery poured out of him in palpable waves.

Andi made the decision right then and there to give him an out. She'd made her point; she could afford to be generous. Tim and Jeff were another story, but she'd cut Mike some slack.

When 9:00 rolled around, she gave the choir the final cut off. A moment of silence passed, then she smiled. "And that's a wrap. Good work, and good night!"

The choir started talking all at once. Mike scowled at the music in his hands. He looked adorable.

"Mike." Andi weaved through the gang to where he still sat. "You were a real sport tonight. Want to come out for a drink?"

Mike lifted his eyebrows and looked at her as if she had asked him if he wanted to be bitten by a rattlesnake. He stood. "A drink?"

She supposed he had a right to be suspicious. "Yeah, a drink. Look." She put a hand on his arm. "I want to talk to you. Please."

Mike glanced at his watch, squinted back at Andi. "Yeah, I guess that would be okay."

"Don't sound so enthusiastic."

He exhaled heavily then contorted his face into the fakest Cheshire Cat grin she'd ever seen. "A drink would be dandy."

She laughed. "I'd be daunted by your attitude, but you're cute when you're miserable. Please come. My treat. I really want to talk to you about all this." She gestured around the room.

Mike's gaze followed her gesture then settled back on her face. "I already said I'd come."

"Great! How about Esmeralda's?"

"Is that the place with all the ferns over on Eighth Avenue?"

"That's the spot. Is that okay with you?"

"Sure."

****

Mike cursed himself to hell and back again on the drive to Esmeralda's. He was going to a fern bar. He'd once been a guy who would never be caught dead in a fern bar. What had become of him?

The answer was obvious. He had been sucker betted by a sneaky chorus teacher, and now look at him. He was going to have a drink in a fern bar with Cruella de Ville.

He'd just bet she would order some fancy, tasteful, and unpronounceable French wine, white, probably, and stick her pinky out while she sipped it.

Was holding the pinky out for wine or for tea?

Why did he even care?

The whole evening had been a nightmare. He supposed it was only fitting he end it at Esmeralda's Cafe.

He pulled into the parking lot and parked next to Andi's car. She was already inside.

Mike had given her a headstart *and* taken the long way there. No way was he waiting inside for her. He'd go in, have a beer, listen to her say whatever it was she wanted to say, then go. No harm, no foul.

It was fairly quiet inside. *Good*, he thought. Not very many witnesses to his being there. Classical music played soft and low. People spoke in muted voices, and there were several single people sitting alone at tables, reading newspapers.

He shuddered. What a way to spend an evening.

It was easy to find Andi. She was at a table in a

back corner, chatting with a waitress. The waitress laughed at whatever Andi had said.

Andi looked up, and her eyes danced as she noticed him and motioned him over. She smiled, and just like that, his heart turned over in his chest.

Unh-unh. No way! He refused to be attracted to her, never mind like her. He would fight it kicking and screaming.

"Good, you're here," Andi said to him as he reached the table. She introduced the waitress. "This is Clarisse. Clarisse, meet Mike."

Clarisse smiled. "Hello, Mike." She had some kind of foreign accent. Didn't that just figure? "What may I get for you this evening?"

"What kind of beer do you have on tap?" He took off his jacket and put it down on a chair next to him. Then he pulled out another chair and sat down.

"None. We only have imported beer in bottles."

He should have seen that one coming. "Do you have Heineken?"

"Yes."

"I'll have that, then. Please."

Clarisse smiled and left with their order. Mike looked across the table at Andi, leaned forward on his forearms, and clasped his hands in front of him. "So, shoot. What do you want to talk about?"

"I'm letting you off the hook. You don't have to come to choir if you don't want to."

"What?"

She grinned at him and put her hands over his. "I'm letting you off the hook. You don't have to come to choir if you don't want to."

He didn't want to go to choir, that was for sure. This was an offer that was too good to refuse. There had to be a catch. "Why?"

Andi took her hands back and blinked. "Why?"

"Yeah. Why?"

"Can't I just say we're even and leave it at that?"

"No. I don't trust you."

She opened her mouth to say something, but Clarisse came with their drinks and a plate of crackers, fruit and cheese. Andi murmured a thank you to the waitress, as did he when Clarisse put down his beer. He took a long swallow. "So?"

She had taken a dainty sip of her wine. Since she didn't hold her pinky out, he figured it was a gesture saved just for tea. Live and learn.

Then she did something truly odd. She took six crackers out of the basket they came in and placed them very precisely on her plate, like little soldiers lining up to be reviewed by a general. She then took a few apple slices and put them on the plate as well, taking great care that they didn't touch the crackers. It totally absorbed her attention for a moment. She looked up, caught him staring at her, and blushed beet red.

Andi cleared her throat while she wiped her fingers with a napkin. "Okay. It was really clear tonight you weren't having a good time."

Got that right, he thought. He waited for her to go on.

"I just felt bad you were so miserable. You've been to choir. You've seen that it's about working hard as an individual as well as a team. I figure I've made my point."

"But what about the bet?"

"What about it?"

"You won."

"Yeah, and your point would be?"

Mike took another slug of beer. There had to be a catch. Wait... "What about the boys?"

"What about them?"

"Do they get a get-out-of-jail-free card too?"

Her eyes widened. "I have to say no. They stay in chorus until the end of the school year."

His heart sank to the bottom of his chest like a

stone. Mike had no choice. "Then I stay in the church choir."

She looked perplexed. "But..."

He sat back, taking note of the confusion in those pretty, blue eyes of hers. He felt good for the first time that night. "It's really simple. I made a promise on behalf of those boys, and I'm going to keep it. As long as they're in chorus, you're stuck with me."

She just sat there and looked at him. "But you don't have to."

"Yes, I do. I made a promise. I'm going to keep it."

Andi studied her glass of wine, snaked a hand to her plate of crackers and fruit, sliding it back across the table without taking anything off it. She appeared to be fighting with herself, but then she looked back at him, and the smile she sent him was pure magic. "I really admire you for that."

Whatever Mike had expected Andi to say that was not it. "You admire me?"

She laughed, and the sound was more musical than the classical crap coming from the restaurant's sound system. "Yes. I admire you. Is that so hard to believe?"

"Well, yeah." Boy, oh boy. He could sure get used to her looking at him like that. He felt ten feet tall. "I'm just keeping a promise. No big deal."

"But it is." She leaned forward. "It's a very big deal. It's my experience that honor is as rare as hen's teeth."

"I, um, I don't know what to say." When was he ever tongue-tied? He was usually smooth with the ladies. He looked at her, and his heart pounded a little faster. "Wow."

She picked up her glass and toasted him. "Wow."

He laughed. She flashed him that saucy smile of hers, and he wanted to kiss her. Just like that, he wanted to reach across the table, cup her face in his hands, and kiss her. His throat felt suddenly dry, and he finished off his beer in one big gulp.

"Do I have something on my teeth?" Andi asked him.

"Uh, no I don't think so. Why?"

She shrugged. "You're looking at me funny, that's all."

Boy, Kelly, he told himself. That's real slick, mooning over her like a lovesick adolescent. Get a grip. Then, inspiration struck. "I was wondering if you could do me a favor."

"Depends on the favor. If I can, I will."

"It's not for me, exactly. It's for the team's morale."

Andi frowned. "If it's got anything to do with Tim, Jeff and the chorus, then you're out of luck. I-,"

"No, it's nothing like that," he hastened to reassure her. "I was wondering if you could maybe talk to your dad and your brothers and see if they would come to a practice and talk to the team. You know, a pep talk to boost morale."

Andi's smile froze on her face, and her eyes got as cold as glaciers. "That's the favor you want? To get my father and brothers to visit the team?"

"If it's not an imposition."

****

Andi couldn't believe what she was hearing. One minute he was looking at her like he could eat her up. The next, he wanted to use her to get to her father.

Well, she should be used to it by now. It was the only reason she had gotten any dates in high school. She had learned the hard way to stay away from athletes, no matter how hunky they were.

She glanced at him, at his clearly expectant face. Suddenly he looked like every guy who had ever used her to get in good with Deke.

He looked like Bobby Maclenden, who had asked her out in the seventh grade, only so he could go to her house, pretending to do homework. What he really wanted was to meet Deke and get advice on how to improve his game.

He looked like Brody Collins, who had asked her to the prom, just so he could meet Deke and impress him enough to get him to write a letter of reference for a college program Brody wanted to get into.

He looked like Tom Otis, who had dated her in college and had even asked her to marry him just to get to Deke and get a pro try-out.

She grimaced. Andi Otis would have been an ugly name. Good thing she found out in time that Tom didn't love her, had never loved her. At the time, though, Tom's betrayal had hurt like crazy. It had taken her a long time to get over it.

And now, sitting right across the table from her, was good ol' Coach Mike, looking cuter than an over-eager puppy, wanting her to introduce him to Deke, so his team could maybe win a ball game.

She would refuse, no matter how cute she thought Coach Mike's butt was.

She took a sip of wine, but it tasted like vinegar. Worse than vinegar, actually. She popped a cracker in her mouth and chomped it vigorously. It was just something to do to help her control her temper, she promised herself. She looked over at him. His eyes were still as eager as a young pup's. She reminded herself of how miserable he had looked at rehearsal. Nope. It wasn't going to work. She hated asking her father for anything. She just couldn't do it. "I'm sorry, but no."

Mike's face fell. "No? But it would mean so much to these kids."

She glared at him. "I just can't do it."

"Can't do it, or won't do it?"

"What difference does it make?"

"Lots. If you can't do it, because it's an imposition and I'm stepping over the line, then, okay. But if you just *won't* do it out of stubbornness or spite, then the kids will be the ones who'll pay. It'll be no skin off my teeth."

Andi looked down at the table, then up again, but she focused on some spot behind him. "Let me think about it. I've been commanded to go to my parents' house this Sunday for dinner. The twins will be there too, since they're home for a while. It'll be a good time to ask." She ran her finger around the rim of her glass. "I'm not promising anything."

"Thanks for considering it."

She wanted to scream and shake him. "Yeah, well..." She could think of nothing else to say.

"Don't forget how much it will mean to the kids."

"I'm sure." She looked at her watch. Nothing killed an evening more effectively than being used to get close to her father. "It's getting late."

Mike nodded. "Yeah. I guess."

She grabbed her purse and stood. "Thanks for keeping me company."

Mike stood. "Thanks for the drink." He looked at her as if he were trying to read her mind.

"You're welcome." His hands reached for her jacket, warm where they covered hers. Without a word, he held it up, waiting for her to slip her arms into the sleeves. His look was probing, but he remained silent. Foolishly touched by his unexpected gallantry, she murmured her thanks.

Andi wanted to escape. She needed solitude to close over the newly reopened hurts of her past.

"I'll walk you to your car." His tone brooked no disobedience.

"Fine."

They left Esmeralda's after Andi had a brief consultation with Clarisse. In the parking lot, Andi fumbled around in her bag for her keys, a fact which made her feel clumsy and ditzy. "Well, good night."

Mike looked at her, and for a brief, intense second she thought he was going to try to kiss her. She told herself she was relieved when all he did was take her keys from her and open her car door. "Good night," she said as he handed the keys back to her.

"Good night. Thanks again for the drink."

Andi nodded, pulling the door from underneath his hand then closing it. Turning the key in the ignition, she ground the car into gear, gravel spraying into the air as she gunned the engine.

She couldn't help herself. Checking the rearview mirror to see if he was watching, she cursed.

He was.

## CHAPTER FOUR

Mike looked up at the scoreboard. Despair, dark and deep, welled in his chest. With only two minutes left in the game, the Bayside Fishermen had forty, the Addington Minutemen zip.

It was cold. His breath swirled out in a fine white vapor, and his hands were getting numb. The clouds overhead looked ominous, and his team was getting their butts whipped. At this point, even the cheerleaders had trouble drumming up enthusiasm.

Since the team had no chance of winning, Mike cleared the bench to give the second and third string players some time on the field. The last two minutes ticked away slowly. God must be taking some perverse pleasure in prolonging Mike's agony.

The final whistle shrilled, sealing their fate. Mike hung his head. Somehow, he had to put a positive spin on this for the kids so they wouldn't feel like total losers. But what could he say? He knew they'd done their best. They weren't dumb, and they had their pride.

There were ceremonies and rituals to be attended. He did his duty and sought out the opposing team's coach to shake his hand. He conferred with his coaching staff, making sure the game video would be available for him to watch on Sunday night—though reliving this game wasn't an experience he was looking forward to.

The principal, the superintendent, and the school board president found him and demanded a meeting on Monday morning.

Oh, goody.

And then, to top it all off, he'd been unable to stop himself from checking out the crowd to see if a certain blonde was there.

He shook his head while he brutally thrust thoughts of Andi Nelson out of his mind. He had to focus on saving his career. He couldn't afford to become distracted with anything that got in the way of that, no matter how cute a distraction she was.

****

"Omigod, Beth! He's coming over here!"

Beth looked over her shoulder to see what her friend Katie was seeing. Jeff. Walking towards her. Her heart threatened to pound out of her chest, she was so nervous. She turned back to her best friend. "Do I look okay?"

"You look great. I am sooooo jealous."

"I am sooooo nervous. Remember, now. This is important. You and I are going to the movies, right? That's what you told your mom."

Katie rolled her eyes. "Don't worry. As far as my mom knows, we're at the movies." She smiled over Beth's shoulder. "Hey, Jeff."

Jeff nodded at Katie. "Hey." He looked at Beth as she turned to face him.

He seemed distant and closed off. He was probably upset about the game. "Hi, Jeff." Her mouth suddenly felt dry, her palms damp.

"Beth." Jeff looked at her, and she thought she saw something flicker in his eyes.

Just as the silence became awkward, Katie blurted, "Well, I've gotta get going before I get in trouble. See ya' later." And she was gone.

Jeff looked down at the ground, then up at Beth. Oh, no, she thought as her stomach lurched downward. He's going to try to ditch me.

They both started talking at the same time.

"You go first," Jeff said.

Beth took a deep breath. The air was cold

against her throat. "I just want you to know that if you've changed your mind about taking me to the party, I understand."

Jeff shook his head. "It's almost as if you can read my mind or something. I have changed my mind about the party."

Beth's heart shattered into a million pieces. "Okay. Well, I'll see you around."

She started to leave, but he took hold of her arm. It tingled where he touched her. "I've changed my mind about the party, but not about being with you. If it's okay, can we just go someplace quiet and talk?"

She whirled around to look at him. "You want to go and talk? You don't want to go to the party?"

"I will if you really want to go. But honestly, I really, really don't want to go. I feel bad enough about what happened at the game today, and spending time listening to the other guys bitch, watching them drink, is not my idea of a good time." He moved his hand down her arm and held her hand. "I'd just like to be with you and, you know, talk."

Beth's head started to swim. "I'd like that."

He smiled. "You don't mind about the party?"

"No, not at all."

"I've got my mom's Volvo. We can go out to the old quarry if that's okay."

She gulped. The old quarry was, like, make-out central. She looked at their linked hands. His felt so warm and thrilling around hers. She was suddenly desperate for him to kiss her. "That's okay."

They walked off together, hand in hand.

\*\*\*\*

"Hey, Mike. Tough game." Dave Mason sat back in his chair as Mike came up to his table at The End Zone.

Mike gave a curt nod, sloughing his wet jacket

and wishing he could shed his darkness as easily. It was pouring rain outside, mirroring his mood. The warmth generated by the crowd in the bar was humid, but welcome. "You don't know the half of it. The team morale is in the toilet, and to top it all off, I've got a meeting with George, Steve Windley and Betty Kincaid, first thing Monday morning."

Dave let out a low whistle. "You hit the jackpot, buddy. The principal, superintendent, *and* the head of the Board of Ed all in the same room at the same time."

"That's me. Lucky as the day is long." He took a look around. "Gina working tonight?"

"Yeah, she's around here somewhere." Dave popped a pretzel in his mouth and bit down on it with a loud crunch. "What are you going to do about Monday morning?"

"I don't have a clue." He ran a hand through his damp hair, more a gesture of frustration than to put it into place. "How easy would it be for them to fire me?"

"I don't think..."

"Hey, Mikey! What can I get for you?" Gina came up to the table and put her hand on Mike's shoulder.

"Gina. Hi." Mike cleared his throat. "What's up?"

She laughed. "I'm working. What do you think is up? Never mind, don't answer that question." Her face turned solemn. "I'm sorry about the game today."

Mike nodded, but tried to keep the atmosphere light. "Stuff happens."

Her face darkened. "Are you in trouble?"

"Me?" He saw no reason to worry her with his problems. "Nothing I can't handle. What's good tonight?"

"The special is vegetarian pasta Alfredo." She grinned when he shuddered.

"How about my usual, then."

"Want fries with that burger?"

"Is Bobby making onion rings tonight?" Mike loved Bobby's made-from-scratch onion rings.

"Nope. Sorry."

"Too bad." His sigh was heartfelt. He had been looking forward to those onion rings. "Guess I'll take the fries."

"Coming right up. Do you want a refill, Dave?"

Dave looked at his glass, considering. "I'm good for now. Thanks, Gina."

"No problem." She bustled off to the kitchen to place the order.

Mike watched Gina go, then turned back to find Dave staring at him. He got serious again. "You're closer to George than I am. Can I trust him to be in my corner on Monday morning?"

"I think so." Dave grabbed another pretzel. "He knows what you've had to work with, seeing how the school is so small. He's also behind Andi Nelson's tough line with Jeff and Tim." He chuckled. "You know, I've had my problems with some of his decisions, but bottom line, he's a decent guy and a good principal. Windley and Kincaid will be the problem. After sinking all that money into improvements to the field, they'll be looking for return revenue. They think a winning team will guarantee that return."

"This is high school, not the pros. The game is supposed to be fun and teach them something." Mike grabbed a pretzel of his own. "No one wants these kids to win more than I do. No one works harder for them."

"I know that. George knows that. I'll call him to see if I can sit in on the meeting. There's not a whole helluva lot more I can do for you."

"It's enough. Should I call Sandy?"

"It probably wouldn't hurt to have the union rep

with you."

Gina came by with Mike's beer. "Your burger will be out in a couple of minutes."

"Thanks, Gina." The beer foamed over the top of the mug as she put it down in front of him. He shot her a grateful smile.

The smile she gave him back was warm. It let him know she was interested in doing more to cheer him up than bringing him his burger. She gave his shoulder one more squeeze and went off to wait on another table.

Mike lifted his beer and took a long, hard swallow. Over the top of the mug, he saw Dave watching him. "What?"

"Is there something going on with you and Gina that I don't know about?"

"No. But even if there was, I don't kiss and tell."

"She's a beautiful woman."

Mike grinned. "She's gorgeous."

Dave grinned back. "I'd noticed."

Both guys stopped to watch her lift a tray of drinks. Gina's body was a sweet one, with generous breasts and a really cute backside. Mike wondered how difficult it'd be to get her into bed. He didn't think he'd have to work that hard.

Not as hard as he'd have to work to get Andi Nelson into bed.

And, damn, just the thought of Andi put him off the idea of Gina.

Damn female was ruining his life.

Later that evening, as Mike was going home, alone, he swore a blue streak as he fiddled with the radio for a station that was playing some decent tunes. What he wanted was some metal, head-banging tunes that sounded as mad as he felt. All he could find was some fruity, classical crud that only reminded him of Andi Nelson and how she frustrated him.

He hated the way Andi Nelson tied him up in knots like he was some school kid with a crush on the teacher. He had to get a grip.

Right now, his first priority had to be hanging on to his job. Quite simply, he loved the job, he loved the kids. If he had to put his pride on hold and ask Andi to get her dad for a little help and encouragement, well, it was worth it.

He hoped she would come around. It was so weird on Wednesday. One minute she was laughing with him, telling him that she *admired* him, and the next she was hostile and cold. What was up with that?

He had felt he could move mountains when she told him she admired him. He'd felt lower than dirt when she'd said she wouldn't ask her father to visit the team. What a roller coaster ride she had put him on that night. The choir rehearsal had been beyond terrible, and then she made him feel higher than the angels with all her so-called admiration. That final snub of hers had capped the evening.

Still, he couldn't get past how she made him feel when she smiled at him with such approval, how warm he felt when her eyes looked at him with such interest.

And damn, in spite of himself, he had been interested. It was like a switch had been turned on, and he felt protective and proprietary towards her. Man, he had even done the get-the-coat and open-the-door routine for her, when usually he respected a liberated woman's right to get her own coat and open her own door.

What was wrong with him?

Okay. Andi Nelson was beyond pretty, in that don't-touch-me, I'm-better-than-you way. Of course, that made him want to touch her in the worst way. Just to mess her up a little bit.

And he didn't just want to touch her, Mike

realized. He wanted to kiss her mouth, bare her breasts, and suck at her nipples until she cried out with pleasure.

He was a man with simple and direct passions.

A wave of loud, screechy violins suddenly blasted from the radio. He swore again, and snapped the radio off.

He wished he could do the very same thing to his obsession with Andi Nelson.

****

Andi sat on the piano bench, staring out into the empty church. She had spent half the previous night speculating on one question. She yawned, put a hand up in front of her mouth to cover it, and ran the thought that had plagued her all last night one more time, in spite of herself.

The hope Mike would make it to mass consumed her. She was sure he wasn't going to come. Call it intuition, whatever; she just couldn't see that big, gorgeous guy taking up space in her choir loft.

Andi shook her head at herself. Why did she even want him to come? He didn't know the music. Even though he'd gone to rehearsal, she didn't even know if he could sing. Their deal had nothing to do with him showing up for church. They'd said nothing about it. They hadn't spoken of commitment beyond going to the rehearsals, although, hindsight being 20/20, she probably should have insisted on it.

He probably didn't get up before noon on Sunday morning, sleeping in after a night of carousing. She had no doubt he didn't wake up alone.

She cursed as she jammed her finger and broke a nail while trying to open the piano lid. This was not shaping up to be a good day.

"Hurt yourself?" Angie came into the choir loft and dropped her tote bag onto the pew.

"I jammed my finger and broke a nail. No big deal."

Angie just looked at her with those mom eyes that didn't miss a trick. "You're not usually clumsy."

"So?"

"Maybe you're nervous about something."

"I'm not nervous about anything."

"No?"

"No. What would I have to be nervous about?"

"Oh, I don't know. Maybe about whether a certain, very good looking, football coach is going to show up for mass this morning." She raised and lowered her brows three times in a row then wiggled them suggestively. "Hmmmm?"

"And why would that worry me?"

"You tell me."

The arrival of Jack Canard and his son Danny saved Andi from answering. Danny was cute as a button and loved to sing with his dad. Loudly. One always knew when Danny was around. At any rate, Angie and Jack traded wisecracks, and Andi took advantage of that opportunity to go downstairs and put the numbers up for the hymns. Then she had to check in with the priest. This took a little longer than usual, which was fine with her. By the time she made it back to the choir loft, most of the choir was assembled and ready to warm up.

Mike was among the missing members. She should have figured he wouldn't come. She shouldn't be disappointed at all.

People were arriving, filling the pews, and blocking further thoughts of Mike Kelly. The opening hymn was announced, and the choir and congregation launched into it. Mid-way through the second verse, Mike slipped into the back row and sat in between Wally and Heinrich.

Her eyes met his, and she hoped she kept the feeling of delight out of her expression. For his part, Mike seemed defiant and hesitant at the same time. He looked adorable. He took the hymnal Wally passed him and glared at it.

He glanced up, catching her looking at him. She looked away, but not in time to miss the sizzle in his eyes.

Angie caught Andi's attention and winked at her. Andi was mortified to feel herself blush.

Used to only seeing Mike in warm up suits or jeans, seeing him wearing a sport coat and tie surprised her. She had to admit he cleaned up very well.

Of course, not that she had any complaints about how he filled out a pair of jeans. *Stop that,* she warned herself. *Remember he's using you to get to your father!*

She managed to ignore him for most of mass. She did notice he sang when the music was very familiar, and his voice wasn't half bad. Low and warm, it rumbled through her. Sexy, she admitted. It would be a great voice to wake up to.

*Better not go there, girlfriend,* she chastised herself.

She couldn't avoid him during the sign of peace. The choir was a close group, and so hugs were traded around the choir loft. She moved through them, giving each person a little squeeze. Then she found herself face to face with Mike.

The bright light in his eyes made her stomach feel fluttery. She held out her hand for a handshake, and was embarrassed to find it trembling. "Peace be with you, Mike." Was that whispery voice really coming from her?

He smiled that lady-killer smile of his. "Only a handshake, Andi? When everyone else gets a hug?" He shook his head, ignored her hand, and pulled her into his arms. "I don't think so." He brought his lips close to her right ear. "Peace be with you," he whispered. He brushed a kiss on her temple, and released her.

She just stood there for a moment, looking up at him. Beth launched into the *Lamb of God* response, which brought Andi to her senses.

She was acutely aware her nipples had hardened into achy points. Her lips actually tingled with the desire to plant a hot steamy kiss right smack dab on his gorgeous mouth. The man was potent. This was not good, she told herself. Not good at all.

Mass ended, and, poof, just like that, Mike was gone, which was just as well, she told herself. She really didn't know what she would say to him. She *had* expected him to ask her again about Deke and her brothers visiting his team. She had an answer all prepared for that question, but his not asking it really caught her off guard.

No doubt about it, the man was a menace to her sanity.

****

"Thanks again, Ian, for coming along with me to my parents' house." Andi said. "I really appreciate it."

"Not a problem, darling. You know I love to spend time with you."

Andi looked at Ian from the passenger seat of his Lexus. Ian Ross was a professor of French Literature at Barrett College, a small, private, liberal arts college near Addington. He served on the ballet board with her, and she considered him a good friend. He was cute in a scholarly kind of way, like Mr. Giles on *Buffy the Vampire Slayer*. He also loved to demonstrate his prowess driving on what he called the wrong side of the road, which was the reason he was driving her to her parents' house.

"Well, I know this time of year is difficult for you with the semester in full swing and papers and mid-terms to grade. I feel guilty tearing you away from your work."

"Oh, *please* tear me away from my work. This last batch of papers from my senior seminar is just awful. Terrible. I might as well have spoken Greek for all the attention they paid me."

"Can you speak Greek?"

"Well, yes I can, but that's hardly the point. It's getting to the-,"

"How many languages do you speak?"

"French, of course. Greek, like I just told you. Latin, Spanish, Italian and German." He took his eyes off the road to give her a quick smile. "I'm still learning American English."

Andi studied him as they drove along. He looked professorial, as usual, with his tweed jacket and wire-rimmed glasses. He really was nice looking. She tried to conjure up the same feeling for Ian that had jolted through her when she looked at Mike that morning at church.

No luck.

Damn.

It wasn't fair.

"Do you mind if I turn on the radio?"

Andi blinked, and shook her head to clear it. "I'm sorry. What did you say?"

His smile was one of infinite patience. "I asked if you would mind if I turned on the radio."

"Oh, no. Not at all."

Ian hit the radio's control panel and classical music from the local NPR station came on. He sighed. "Mozart, right?"

She nodded. "His *Jupiter Symphony*."

"Beautiful. Simply beautiful." This last bit he said, looking at her again with heat in his eyes.

She gave him a weak smile, turning to look out the window again. "Mozart is always beautiful."

## CHAPTER FIVE

Her brothers were already at her parents' house when Ian and Andi pulled into the drive. He turned off the engine and pulled up the parking brake. "Here we are. Are you ready?"

"I should be asking you that question."

"Absolutely. I thrive on challenges."

Andi gave a soft little chuff of a laugh. "Let's go, then."

He got out of the car, moving around to open her door, but she was already out and waiting for him. Gesturing widely with one arm to the walkway leading to the front door, he said, "Lead on, MacDuff."

"Keep saying things like that. It'll drive my father crazy."

He chuckled. "I aim to please." Touching her elbow lightly with his hand, he led her up the walkway to the house.

The house was a large, old, New England farmhouse, made of stone, and surrounded by maple trees. The lawn was obviously cared for with diligence and love. Mums and marigolds tenaciously held on to life, even though Indian summer was over and the first frost was imminent.

This was not the house Andi grew up in. They had lived in Texas when she was growing up, just outside of Fort Worth. Her father had been on the road most of the time, but he did manage to make it home more often when the twins started playing football.

He'd never made it to any of her concerts or

ballet recitals.

Her mother, Pamela, had tried, really she had, but Andi knew in her heart her father was disappointed his first-born was a mere female. Not only that, but she was a real girly-girl, into dolls and tea parties and ballet. Deke Nelson just didn't do dolls, tea parties, or ballet.

Especially ballet.

Then she'd gotten sick, her life had fallen apart and Deke had taken no more notice of that than he had while she'd been dancing. She was always the outsider, always the afterthought. She should be used to it by now.

When he retired five years ago, he and her mother had come to her mother's hometown, Addington, Massachusetts. They bought the 100-year-old farmhouse and settled in, gardening, golfing and generally puttering around.

The problem was, her father really wasn't a putterer. Nope. Deke Nelson was a man of action. Being restless and missing football, he managed to convince the twins to move to New Rochester, which was close enough to Addington so as not to uproot Pamela.

It was sheer happenstance Andi had gotten the teaching position at Addington High. She took it with the notion maybe she could mend fences with her father, that the two of them could find some common ground. So far, it wasn't happening.

"Here we are. Shall we ring the bell?" Ian pulled down on his jacket cuffs.

"No. The door's open." To prove it, Andi took the handle, turned it, and pushed it open. "See?"

Ian followed her into the house and sniffed the air appreciatively. "Something smells heavenly."

"Mom loves to cook. Everyone must be out back." She motioned with her head and affected a thick cowboy drawl. "Let's go that-a-way."

Sure enough, they found her mom in the spacious, sunny kitchen. Pamela smiled when she saw them. Throwing down the oven mitt she held, she bustled over and folded Andi in a welcoming hug. "Andi! Finally." She stepped back and looked at her. "We expected you an hour ago."

"I got hung up at church." She gestured to Ian. "You remember Ian Ross, don't you?"

"Of course." Her mother held out her hand for Ian to shake, which he promptly did. "It's nice to see you again, Ian."

"Thank you for having me." He extricated his hand so he could push his glasses back up on his nose. "Whatever you're cooking smells absolutely delicious."

"I'm trying out a new recipe. I hope you don't mind being a guinea pig."

"Not at all." He put his right hand over his heart. "In fact, I'm honored."

Pamela's face glowed with pleasure at his compliment. She looked at Andi. "Don't worry. I made something special for you."

Andi smiled. "Thanks, Mom. But you didn't have to go to the extra trouble." She didn't need Deke to make a scene in front of Ian.

"You know it's no trouble." Pamela reached out and put her palm to cup Andi's cheek. Her smile was gentle. She looked back to Ian. "I hope you like pot roast."

Andi winced. "I thought I'd told you. Ian's a vegetarian."

Pamela blinked. "Oh." A pot on the stove clamored for attention. She made a lunge for it. "Well, no problem. I have plenty of salad, and I've steamed some broccoli for Andi. There's plenty of that..." She kept her back to them as she stirred the boisterous pan. She looked over her shoulder and smiled. "Why don't you go and say hello to your father. He's with the twins in his study, watching a video of last week's game."

"Why am I not surprised?"

"Andi, be nice."

Andi rolled her eyes, but heeded Pamela's look. "Yes, Mother. Come on, Ian. Let's go beard the lion in his den."

"I'm right behind you. And please-" He flashed Pamela a smile. "Please don't go to any extra trouble. I'm sure I will be absolutely fine with whatever you've already prepared." He touched Andi's arm as they left the kitchen. "I don't want to be any trouble."

Andi shrugged. "Don't worry about it. It's my fault, I forgot to tell her. I'll make it up to her later on."

Her father's study was the only room in the house that bore no sign of her mother. While the rest of the house was filled with antiques, fresh flowers and real art, football trophies and pictures of the twins at various stages in their careers created Deke Nelson's domain. A wide screen plasma TV dominated one wall.

Three recliners were lined up in front of the 'wall o' TV', just like the bears' chairs in *Goldilocks*. And right now, three football legends, Deke Nelson and his twin boys, Buck and Brock, occupied those chairs.

Deke sat in the recliner between the twins, using the VCR remote to point out different things here and there. The twins listened intently, nodding every now and then as they absorbed their father's infinite wisdom.

Jealousy burned in Andi's chest. She knew her mother had taken video after video of her concerts and recitals and ballet performances. Her father had, to the best of her knowledge, never looked at one.

"Hey, Coach."

Deke twisted in his recliner to see who was there, brought the footrest down with a thump and rose to greet her. "Andi, girl, it's about time you got here. Your mother made us hold dinner for you." God forbid Deke Nelson had to wait to eat. Andi rolled her eyes as she looked away from him.

"Sorry. I got hung up at my church job. Hey, boys," she said to the twins. "How's it going?"

"Pretty good," Brock said. He was the flashier of the twins. Right that moment, he was dressed in jeans and a Hawaiian shirt that would make Heinrich envious.

Buck stood. The quiet one, he came to his sister and gave her a hug. "Hey, Big Sis." He draped one enormous arm over her shoulders.

"Deke, I don't know if you remember Ian." Andi smiled at her father after she extricated herself from her brother's bone crushing embrace. "He was with me the last time I was here. Ian, I know you remember Deke."

Deke and Ian shook hands. "Sure I remember Ian. You teach some frou-frou subject at the college, right?" Andi could tell her father was doing the macho jerk thing, squeezing Ian's hand with far more force than was necessary.

Ian's expression remained stoic. "French language and literature."

"I thought it must be something like that." Apparently, Deke decided to have mercy and gave up his death grip on Ian's hand. "I'm starved. Let's eat."

****

"Why can't you eat normal food like the rest of us?"

Andi looked up from her plate to meet her father's eyes. "This is normal food." A wedge of Greek-marinated and broiled tofu with steamed broccoli and brown rice, all strategically placed on her plate to not touch each other was normal food for Andi. In fact, it was the only way she could eat.

Her father pointed to his plate heaped with pot roast, potatoes, carrots, and pearl onions. He had poured gravy over everything so one couldn't tell where one food started and the other stopped. "No, this is real food. I don't see why you make your mother go to all the trouble of making an extra meal."

"I don't mind making special food for Andi," Pamela quickly interjected. "I love to cook, Deke. You know that."

Deke snorted. "She should eat the same food the rest of us eat."

Andi clenched her jaw. This was an old argument. He'd been railing at her about it since she was sixteen. She should be used to it. Looking back at her plate, she scooped up a fork full of brown rice.

"The salad is delicious, Pamela," Ian piped up courageously.

Deke muttered something that sounded suspiciously like "A real man wouldn't be caught dead eating salad."

"What did you say, Coach?" Andi asked.

Deke looked at Andi, his face suddenly bright red. "I suppose he eats quiche, too."

One of the twins, Brock, snickered.

She smiled. "Only if there's lots of broccoli in it."

Deke harrumphed, silenced. He focused on attacking the slab of beef dominating his plate.

Pamela stepped into the breach. "How are the rehearsals going for your choral competition?" she asked Andi.

"Really great. The kids are excited about the music and are working very hard. I'm hopeful we'll place high."

"That's wonderful." She looked at her husband. "Don't you think that's wonderful, Deke?"

He grunted. "Sure. Wonderful." He put down his fork and leaned back in his chair. "Gotta say, though, the school has one poor excuse for a football team. The administration should put money and effort into shaping up that team instead of wasting money on frivolous stuff."

Andi stiffened and got very quiet. "And I suppose my choral competition comes under the heading of *frivolous stuff?*"

Deke seemed to realize he had made a mistake. "Now don't take it that way, Andi. But everybody knows sports build character." He picked up his fork again and gestured with it. "A chorus just doesn't do that the way a football team does."

Any thought Andi might have entertained about hooking Deke and Mike Kelly together flew out the window. She conjured this wild fantasy of Mike and Deke getting along famously, watching football, ensconced in a couple of ratty old Barcaloungers, scarfing down red meat, scratching their armpits and belching after a good swig of beer. Oh, yeah. They'd be soul mates.

She'd be damned if she let that happen.

\*\*\*\*

Many hours later, exhausted and alert, Andi punched her pillow one last time before sitting up. After tossing and turning for most of the night, she gave up trying to sleep at 4:30 and went to the kitchen to make coffee and watch the sun rise.

The day had been a doozy, she reflected as she ground coffee beans. The pungent nutty aroma of the freshly ground beans made her tired eyes water. After dumping the coffee in the filter, she poured water in the coffee maker and flipped it on. She stared out the window, waiting for dawn, thinking about Deke.

Thoughts of her father brought a frown to her face. She would be a whole lot happier if she just accepted he would never be the father she wanted, would never accept her choices, would never love her like he loved the twins.

Tears filled her eyes, as her throat choked up. She swallowed, and it hurt. The coffee maker gurgled. Pulling a black ceramic mug with a bright orange quarter note handle from an overhead cupboard, she filled it, absently wiping at a drip on the countertop with one finger.

She forced herself to think of her work. The competition music was going well, so she needed to turn her attention to the pieces for the holiday concert. Fine. And for church, they had to dig in and really start to put the finishing touches on the Christmas Eve music.

The church choir.

Mike.

Sigh.

That kiss he gave her had been in the back of her mind all day. Why couldn't she feel that attracted to Ian? Maybe she should try harder. Closing her eyes, she imagined Ian standing in front of her, his eyes hot and eager. He came closer and she raised her face and parted her lips for his kiss...

Brown eyes morphed into green and gold-flecked eyes. It was Mike's lips that touched hers. Mike's mouth taking hungry possession of her own.

She opened her eyes and walked to her kitchen table. She pulled out a chair, sat down, and bonked her forehead on the tabletop three times.

****

Since his meeting earlier with the principal, superintendent, and chair of the school committee was an exercise in futility, Mike worked out his frustrations in the weight room. He pushed his body through endless reps. It didn't help.

"I take it the meeting didn't go well."

Mike stopped in mid-grunt to look at Dave. "I

thought you were going to be there."

"George and I agreed it would go better for you if I stayed away. What's the bottom line?"

Mike oomphed as he sat up. "The bottom line is I deliver a win soon, or else I find a new job." He stood and started to pace. "Even if Jeff and Tim could play, winning next weekend's game is a long shot. East Bennington is a more experienced team. I've got a total of five seniors, no more than seven juniors, and a whole passel of sophomores and freshmen. Most of them are still a whole lot smaller than anyone from East Bennington." He plopped down on the weight bench. "I'd better get my resumé in order."

Dave frowned. "Don't give up yet. The whole school board can't feel that way. Besides, what else do we have a teacher's union for? Have you talked to Sandy yet?"

Mike shook his head. "No, I didn't get the chance. I guess I should."

"I would if I were you."

Mike stood. "I'm gonna catch a shower before practice. Thanks for the ideas."

"We'll fight this, Mike. You're not going to lose this job. You're too good for the kids."

Mike gave a weak smile, put his hand on Dave's shoulder, and squeezed before turning to go to the showers. There stood Tim and Jeff, and they had obviously heard every word. "You two, not a word to anyone about what you heard, got it?"

The boys nodded, but murder was in their eyes. "'Course Coach," Jeff assured him. "We won't say a word."

****

Andi couldn't help but overhear Jeff and Tim discussing the possibility of Mike losing his job as they entered the rehearsal room. The angry accusing looks they continued to shoot her throughout the warm-up exercises would have alerted her if she hadn't. The whole chorus was stirred up about it, even Beth. While she didn't like football, she didn't like people being treated unfairly, either.

In the end, the choice was easy.

Andi didn't know if it would do any good, but it was the only thing she could think of to do. She called her father and asked him to help. If she didn't know better, she might have thought he sounded pleased she had.

## CHAPTER SIX

"Hey, Andi. Got a minute?"

Andi turned to see Mike walking down the auditorium aisle towards her. Her heart tripped a little at the sight of him. No man had a right to look that good in sweats and a tee shirt. "Sure. What can I do for you?"

He smiled a sheepish grin. "Actually, it's about what you've already done. I don't know why you changed your mind about asking your father to come talk to the guys, but I appreciate it. It ought to really psyche 'em up." Mike shrugged. "Who knows? Maybe he'll watch a couple of practices and see something I'm missing."

"Maybe." Now, why did he have to look at her that way? It made her feel too good and all shivery inside. "When is he coming?"

"Thursday. I haven't told the guys yet. I thought it should be a surprise."

Andi nodded and tried to look like she didn't care. "Are Buck and Brock coming?"

"Not this time. They're out of town. But your father said he'd arrange for the team to go to the next Ranger home game and then go back to the locker room to meet the twins and the rest of the team. Listen." He cleared his throat. "I know you had some sort of problem with this, and I want you to know how grateful I am and how much it will mean to the boys."

"It's not a big deal."

"To me it is. Maybe you'd let me take you out for a drink tonight after rehearsal? To say thank you."

"I don't know. I've got so much-,"

His smile beseeching, he almost groveled. "I'll even take you to Esmeralda's." She laughed, and he evidently took it as a sign of encouragement. Reaching out, he clasped her hands in his. "Please."

She let out a breath she didn't even know she had been holding. "I'd love to go out for a drink with you tonight."

He beamed. "Great. I'll see you at rehearsal." He started to leave, stopped. "About rehearsal tonight?"

"Yes?"

"Those exercise things just about killed me last week. Do you mind if I wait out in the hall until you're done with them?"

Her laughter was the music he took with him when he left the auditorium.

****

"And that, gang, is that. Good rehearsal. See you on Sunday."

"At 9:15?" Angie asked in a very loud voice. Angie probably knew very well that the choir was supposed to convene at 9:15. It was just her subtle way of reminding choir members who had a tendency to be late. Andi looked grateful for it.

Mike supposed he was one of the ones being reminded. Ah, well.

He was still so confused by this choir stuff. In fact, he was sure he would never get the hang of it. But that didn't mean he couldn't sit back and enjoy watching Andi work the crowd.

He thought the group sounded awful, but she was so positive and so upbeat, he could almost start to believe they had a shot at making this work.

The sheet music was so far beyond him. He knew he would never have a chance to figure it out. Maybe if he had encountered it when he was younger, he wouldn't feel so far out of his league. To go from bad to worse, the words were in some foreign

67

language. Wally said it was Latin, and Mike guessed Wally would know.

Mike sure as hell didn't. He had a hard enough time following English, never mind Latin. The sad reality of his life was that all he really understood was football. If sitting in this choir feeling like a fool helped him keep his job, he'd do it.

He didn't know what made Andi decide to ask her father to visit the team, and he didn't want to know. He was too damn grateful she had. He held few illusions it would help the team win the game, but the kids would get a thrill.

Mike watched Andi give Beth some last minute instructions. The kid listened intently, nodding every so often. Then, as if Andi felt him watching her, she looked up and met his gaze.

Snap, crackle, pop, just like that, there were only two of them in the room. She looked at him, and her smile was sweet. She murmured something to Beth, who shook her head in reply. Andi nodded, patted Beth's arm, then walked towards Mike. Suddenly, the evening didn't seem so bad.

Hoo, baby, come to papa.

The smile she gave him was electric. "Let me get my coat and my purse."

"Take your time."

Her movement was fluid, graceful. He really could get used to watching her. Of course, after seeing her brothers move on the football field, he shouldn't be surprised.

"Let's go." Andi was there, coat in hand. He took it from her and held it up for her to slip into. "Thanks," she said. "Where are we going?"

"I promised you Esmeralda's, so Esmeralda's it will be."

"We can go somewhere else if you want."

"I'm a man of my word."

They walked out of the church basement and

into the parking lot. The air was brisk and smelled of wood smoke. They got to their cars and she fished in her bag for her keys. He put his hand on her arm. "Let's take mine. I'll drive you back here when the time comes."

"Oh." Andi blinked. "Sure. Why not?"

He escorted her to his car and tucked her safely inside. "That was a good rehearsal," she said, once he was inside and started the car.

"How could you tell?"

"I *am* a trained professional." She sighed. "Some nights are better than others." She smiled again, a sudden, unexpected ray of sunshine.

His heart thrummed at the sight of it. "They're quite the group."

"True. But they're my group, and I love 'em."

"Along the lines of it's a dirty job but somebody's got to do it?"

Her chuckle was low and husky. "Something like that."

He guided his car into Esmeralda's parking lot. Cutting the engine and palming his keys, he glanced over at her. Knowing a liberated woman when he saw one, he ordered, "Wait for me."

Her puzzled look pleased him. He got out of the car and moved around to her side. Opening her door, he leaned in, offering her his hand. "Ma'am."

She laughed, full out and hearty, but took his hand and let him help her out of the car. "Gosh, Mike. I didn't know you had it in you."

"I'm just full of surprises."

"Do tell?"

"If I told you, then they wouldn't be surprises."

"A man of mystery?"

"Damn straight." He opened the door to the restaurant and let her in ahead of him.

Greeted at the door by the hostess, Andi exchanged small talk with her while she led them quickly to a table. Clarisse waved to them, indicating she'd be right there. They settled in. "I know this isn't your usual type of place, but I-,"

"Jeez, how could you tell?"

She stared at him, then laughed. "The look of panic on your face last week when you were looking around for me."

"I was that obvious?"

"Mmmm-hmmmm. But I'm intrigued. Where do you usually hang out?"

"The End Zone."

She slapped the table as she leaned forward. "A sports bar! I should have known. I've driven by there a couple of times. It looks okay."

"Oh, yeah." He could eat this woman up with a spoon, she was that appealing.

Clarisse came up to the table. "Hey, you two! How are you tonight?"

Andi smiled, and for Mike, the world tilted on its axis. "Clarisse. How are you?"

"I can't complain. The usual?" She scratched away at her order pad when Andi nodded, then turned to Mike. "And what about you? A Heineken again, or are you going to live a little?"

"I'll stick to the familiar for a while. A Heineken sounds great."

"Okay. A chardonnay and a Heinie. Be right back."

Andi watched her go, then looked at Mike, and got right to the point. "Does the team have a chance at winning this weekend?"

Mike sucked in a breath. "Don't be shy. Say what's on your mind."

"I find honesty and directness are best."

"Right. You, the sucker bet queen, are the poster child for honesty and directness."

She narrowed her eyes at him. "When it comes to that bet, you're as guilty as I am. Now, don't dodge the question. What are your chances?"

"Not good." He shrugged. "Small school, small team. Plus, we're in a building phase. I inherited a team in a slump, and it's only gotten worse. We've got some talent coming up, but they're still little guys. My freshmen and sophomores can't hold back juniors and seniors on other teams."

"I see."

He supposed, because of how she grew up, she really did understand, whether she wanted to or not.

"How many juniors and seniors can you field?"

"Seven, with Jeff and Tim. But they're the two that count. Without them, well, try to imagine running the choir without your best singers. Do you see what I'm saying?"

Andi looked down at the table. She looked like she wanted to say something but Clarisse interrupted, choosing that moment to show up at their table with their drinks. After Clarisse left, Andi rearranged her wine glass so it was dead center on the cocktail napkin and placed exactly ten pretzels in military formation on another napkin.

Reminded of the crackers from their last visit, he desperately wanted to ask her about the pretzels but was equally afraid of offending her. Mike cleared his throat and scraped a fingernail at a loose edge on the label of his beer bottle. "That's the reason I'm so grateful you talked to your dad for us. I have a feeling in my gut if he takes an interest in the program, it will buy time for me to train the talent in the wings." He took a drink. "I need a year to let the younger kids get bigger and some experience."

"You mean all these littler guys who just need to grow up."

"Yes! I can teach them the basics, and they already love the game. I can turn this program around. I know I can. I just need time."

Sipping her wine, Andi looked at him, nodded,

and licked her lips.

Mike couldn't breathe. It was all he could do to keep from reaching across the table, dragging her out of her seat, kissing her and touching her until she begged him to take her to bed. He pictured himself feasting on her, lifting her up in his arms, and carrying her out of the bar. Once he got her alone, he would explore her mouth with his tongue, he'd touch her breasts, kiss them, he'd make her so hot she'd scream with...

"Andrea. What a surprise to see you here."

A very crisp, very British, very cultured voice startled Mike out of his fantasy.

"Ian," Andi said. "This *is* a surprise. Umm..."

Mike noted that Andi was genuinely flustered. He might not be able to read books very well, but he had a good grasp on how to read women.

If he didn't miss his guess, and he rarely did, Andi Nelson was mighty uncomfortable at the moment. The thought had him twisting in his seat, trying to avoid the unpleasant punched-in-the-gut feeling Ian's presence at their table created.

Mike wanted to be the only one who made Andi Nelson sweat. He shifted again as he felt a little too big for his shirt collar, not to mention his jeans, which had managed to get more than a bit uncomfortable while he had been indulging in that hot fantasy of Andi Nelson naked.

He just bet ol' Ian here had a few fantasies about Andi of his own. Mike scowled.

"I've wanted to call you," said Sir Ian of the tweed blazer. Man, were there even suede elbow patches on that thing?

"Ian, have you met Mike Kelly? He's the football coach at Addington High."

Ian looked annoyed, but offered his hand. "Ian Ross." His expression was hostile and suspicious.

Mike rose out of his seat to shake Ian's hand.

"Nice to meet you." He hoped God would one day forgive him for being a big, fat liar.

Ian looked at Andi. "As I said, I've been meaning to call you."

"Please, Ian, don't worry about it." Was Andi blushing?

Ian slid his eyes over to Mike. "Well," he said, holding out his hand again. "Nice to meet you." He bent down and kissed Andi on the cheek. "Expect to hear from me soon." Ian straightened, then vanished.

After a short debate with himself about the wisdom of slaking his curiosity, Mike looked at Andi. "Am I poaching here?"

She grimaced. "Poaching? That's insulting. You make me sound like a big game trophy or something." Shaking her head, she reached for her drink and took a sip.

"Are you dating Joe Professor there?"

"No, not really. Ian and I go out every now and then. It's not serious. He's on the ballet board of directors with me." Her face blossomed into a lovely shade of pink.

"I have a feeling he wouldn't agree with you."

"Don't be ridiculous," she sputtered.

He smiled. It felt good to see Andi's oh-so-proper exterior crack just a bit. Of course, it had nothing to do with Andi denying having a thing with tweed boy.

Right.

"About the choir. Jeff and Tim are holding up their end of our deal. You should be pretty proud of them," Andi said in an obvious attempt to change the subject.

"That's good to hear. The sooner I can have them back, the better."

"They're doing some extra credit work to bring up their grades. I think it was Jeff's idea, but Tim is doing it too."

"You gonna make them sing solos? I'd pay money to hear that."

Andi laughed. "They'd die if I made them sing solos. No, I'm not *that* cruel. I've assigned them to do some research on the composers of the pieces we're preparing for the competition. Their papers are due tomorrow, actually. If they get them in on time, and if what they've done is any good, then maybe they'll have brought their grades up enough to get off the ineligible list." She sipped her wine again, being very careful to put it back in the wet circle on the napkin. "I'd have to crunch the numbers."

Mike went very still. "You wouldn't be putting me on about this, would you?"

"I wouldn't do that to you. If they've done their part, then they can suit up for practice on Thursday."

Man, did he dare hope? "That's pretty decent of you." He stopped himself from falling at her feet and genuflecting, but it was a close thing.

"I have my moments."

*Did she ever.* Right now, her eyes were sparkling at him, and her mouth was smiling *just* for him. He felt ten feet tall. He reached across the table and covered one of her hands with one of his.

Her tongue flicked out to wet her top lip. The gesture unconscious, he ran his thumb over her knuckles. Some pretty music twinkled around them, and Andi's eyes were wide and bright as she studied him in the bar's muted light. The attraction sparkled like fairy dust between them.

She tilted her head, looking at their joined hands, then at him. "What about you? Are you involved with anyone now?"

He shook his head and lifted her hand to his mouth. He felt her tremble in his easy grip. "There's no one in my life right now." He brushed her knuckles with his lips.

Her lips parted as she watched him kiss her hand. She looked frozen in place, afraid to move, afraid to breathe. Then, she shook her head and pulled her hand back. Her eyes narrowed. "Are you coming on to me because of my father?"

The abrupt shift in mood hit him like a cold slap in the face. Mike sat back in his chair and crossed his arms across his chest. The lady sure knew how to ruin a mood. "Talk about insults..."

She bowed her head. "It's a valid question."

Debating whether or not to just walk out on her, he counted to ten, gave it a moment of thought, and supposed that from her point of view, it was a valid question. Maybe. "No. I can guarantee you right now, your father is the last thing on my mind."

She looked back at him, and her eyes were filled with regret. "I'm sorry. I had to ask."

It was too bad, because the amazing mood was gone, popped away like a pin in a balloon.

Looking miserable, she picked up a pretzel and tapped it on the table. "Maybe we should just call it a night. I've got bus duty in the morning."

"Sure. No problem." Trying to be cool, he pulled out his wallet, selected a twenty, and threw it on the table. "Let's go."

They left in silence. As previously arranged, Mike drove Andi back to her car. This time she waited for him to come and open her door, he noted with surprise. She seemed to bring out this gallant side he didn't know he had inside him. He took her car keys and opened the door for her.

"Thanks for the drink, Mike. I had a good time."

"Me too." While handing her back her keys, he managed to take her hands in his and hold them there. He tugged on their linked hands and brought her closer to his body. She raised her face to look up to him.

"Just to be real clear here, I am *not* thinking of

your father right now." Mike figured he needed to make that clarification.

Slowly, oh so slowly, he brought his lips down to hers for the gentlest of kisses. Though it was the barest breath of a kiss, soft and beguiling, it packed the emotional wallop of a freight train. When his lips left hers, she lifted her mouth in an effort to bring his back, and he obliged her, just barely increasing the pressure and prolonging the kiss. She tasted of chardonnay and all his dreams come true.

More than a little wobbly, he pulled away. She looked at him and whispered, "Third time's the charm?"

He let go of her hands to put his on her waist. She twined her arms around his neck, snuggling in closer to his body. Their kiss was deeper, hotter this time, their tongues getting into the act. It was a long time before they surfaced for air.

"Wow." Andi was breathing hard.

"Yeah." If he didn't get her in her car very soon, they were going to end up making out like two horny teenagers in the parking lot. Reluctant, he pulled away from their embrace. "You need to get in that car and go home before it's too late."

Andi stared at him with wide eyes. "I suppose I do." Her throaty whisper told him she was just as aroused as he was. Pulling out of his arms, she managed to fold herself into her car. "Thanks again for the drink."

"Anytime."

Mike found himself standing in the night, watching her taillights disappear. He took a detour on his way home, deciding to go by way of the Old Quarry Road. He was restless and more than a little frustrated, needing to think. He pulled into the parking lot that overlooked the lake on the border of the quarry.

It didn't please him to find Jeff Myers' mom's

car parked in a secluded spot. Checking his watch, he was really ticked to see that it was after Jeff's curfew. A certain quarterback had some explaining to do.

Mike turned his lights down to parking lights and drove slowly by the car. The windows were pretty fogged up and from his vantage point, it looked like two shadowy figures were going at it hot and heavy.

He really didn't need this. He honked his horn to give them some time to pull themselves together, then got out of the car and walked slowly to where Jeff was parked.

Heaving a sigh, he put on his best coach face and knocked on the window. After a brief flurry of whispers and frantic *thonks* from inside the car, Jeff finally rolled the window down.

"Coach!" he yelped.

"Be glad it's me and not the daddy of the girl you've got in there." He looked past Jeff and was shocked to see Beth Pritchard. Just what he needed, Jeff fooling around with Andi's pet student.

"I was just giving Beth a ride home from her choir practice."

"I can see that. But, you know what? These roads aren't very safe at night. So, here's what we're gonna do. You're gonna drive Beth home, and I'm gonna follow you to make sure she gets there all safe and sound. How's that for a plan?"

"Uh, fine, Coach. It sounds like a great idea."

Mike nodded. "I thought you'd see it that way." He nodded once more and went back to his car. He got in and flashed his high beams twice to let them know he was ready to follow them.

Jeff and Beth, he mused. Mike barely knew her, but from what he did know, she was a sweet kid, quiet and shy. He didn't think she was the type of girl the captain of the football team would go for. It worried him. He knew Beth was special to Andi. He should talk to her; let her know what was going on.

But what if Andi got all protective of Beth? She already had a chip the size of Montana on her shoulder about football players. What if she changed her mind about Jeff? What if she didn't give his paper a good grade as some sort of payback for messing with Beth?

Man. Thinking about it made his brain hurt. He truly didn't need this. The stakes were too high. Taking the coward's way out, he decided not to say anything to Andi unless it was absolutely necessary. He wouldn't do anything to adversely affect Jeff's chance at eligibility.

## CHAPTER SEVEN

"This is good work, guys. You really did your homework." Suffused with pride in a job well done, Andi beamed at Jeff and Tim. She'd really turned these boys around. "I'll figure the grades for these with your participation grades. If the numbers add up, I'll go down to the office today and take you off the ineligible list."

Tim grinned. "Thanks, Ms. Nelson. We really appreciate it."

"You're welcome! Thanks for doing such a super job."

"See ya' later." Tim practically danced out of the auditorium. Jeff looked like he wanted to say something and then thought better of it. He nodded at Andi, and then followed Tim at a much slower pace.

Though puzzled at Jeff's attitude, Andi didn't say anything. She felt vindicated. The triumph of it fizzed in her veins. This was her first serious hurdle as a teacher in this school, she had taken a hard line, and it had paid off.

Life was sweet.

****

"Score!" Tim put out his hand for a high five from Jeff. "You are the man."

Jeff slapped Tim's hand, then shoved both his into his pockets. "I don't feel so great about this."

"What's not to feel good about?"

"We just got credit for something we didn't do."

"Dude! That all? Think of this as your reward for spending time with the music nerd."

"It's cheating. And don't call Beth that, especially after she helped us out."

Tim shrugged. "Did *Beth* have a problem writing those papers for us? Didn't she offer to?"

"Yeah, but... I dunno. I just don't feel good about it."

"Then think about this. Think about how great it will feel to be playing football again."

Jeff didn't say anything. He could tell Tim was getting mad at him, but he didn't know what to say.

Tim stopped in the middle of the hall, a queasy look on his face. "You're not thinking of turning us in, are you?"

Jeff shook his head. He wasn't. Not really. "I guess not."

"You better not."

"I said I wouldn't."

"Yeah, but you're acting all crazy lately. It must be the time you're spending with the music... Uh, with Beth."

Jeff looked at the floor. "Just shut up about her, okay? She did us this big favor, and we owe her."

Tim stared at him, then shook his head. "Whatever." He looked at his cell phone. "I gotta go." He gave Jeff a huge grin. "See you at practice."

"Yeah," said Jeff without enthusiasm. "See you at practice."

\*\*\*\*

"Well, this is good news for Mike." Dave looked at the papers Andi gave him. "Are you sure about this?"

"Absolutely. These papers show really good research and writing. I'm amazed, actually. I didn't expect this from those boys."

"Hmmmm."

"It restores my faith in my decision to stick to my guns. I really think the boys have learned their lesson."

"It sure looks that way."

"Anyway," Andi burbled on. "I'm sure we're over the hump with this. The boys know I mean business. They've lived up to their obligations, and we'll go on from here. This has really worked out. I was worried, I have to confess. I mean, to some people sports are the most important thing in life. It's not easy to take on the football team. Believe me, I know what I'm talking about." Laughing, she glanced at the clock. "I've got to set up for general music. You'll tell Mike the good news?"

Dave nodded as his eyebrows crashed together in the middle of his forehead. "You can be sure I'll talk to Mike."

****

"Mike Kelly?"

Mike looked away from the field where his team was running drills and faced the man who had come up beside him. Recognition was instant. He held out his hand. "That would be me. And you're Deke Nelson."

The tall blond man nodded and shook Mike's hand. "I am." Deke looked past Mike, out onto the field. "These your guys?"

Mike was thrilled right down to his toes. Deke Nelson was a freakin' football god. "Yeah. Thanks for coming out to talk to them. It's gonna mean so much to them." It was unsettling seeing Andi's eyes looking at him from his hero's face

Deke acknowledged that with a smile and a nod. "It's not every day that Andi calls me up and asks me for something."

"I appreciate that."

"Apart from that, I did some research, and I can't resist a challenge. Turning these kids into winners..." He shook his head.

Mike bristled. These were his boys, after all. "They're young."

Deke laughed. "They're shrimps."

"They'll grow."

Deke brought a hand up and rubbed his chin. "That they will."

The two men lapsed into silence while they watched Mike's team practice. Mike would log some things onto his clipboard and yell out instructions or encouragement to this kid or that kid as they tore up the field. Then, he split the kids into two teams and had them scrimmage. Through it all, Deke was quiet, but his eyes were busy, taking in all the action.

The guys were beside themselves when Mike brought Deke into the locker room after practice. Deke had deity status. His visiting them, talking to them, learning their names, was a thrill beyond belief. He answered all their questions and signed some autographs before he was done.

After all the fuss was over and all the kids had gone home, Mike took Deke to The End Zone for a beer. They settled into one of the few booths.

"You were right about those boys of yours, Mike. They've got heart."

"Right. They just need to grow up some."

Deke laughed. "The curse of high school football." He got serious. "Those two stars of yours looked a little off their game."

It took Mike a minute while he figured out who Deke was talking about. "You mean Jeff and Tim."

Deke nodded. "They played like crap today. Looked like they hadn't been on the field for a long time."

"They haven't. They were ineligible until today."

Deke snorted. "What fool teacher would flunk the only two players who can really play ball?"

"Your daughter."

Deke was momentarily stunned, then with a snort he came around. "Damn fool girl. Never had the proper respect for the game. It was all that ballet crap she was involved with." He shook his head. "Damn shame if you ask me."

Gina came with their beers, saving Mike from answering. It didn't take him long to figure out Deke Nelson was on a roll.

"I have never understood that girl. Ballet! I told her mother if she wanted to dance so much, she could be a cheerleader. Her mother said I just didn't understand. Hell no I didn't understand. I haven't had a clue what that girl was going to do since she was born Andrea instead of Andrew." Deke slugged down some beer.

Mike felt an inexplicable need to defend Andi. "She runs a tight choir."

"As well she should! I taught her everything she knows about being a leader." Deke stopped to gulp down some more beer, then looked at Mike with suspicion. "How do you know what kind of choir she runs? I didn't take you as a choir type of guy, if you know what I mean." Deke made a loose wrist kind of motion.

Mike *really* hated telling this story. "She got me to make a bet with her on the Rangers game a couple of weeks ago. This was before I knew about the deal with the twins. Not being stupid, I took Toledo."

Deke chuckled. "You lost big on that one."

"You're telling me. The boys had to stay in choir and behave until they did some extra credit stuff. I've got to sing with her church choir until Christmas."

"She really snookered you. I didn't know she had it in her. Maybe there's more of me in her than I thought." He seemed really proud.

"So Tim and Jeff did this extra credit stuff for her and are back on the team, and while I'd never admit it to Andi, I think they've learned a valuable lesson."

Deke hooted. "I bet you want me to keep that last little bit to myself."

"Please. I don't bet with anyone named Nelson anymore."

\*\*\*\*

Andi got a call from her mother that night, right as she was getting ready to dance off a little nervous energy. Though she had been at her parents' house for Sunday dinner last weekend, she was to be there again the next weekend. Oh, and, by the way, her father had invited Mike Kelly. Could she give him a ride?

Oh, yeah. She could easily do that. But did she really want to?

With a heavy sigh and an almost as heavy heart, she clicked on her music, Debussy's *La Mer,* and started to move and warm up. She only danced these days to keep in shape. It wasn't the force that drove her anymore, but she still had to be careful it didn't begin to take over her life like it had once before. Right now, she hoped the ritual movement would drive those pesky thoughts of Mike Kelly out of her head. He was exactly the type of man she'd sworn never to get involved with. She shouldn't let a few kisses change a very important lifelong rule: Never, ever get involved romantically with a football player, no matter how great he kissed.

But holy Hannah, could the man kiss! Her heart skipped a beat just thinking about it. Besides, if she were honest with herself, it was too late not to get involved. She'd been involved since making the decision to ask Deke to take a look at Mike's team.

She moved to the ballet barre she'd had installed in the spare bedroom of her condo and dipped into a rhythmic series of pliés. It also didn't hurt that Mike Kelly himself was extremely easy on the eyes and had more sex appeal than any man had a right to. The man was just way too distracting.

She shook her head. She just couldn't afford to be distracted right now. Making this high school choir an award winning choir and gaining the respect of the students, parents, and other teachers was paramount. If she could do that, then Deke would have to be proud of her, her life, and her choices. Nothing else should matter.

She lifted her leg onto the barre and pressed her forehead to her knee. It burned a little, and that was good. A bittersweet reminder of all she had lost and found. She supposed she had been as close to death as a person could get and come back from it. Her hospitalization after her collapse had been frightening and profoundly life changing. At one time, she would have thought the loss of her professional dance career was the end of the world. She'd been given a second chance with this new career, a chance to make a difference in the lives of kids, a chance to make her life over and celebrate what was right with her.

Her rag tag band of merry church singers was a huge part of that as well, part of what she needed to do to exorcise her demons. She pulled her leg down and switched sides, humming along with the CD. Mike was a part of that church group by her instigation. What had she been thinking?

Plain and simple, she *hadn't* been thinking.

She pulled her leg down and sat on the floor. Mike was all tangled up in her life now, not just the church choir, but with Deke and that whole mess. It was a problem, that was true, and she didn't usually have the patience to wait and see how things were going to work out. She had the feeling that this time she wasn't going to get a choice.

Andi walked into the faculty room the next morning to be greeted by a huge bouquet of flowers and Mike Kelly. He was signing for the flowers and tipping the delivery boy. He looked up when she walked in. "Just in time. These are for you."

She felt herself turn red, remembering those damn kisses. Managing to not swallow her tongue, she said, "Oh?" He flashed a grin that made her tingle all the way down to her toes. He looked better than any man had a right to look, and what his truly amazing butt did to a pair of sweatpants should be outlawed. "Thank you."

"Don't thank me; I was just here to get the delivery." He nodded to the delivery boy as the kid left, and put the flowers down on the Xerox machine. "There's a card." He plucked it out of the greenery and held it out to her. "Why don't you read it?"

The flowers must be from Ian. She took the note with caution. "Thanks." If this was what she thought it was, then she wished with every fiber of her being that Mike was not there right now. She opened the envelope and pulled out the card. She read it, then looked back at Mike. "Thanks."

Mike was looking at her as if she had just grown another head. He shook his own head and said, "Since I tipped the delivery boy, I should get to read the note."

"No way."

"C'mon. Be a sport."

"No!"

"Please?"

"No. It's personal."

Mike's eyes glittered with something she couldn't read. "Give me the card, Andi."

"I don't think... Hey!" she sputtered when he plucked it out of her hands. "Give that back!"

He held the card out between them and stared hard at her. It made squiggly type sensations run up and down her spine. Then he gave her his best bad boy smile. She shook her head, accepting the inevitable. She had two brothers, she knew that smile. There was no way she was getting that card back until Mike was done teasing her. "Go ahead and make your day, Mike. Read the card."

Mike's smile grew even bigger. "Dearest Andrea," Mike read. "Please accept this in the spirit in which it is offered. I never meant to push or offend you. Love, Ian." The smile left his face. "Is this the guy who was at the fern bar the other night?"

"None of your business."

"I beg to differ. Is this the same guy?"

Andi closed her eyes and gave in to the inevitable. "Yes."

"He wrote you some kind of poem or something on the back of the card."

"I'm not surprised. Ian is quite an accomplished poet."

"You could have fooled me. This poem is only three lines long. If this Ian is such a good poet, you'd think that he could come up with more than just three lines."

Andi gave him the most evil eye she possessed. "It's probably a Haiku. They've only got three lines."

"A Haiku."

"Yes."

"As in, 'There was an old man from Nantucket...'"

"That's not a Haiku."

"It isn't?"

"It's a limerick."

"Whatever."

Andi slumped. "Give me the card, Mike."

"You didn't say the magic word."

"Give me the card, Mike, before I punch you in the face."

He laughed. "You're cute when you're violent."

"Give me the card."

"Okay, okay. You win." He waved the card in

front of her face. "But you've got to admit that three lines is a pretty cheap poem."

She snatched the card out of his hand. "Cheap it may be, but it's mine. Get your grubby mitts off it."

"Done." He flicked a daisy with his finger. "What time are you picking me up on Sunday?"

"What?"

He didn't even blink. "What time are you picking me up on Sunday? For dinner. At your parents."

"Oh, that."

"Yeah. That."

Again, Andi couldn't read what he was thinking. "We can leave right after church." She paused. "That is, if you're coming to mass again this week."

"Isn't that my responsibility as a choir member?"

"If you were a typical choir member, I'd say yes. But you're not."

"While I'm in the choir, I'm in it for the whole enchilada. I'll be at mass on Sunday."

"Are you even Catholic?"

"With a name like Kelly, you have to ask?"

She snorted. "Right! You're probably more Catholic than I am."

"I was the head altar boy at St. Aloysius Ignatius the Impatient for five years straight."

"There is no saint named Aloysius Ignatius, impatient or otherwise."

"No? Maybe it was St. Alouette-gentille-Alouette."

"Right. And you sang every hymn as a round."

"Oh yeah. Is there any other way to sing them?"

"You've heard the church choir sing. They don't do rounds."

"I sit between Wally and Heinrich. You could have fooled me."

"Right. How silly of me to forget."

The bell rang to start the next class. Did she see

regret in his eyes? "I'll see you on Sunday."

"See you on Sunday."

\*\*\*\*

The Minutemen lost again on Friday, but the game had been close. Mike could tell Jeff and Tim were disappointed about the loss, but the younger kids were surprisingly upbeat. He chalked it up to Deke Nelson's visit.

Speaking of visits and Deke Nelson, Mike was very much looking forward to Sunday dinner. More important, he was looking forward to the drive to the Nelson homestead with Andi.

After that little episode in the teachers' lounge, he thought that his relationship with Andi would go nowhere. He was good enough for some hot kisses and some fun, but she was used to guys who wrote *poetry*, for chrissakes. He could barely read poetry, much less write it.

No. Not poetry. *Haikus*. Whatever the hell they were.

He shuddered.

In the scheme of things, writing Haikus was worse than singing in a church choir. Right?

It had to be.

\*\*\*\*

"I thought the music went well today."

Andi looked sideways at Mike before turning her attention back to the road. She had insisted on driving. "Really? What did you like about it?"

He shrugged. "It just sounded okay to me. And I knew where I was in the sheet music, most of the time. Wally only had to help me out three times."

Andi grunted. "You did a good job. I'm glad it's getting easier for you."

"Your excitement overwhelms me."

She kept her eyes on the road. "I'm sorry. You did fine. There were a lot of other problems, but you were just great."

Mike was intrigued. He hadn't noticed any problems. "What went so wrong?"

"Nothing, really. I just hate surprises, and the baptism today didn't go according to script. They should have let me know about several things."

"Like..."

"Like the mother's brother was going to do a special song."

"It was a good song."

"That's beside the point. I should have been told. And then there's the Ecumenical baptism, and getting two pastors for the price of one."

"I thought that part was kind of cool. We only ever got the Catholic point of view at St. Aloysius Ignatius the Impatient. Sister Mary Margaret wouldn't have allowed anything else."

Andi arched a brow. "I would bet there was never a Sister Mary Margaret. You're making her up."

"Am not. Sister Mary was one hell of a basketball player. She had a killer jump shot."

"You are so full of bull."

"Yes, I am. But at least I got you to smile."

He watched her face shut down.

"About Sunday dinner. You've met the Coach. He can be pretty opinionated."

Mike laughed. "Yes, he can. He practically accused me of being gay because I was singing with your church choir."

"He didn't!"

"He did. It was funny."

"What did you tell him?"

Mike wanted to ask her why she cared what he told her father. "I told him about how you played me for a sucker."

"What did he say?"

"That there was more of him in you than he thought. I think he was proud of you."

Her laughter sounded bitter. "Right. I can get a master's degree in music, and he says nothing. I con you, I get you to make a bet you have no business making, and he's proud of me. Go figure."

"I didn't have to make that bet. Truth be told, I was more than willing to con you. I got what I deserved."

"Tim and Jeff have really gotten their acts together. Especially Jeff."

*Riiiight.* Jeff was getting something together, but Mike wasn't sure it was his act. More likely, he was getting *the* act together, with sweet little Beth Pritchard. Guilt swamped him. He knew he should tell Andi about his suspicions, but he just didn't know what to say. He looked at her. She was beautiful, inside and out, and he wanted her. He cleared his throat, ready to do the manly thing and 'fess up. "About Jeff-,"

"He's really working hard. The paper he turned in was dynamite. It's a tribute to your leadership skills that he just buckled down and did that kind of work to get back on the eligible list."

Mike was dubious about the kind of work Jeff did to get back on the eligible list. "Yeah, well..." He just couldn't find the words to tell her. Time to change the subject. "What was it like growing up as Deke Nelson's daughter?"

Her frown immediately came back. She seemed to struggle with herself. "Deke wasn't around much. You know pro football. He was always on the road. Mom was always there for us, though." She checked the rearview mirror before putting her blinker on and pulling into the left lane to pass a semi. "What about you? What's your family like?"

"I had a hopelessly normal childhood. Dad was a construction worker. He died about two years ago."

"I'm sorry."

"Yeah. Lung cancer. Mom stayed at home while

we were kids, but she went to work when I went to college."

"Brothers? Sisters?"

"One sister. Evelyn. She's married, got a couple of kids. They're great."

"Do you see them often?"

"Not as often as I should. Thanksgiving, Christmas, Mom's birthday."

She didn't ask any other questions, and Mike couldn't tell what she was thinking. It bugged him.

"Nice place," Mike said as they pulled into Andi's parents' driveway.

"I guess. I didn't grow up here. We lived..."

"In Texas. I know. Deke was one of my idols when I was a kid."

\*\*\*\*

Andi looked at Mike and saw the anticipation on his face. She bit back a sigh, opening the front door. "Come on in. I'll take you to meet Mom and then we can round up the Coach."

"Mike! It's about time Andi got you here." Deke boomed as he hurried over to greet them. He and Mike exchanged vigorous handshakes. "Come on into the den, and I'll get you a drink." He looked at Andi for the first time. "Your mother's in the kitchen. I know she wants to see you." Andi stood and watched her father lead Mike down the hall.

Now, wasn't that just dandy? The boys were bonding.

She made her way to the kitchen, getting there just as her mother was pulling a massive lasagna out of the oven. "Hi, Mom."

Pamela straightened and turned to face Andi. There was a huge smile of welcome on her face. "Hi, sweetie." She put the pan of lasagna on top of the stove and crossed the room to give Andi a big hug. Andi met her halfway. "I thought you were bringing a guest."

"I was told to deliver Mike Kelly here today. The Coach has absconded with him, into the inner sanctum."

Pamela stood back and studied Andi's face. "Please don't start a scene with your father today."

"*Moi*? I never start scenes with Deke."

"Andi..."

"Mother..."

They stared at each other for a couple of seconds. Pamela was the first to cave. "Just behave, okay?"

"Call me Saint Andrea."

"Right." Pamela looked for, then located, a bowl of salad greens. She grabbed a bowl of homemade dressing. "Put this on the salad and toss it." She handed the bowl to Andi. "When you're done with that, go get your father and Mike, and tell them we're ready to eat."

"I live to serve."

"Hold that thought."

Andi pushed the door to her father's lair open and couldn't believe her eyes. The Barcaloungers were still in a line in front of the magnificent 'wall o' TV'. Only, instead of the twins being ensconced there, learning of life and football from the master, there was Mike Kelly.

The two of them sat next to each other, mesmerized by the football video flickering on the screen. As they watched, one or the other would point out something of interest.

She felt something inside her shrivel and die at the sight of Mike sitting and watching videos with her father. "Mom says dinner's ready."

Deke didn't turn to look at her, but said, "Okay. Be right there."

Mike got up out of the chair. "Can I help with anything?"

"No." Andi left the room before she said

something rude.

****

Mike stared after Andi, perplexed. His mother would have skinned him alive if he hadn't offered to help, but Andi took off as if he had asked her if he should decapitate some kittens.

Deke saved him further speculation. "We'd better head on in. My wife gets feisty if we wait too long after she sets food on the table."

Mike followed Deke into the dining room. Andi wasn't there, but her mother was. She flashed him a bright smile. "Hi. You must be Mike Kelly. I'm Pamela Nelson."

"It's a pleasure to meet you, Mrs. Nelson. Thank you for the invitation."

"Andi's friends are welcome here anytime. And please, Mrs. Nelson makes me feel old. Call me Pam."

Mike could see where Andi got her stunning good looks. Pamela Nelson had the same classic beauty, except for the eyes.

Andi had her father's eyes, crystal blue eyes that didn't miss a trick.

"Hope you're hungry, Mike." Deke clapped Mike on the back. "My Pammy is one helluva cook."

"It smells great," he said, as he sat down. He meant it. The room filled with the aroma of tomatoes and cheese, of garlic and basil.

"Of course, some people are too good to eat the food that everyone else eats." Deke directed this at Andi, who was coming in with a basket of garlic bread.

"Please don't start this, Deke." Pamela's voice was soft, but brooked no disobedience. After all, this was the woman who had raised the Terrible Twins. She looked back at Mike. "I hope you like lasagna."

"Like the great philosopher Garfield, I never met lasagna I didn't like."

Pamela smiled and went back into the kitchen. Andi took her place across the table from Mike. He waited for Pamela to return before he sat down. She returned almost immediately with a plate topped with some sliced white stuff mixed with spinach, pasta and carrots. "Please, Mike, sit down." She seemed pleased at the courtesy.

Deke grumbled at the sight of that plate, which Pamela placed in front of Andi. "Pammy I don't see why you..."

"Not one word, Deke." She cut a healthy sized slice out of the lasagna. "Give me your plate, Mike."

He tried to be polite and not look at Andi's plate, but he couldn't help himself. She was scraping all the carrot pieces to one side of the plate and all the pasta to another. Was she sick? Did she have to be on some special diet?

Andi glanced up and caught Mike looking at her. "Would you like some of the tofu?"

He barely suppressed a shudder. Ack, tofu! "No, thank you. This is great!" he added to Pamela as he tucked into the food.

"Thank you."

Deke muttered something Mike couldn't make out. Andi must have, because she blushed bright red and kept her eyes glued to her plate.

Pamela jumped into the breach. "Have you lived in Addington long, Mike?"

"Three years. I needed a change, the coaching position opened up at AHS, and I applied. It's really been a challenge, but that's good."

"It's a lovely town, with so much to offer." Pamela smiled. "I was so glad when we moved back here after Deke retired. Now that Andi lives here, I've got my family all close by."

Mike forked up some lasagna and stuck it in his mouth. He'd have sighed, had he been that kind of guy. "This lasagna really *is* great, Pamela. I can't remember the last time I tasted anything this good."

"Thank you. I love to cook."

"My Pammy is a magician in the kitchen. You should taste her pot roast." Deke looked pointedly at Andi. "Of course, some people wouldn't know."

Andi looked at her mother. She was clearly having trouble controlling her temper. "Mother," she said in a tone usually heard coming out of the mouths of annoyed eighth grade girls.

Pamela looked at Andi. "How are plans for the ballet fundraiser coming?"

Andi perked up, her eyes suddenly shining with enthusiasm. "The details are really falling into place. We've found a lovely Big Band for the dancing and have received several extremely generous donations for the goods and services auction. We were having trouble with the caterer, but Nancy Drake managed to find someone really..."

"You should see this team of Mike's, Pammy. Biggest bunch of runts you've ever seen. Getting 'em to even come close to winning is gonna take a miracle."

"That's where you come in, Deke. You're our miracle." Mike snuck a glance over to Andi and got a sinking feeling when he saw how her mouth had formed a thin, bloodless line across her face. He hoped to steer the conversation back to Andi's ballet thing. It didn't look like that was going to happen.

He was dead meat.

Deke was unperturbed. "We'll see. Like I said, they're young and they're small. But, I think I have some ideas about how to get around that. Now, those two seniors of yours, what are their names again?"

"Tim Baldwin and Jeff Myers."

"Yeah, that's right. The twins are in town this week, starting Wednesday. I can get 'em to come to a practice and work some of their moves with your boys."

Mike was momentarily stunned. "Wow. That would be very generous if they could do that. Tim and Jeff would be beside themselves."

"It'll be fun. The twins'll have a blast."

"I hope Tim and Jeff are up to the challenge. Buck and Brock seem to communicate telepathically or something."

"It's eerie, ain't it? Pammy tells me that it's a twin thing. There are times in the game video that I think those kids of yours do the same thing." He waved a forkful of lasagna around in front of him. "I don't think it would take much to get 'em working like that all the time. I think it's worth a shot."

"Well, I know the boys will love it..." Mike was interrupted by the scrape of Andi's chair as she pushed away from the table. Never had Mike seen so much hostility directed at him, not from one woman.

And he had made a lot of women plenty mad at him.

"I think I'll go start the coffee." With that, Andi left her still full dinner plate and went into the kitchen.

Deke shook his head. "You spoil that girl, Pammy. Here you go to all this trouble to make her a separate meal, and she doesn't even have the manners to finish it. I don't get it."

Pamela looked at him, her shoulders slumped and her eyes heavy. "That much is obvious." She winced when she heard a loud crash come from the kitchen. She looked at Mike apologetically. "I'd better go see what happened." She got up. "Please, do keep eating. I'm sure I'll be right back."

Mike was beyond curious about what had just happened. A few more bangs and thuds from the kitchen only fueled his desire to know more.

Deke stabbed the air with his fork as he talked around a mouthful of lasagna. "You should just leave her alone, Pam. She's in one of her moods."

Pamela opened her mouth to say something, then just shook her head and followed Andi into the kitchen.

"Now, Mike, as I was saying about these boys. Here's what I think we need to do..."

****

"Your mother is an awesome cook. I don't think I'll need to eat for the rest of the week."

Andi didn't even spare Mike a look. She kept her eyes glued on the road. "She isn't happy unless she's feeding people."

"Well, she can keep on feeding me. I haven't had an apple pie that good in...ever!"

Andi's stomach rumbled, and she tamped down the familiar, welcome ache. She'd have to force herself to eat when she got home. She had an emergency protein bar in her glove compartment, but she wouldn't be able to choke down a bite in front of Mike. "I'm sure your mother cooks and makes a pie that's just as good."

Mike shook his head. "Not like that."

"Well." Her stomach growled again, and she prayed Mike didn't hear it. "I'll pass on the compliment."

"Thanks. And thank your father again for his incredibly generous offer." Out of the corner of her eye, Andi saw Mike shake his head. "If Jeff and Tim can learn a third of your brothers' moves, then we'll be golden."

"Hmmmmm." Andi needed to end this conversation *now*. "Mind if I turn on some music?"

"Not at all."

Andi turned on the radio, and Wagner's *Ride of the Valkyries* came blasting out. She smiled for the first time that afternoon. Music depicting vengeful women warriors streaking down from the sky and wreaking havoc on too-macho-for-their-own-good men suited her mood to a T. She smiled when she saw Mike try to conceal a grimace.

They rode on without speaking for a while. Andi was grateful for it. Then, Mike reached over and turned down the radio. "You never finished telling about your big fundraiser thing."

"That's right." Her jaw clenched so hard, her teeth almost cracked.

"When is it?"

"November twelfth."

"And you're raising money for the ballet?"

"Yep."

He looked at her, seemingly determined to make amends. If she were going to be perfectly fair, it wasn't his fault her father hated her. She just didn't feel like being fair at the moment.

"If you'd like to tell me about it, I'd like to hear."

*Sure you would.* "It's a dinner/dance with a goods and services auction tacked on. It's $25.00 a ticket, $40.00 a couple. It's the launch party for our new capital campaign. We want to build a home for the company, with enough studio space to expand our education and outreach programs."

Mike continued to look at her, his expression unreadable. Not that she wanted to read it anyway. Shifting so he could reach into his back pocket, he pulled out his wallet. Taking out two twenties, he tossed them on the dash and said, "Leave a couples ticket in my mailbox at school."

She wanted to tell him to save his money. "I didn't peg you for the ballet type."

"I'm not. I hate ballet. But you've done me a favor, and I want to return it. Not," he added, "that buying a couple of tickets to a dinner dance are anywhere near what you've done for me. Getting Deke to take an interest in the team might just save my job. I can't thank you enough for that."

"Don't mention it." *Really, I mean it. The less said the better.*

He grinned, but it was a pale imitation of his usual lady-killer smile, like he lacked confidence, or something.

In her experience, football players, like Deke and the twins, never lacked confidence. Or ego.

"I was wondering, well, if you don't yet have an escort for the evening, if you'd consider going with me."

*Oh, it got worse,* she thought. *A pity date.*

"I'm sorry. I already have an escort for the evening," she said. "Ian Ross. You met him the other night."

Mike scowled. "The guy at Esmeralda's."

"Yes."

She hazarded a glance at Mike. His eyes narrowed before he looked out the window. "Is this the Haiku guy?"

"The Haiku guy?"

"Yeah." Mike scowled. "The flowers the other day. The ones that came with the Haiku. The guy that sent them. He's your date?"

"Yes." Though why Mike should care was beyond her. He should be glad to be off the hook and not be stuck taking her to the gala.

He regarded her, his expression dark. "Forget I asked, then." Turning his head, he looked out his window and didn't try to make conversation with her for the rest of the ride home.

She could have sworn he was pouting.

****

A few hours later, Andi sat on her couch in front of the TV, choking down a cheese omelet and a salad. Each bite was harder to eat than the one previous, but eat she did because she wouldn't lose more of her life to her disease.

She'd been stupid to let her father get her so upset she couldn't eat. Her stomach had cramped up so badly, she literally could not force a bite down her throat, and keeping down what little she had swallowed was a true challenge to her will power.

Most days she had the anorexia under control. She ate on a schedule and made sure she pushed the protein. She didn't own a scale, so she wouldn't be tempted to diet. She kept the name of her therapist from the eating disorder clinic in Arizona in her address book, just in case. She was better, but she knew anorexia was like alcoholism or drug abuse; she could very easily sabotage her own recovery.

She swallowed a chunk of omelet then forked up another one, mentally chewing twenty-five times before she swallowed. Six years ago, when she'd collapsed at dance class and had to be hospitalized, she'd thought her life was over. It took a lot of time, therapy, and trust to get her life back. She'd made her peace with the fact Deke wasn't going to be proud of a mere music teacher for a daughter, but being a professional ballerina was just no longer in the cards.

He hadn't come to her intervention. He'd been on the road, but she knew that was just an excuse. He thought she was a fussy eater because she wanted attention. He didn't know the pressure to be perfect, to be in control of your every movement. He never respected the amount of physical work she'd done to get where she was as a dancer, and she was tired of waiting for his approval.

So, screw him. Let him adopt Mike Kelly and his hapless football team. Andi would be all right without both of them.

CHAPTER EIGHT

"Ballet? You want to take me to the ballet?" Gina chirped. It sounded like she was going to burst into laughter any second.

Mike looked at her, hunched his shoulders, and felt more than a little embarrassed. "Could you announce it any louder?"

"Well, it's certainly not your usual idea for a night out. What's up?"

"Nothing. I bought a ticket for this fundraiser for the ballet as a sort of a favor for a friend, and I thought you might like to go. You know, get dressed up, dance, and drink champagne." Mike shrugged, trying not to look like a fool. "That's all."

She tapped the pen she took orders with against her pursed mouth and deliberated with all the seriousness of a first time voter in the polling booth. "When is it? I'll have to ask Bobby for the night off."

"You've got time. The thing is on November twelfth."

"Okay. I'll let you know." She looked over his shoulder. "Gotta run. Table twenty over there is waving for some refills." Gina hustled away.

Mike turned his attention to his plate, picked up his burger, and took a healthy bite. He was in mid-chew when he realized that Dave was staring at him. "What?"

"I take it the friend in question is Andi Nelson."

Mike swallowed. "Yeah. What about it?"

"Nothing. Nothing at all. She's a nice lady."

"She's a strange lady. I can never figure where I stand with her." He picked up a French fry and salted it liberally. "Take yesterday, for example."

"Yesterday?"

Mike crunched down on the fry, savoring the taste of grease and salt. "I got an invitation to have dinner at her parents', courtesy of Deke himself. She's supposed to be there too, so I catch a ride with her. On the way there, we had a great time. We were really getting along. I'm thinking, that's cool, especially after last Wednesday."

"What happened Wednesday?"

"We went out for a drink after choir rehearsal. And if I was reading her signals right, she was attracted to me."

"Oh really?"

"Don't mess with me. I know when a woman's interested."

"So then, dinner with the great one didn't go so well?"

"It was...interesting. Her mother is a very nice lady, and Deke is really bending over backwards for the team. In fact..." Another French fry went the way of the previous one. "He's going to arrange for the twins to work with Jeff and Tim. You know, teach them some of their moves."

"That's fantastic. When?"

"Hopefully some time before the next game."

"Andi was okay with this?"

"That's a good question. I have no idea. When we got to the house, it was like somebody turned a switch off. She got real quiet. And she was outright hostile on the way home. That was why I bought the tickets to the ballet thing. I wanted to cheer her up."

"Did it work?" Dave was grinning like a freakin' idiot. Mike hoped he wouldn't end up having to punch him.

"If anything, she got more pissed off. I asked her to go with me, but she already had a date."

Dave's grin got bigger. "So you asked Gina to go

instead."

"Well, sure. We're buds. We might get a few laughs out of it."

Dave's smile dimmed a little. "Be careful. Maybe Gina wants to be more than buds."

"No, she doesn't. Gina wants the same thing from me that I want from her—friendship and a few laughs." Mike was absolutely certain on that front.

Dave shook his head. "And what do you want from Andi Nelson?"

Mike wiped his mouth with his napkin. "Good question. Hot, mind-blowing sex would be a great place to start." He was certainly more than willing to hit the sheets with Andi Nelson.

Dave laughed. "And end, probably. You have nothing in common with her."

"Maybe, maybe not. She's fun to be with when she's not ticked off."

"Knowing you, I'm surprised she's not ticked off all the time."

"It's a close call." Mike cocked a brow. "How come we're always talking about my love life and not yours? What's Laura up to these days?"

"Making more hints about getting married than I'm comfortable with. I'm trying to slow things down, like to a stop."

"I'm never getting married. No one could put up with me."

"Sad, but true." Dave chuckled at Mike's muttered expletive, then got serious. "I think I'd like to get married someday. It would be great to have a couple of kids." Dave shrugged, grinned. "I'm just saving myself for the right woman."

****

The arrival of Andi's twin brothers at Addington High was a much touted and heralded event. It drove Andi crazy.

Not that she didn't love her brothers, she did.

104

But they were football players, not deities.

She stood alone in the auditorium, trying to concentrate on the section of music in Thompson's *Alleluia* her choir was having trouble with. It was hard work for the kids to sing so softly for so long. There had to be a new way to help them with that. She looked at the score, but couldn't hear a note. Disgusted with herself, she threw the music on the piano.

An uncomfortable ball formed in her throat, and she worked to swallow around it. Damn. She would not cry. All her life she'd been second-best to the twins. She should be used to it. As far as Deke was concerned, the sun rose and set on Buck and Brock. She had hoped she could escape that here at Addington High, but she couldn't. Most likely, she never could. She was destined to live forever in the shadow of the twins.

"Penny for your thoughts." Mike Kelly had somehow managed to get into the auditorium without her hearing him. He stood in the back of the room like a penitent sinner on the threshold of the Sistine Chapel.

Andi cleared her throat and blinked quickly a few times as he walked down the center aisle. "Believe me, they're not worth that much."

Mike just looked at her. "I want to know what I did the other day that made you angry."

"You didn't make me angry. I'm just fine." She flashed him her biggest, phoniest smile. "See?"

"Well, something made you mad as hell." He crossed his arms over his chest and planted himself right smack dab in front of her, almost daring her not to tell him.

She would put bamboo sticks under her fingernails before she would tell him she was jealous of how he and her father had bonded. "Nothing. Nothing at all. In fact, everything was just the way a visit to my parents' always is."

Mike blew out a breath. "Oooo-kay." He bent his head and rubbed a hand across the back of his neck. "Well, I guess I'd better go back to the gym and try to control the crowd. Everybody's pretty excited about your brothers' visit."

"No kidding." She tapped the music score against the top of the piano.

He narrowed his eyes, studying her. "I don't get it. I'd think you would be proud of their success."

"I am proud of them."

"Then what's your problem?"

Andi slapped her hand down on the top of the piano, crumpling the music. Just like that, years of jealousy, frustration, and resentment rolled up in a wave and slammed into her. "You want to know what my problem is? I'll tell you. It's football."

Mike looked like she'd just told him Santa Claus didn't exist. "Football?"

"Yeah. Football."

"What's wrong with football? It's a great game."

"It's a *stupid* game. The twins are good at playing a stupid, idiotic *game*, and everyone treats them as if they found the key to world peace, a cure for cancer *and* had the ability to tap dance upside down while blowing smoke and whistling *Dixie!*" She closed her eyes, took in a deep breath, and carefully unclenched her hands. "There. You happy?" She opened her eyes.

The stricken look on his face surprised her. Well, he had wanted to know. Be careful what you ask for and all that. She had only told the truth. "Please leave me alone now, Mike. I need a little space."

Mike lifted both hands. "No problem. Consider me gone." Seconds later, he made good on that promise and vanished like a poof of smoke.

She dropped onto the piano bench and leaned

her arms across the music rack. Drained of anger, overwhelmed with guilt, she leaned her head on her hands, cursing herself for caring about Mike Kelly.

****

Stupid! Stupid, stupid, *stupid*! He should have known better.

Mike stormed down the hallway to his office. He opened the door, slammed it behind him, and paced.

Andi had just dismissed his life and his work as stupid and idiotic.

Well, he was certifiably stupid if he thought he could ever have some kind of... of... *thing* with Andi Nelson.

Forget it! No matter how strong their chemistry was he would never get involved with a woman who called him stupid.

No one was ever going to call him stupid again. That he had vowed when he had been held back and had to repeat the second grade. Not promised. Vowed.

And he'd done it, too. He had confessed to his mother about his reading problems, and she had camped out at the school to make sure they got him the support he needed. Then, he'd discovered his talent for reading football plays and for thinking outside the box to come up with maneuvers that were creative and unexpected. He got into college on a football scholarship and worked like a fiend to get his teaching degree. He'd accomplished a lot in spite of his learning disorder. He was proud of that.

But sometimes the angry, humiliated boy wasn't very far away.

He stopped pacing and threw himself into his desk chair. Football was not a stupid game. It was his salvation. Maybe he couldn't read words and numbers so well, but he could read football plays. Because of his dyslexia, he could think outside the box and come up with some creative plays of his own.

On the football field he wasn't dumb. He wasn't *stupid*. He was respected. *Respected*.

Damn it! He picked up a pencil, tapped it on the blotter then snapped it in half. Since it made him feel better, he picked up another pencil and broke that one too.

The only thing that held importance was his team. He would focus on what was right for them and stay clear of Andi and her problems with her father.

****

Because she supposed it was expected of her, Andi went down to the practice field after school to watch her brothers work with Jeff and Tim. It turned out to be a wise call, because her father was there as well, clearly expecting to see her.

"'Bout time you got here, girl. What kept you?"

"Just a little thing called work." She shaded her eyes with her hand. The day was cold but the sun was fierce. "You know, as in my job. I'm not free to come and go as I please." She rubbed at her middle as her stomach started to churn.

Deke noticed the motion, grunted, and turned his attention back to the field, his expression unreadable. They stood side by side in silence.

It *was* a wonder how the twins communicated and moved. She was just sick of hearing about it. Still, they were able to get Jeff and Tim to duplicate some of their easier plays. Andi turned her attention from the field and scanned the bleachers to see who was there.

The entire male population of the school, that's who. Well, duh. What did surprise her was to see Beth Pritchard there. She didn't know Beth followed football.

"The boys are doing pretty well." Dave Mason, looking every inch the harried vice principal he was, came up next to her to watch the team practice.

"Hey, Dave." Andi smiled. She liked him. He was a good guy. "Have you met my father yet?"

"No, I haven't had the pleasure."

"Coach, this is Dave Mason. He's the vice principal here at AHS. Dave, meet my father, Deke Nelson."

The two men shook hands. "It's nice meeting you, sir. I've been a fan for a lot of years."

"Nice to meet you too. Call me Deke. I hope my daughter isn't giving you too much trouble."

"She can be a handful, but we manage to keep her in line."

Deke chuckled. "Well, good luck. I sure couldn't keep her on the straight and narrow."

Andi muttered a curse under her breath. Deke didn't hear it and returned his attention to the team, but the amused smile Dave gave her embarrassed her.

Dave cleared his throat. "It's a great thing you're doing for our boys, Deke."

"They're good kids." Deke didn't look away from the field.

"Yes, they are."

Andi tuned out the conversation. She couldn't bear to hear one more word about Jeff and Tim, never mind Buck or Brock.

A chilly gust of wind tugged on her hair. She looked back out to the field as she pulled her hair back out of her eyes, just in time to catch Mike watching her. He looked away as soon as her gaze met his. She brutally ignored the sense of regret that flashed through her. She had enough regrets in her life. She wasn't going to let Mike Kelly be another one.

\*\*\*\*

Friday dawned dark and damp. No, not damp. Rainy. Monsoons brought less rain, Mike thought as he looked out his bedroom window.

It'd be okay. A little cold, maybe, but okay. Whether they won or they lost, he had done his best. No matter his own future, he would make certain the kids felt good about themselves.

And, if he lost, he hoped the next coach felt the same way.

**\*\*\*\***

Andi refused to go to the game. Her story—and she was sticking to it—was she had ballet board business to take care of. She could come up with all sorts of ways to spend a Friday night.

She lounged around her apartment in her oldest sweats and a tee shirt. Her hair was piled up in a ponytail on top of her head. Thick socks coddled her feet.

She ate mocha chip ice cream for dinner. Lots of it. In fact, she ate the whole half-gallon.

She immediately regretted it and felt sick. To work it off, she cleaned out her refrigerator. Then, feeling ambitious, she reorganized her closets. Plural. She also repapered her kitchen cabinets.

She alphabetized her spice rack.

Eventually, in the middle of the evening, she ran herself a bubble bath with water that was too hot and shaved everything worth shaving. She stayed in until she was prune city, then got out and moisturized and powdered to her heart's content.

She refused to call anyone to find out how the game went.

**\*\*\*\***

"Hey, Mikey! It was close."

Mike nodded to the guy sitting at the bar in The End Zone. "Sure was, Joe. The boys played real hard."

Joe nodded before turning his attention back to his beer and the ESPN channel flickering on the TV above the bar. Mike made his way through the crowd to his usual table.

Dave was already there, and Mike made a mental grimace when he saw Laura sitting next to him. Just what he needed, quality time with the Queen of Snarky Remarks. "Hey." He pulled up a chair and sat down.

"The boys played really well tonight, Mike. I think-"

"Too bad they lost anyway." Laura stretched a hand in front of her to examine her manicure.

Dave glared at her. "Aren't you being a little harsh?"

She looked back at him, the picture of innocence. "It's the truth."

"It's okay, Dave. I can take it." Mike grabbed a pretzel out of the bowl on the table. "The boys played the best they've played all season, and they still lost. Shit happens. But it doesn't make me any less proud of them. They did their damnedest to try to win."

Laura grabbed her purse. "I'm going to the ladies room."

"Have fun."

Both men watched her walk away. "I thought you were cooling things off with Vampira."

"I am. She just showed up here and invited herself to sit down." Dave shook his head. "I'm not having a good time."

"Seen Gina around?"

"Last I saw her was about a half hour ago. Maybe she's taking a break."

"Yeah." Mike caught the eye of a waitress and motioned for a beer. "Man, I've had better days."

"Focus on the good stuff. Focus on how this group of kids is going to get better and better, and in a few years, how they'll be winning more often than losing."

"For another coach. After this season, I might well be out of a job."

"Your losing this job isn't a given. We have ways to fight Steve Windley and Betty Kincaid."

Gina brought Mike his beer. "Hey there, Mikey." She bent down and kissed his cheek. "Sorry about the game."

"Yeah, me too."

She ran a hand over his head, smoothing some hairs into place. "Bobby's making onion rings, though. Want some?"

Mike's spirits lifted a little bit. He sure as hell loved Bobby's onion rings. "That's the best offer I've had all day."

She gave him a warm smile. "Stick around then. You want a burger with that?"

"Sounds great."

"Comin' right up." And she was gone.

He turned back to Dave, who was making short work of a Buffalo wing. Mike's stomach growled as he reached a hand out to snag one.

"Help yourself." Dave nodded at the bowl.

Mike shoved the wing in his mouth. It was hot and spicy, just the way he liked it.

Dave cleared his throat as he wiped his fingers with his napkin. "I need to give you a heads up." He picked up another wing and dipped it in blue cheese. "You can't tell anyone, or else my butt'll be in a sling."

"Great. Just what I need. More bad news."

"Yeah. We just got word from the state that our aid is being cut by about 25%. A bunch of programs are gonna take big hits. No one's decided anything yet, but with today's loss, and the fact that the head of the school board and the superintendent are out to get you..."

"I can kiss my new practice equipment good-bye."

"Maybe not. There are a lot of other projects that could be affected. But I thought you should know."

Dave looked up and beyond Mike, then swore. "Laura's on her way back. Don't say anymore, okay? She can't keep her mouth shut. The last thing I need is her shooting off her mouth in the faculty lounge."

"Yeah, sure." Mike had no trouble ignoring Laura Plunkett. She might be a great math teacher but she could be a real witch.

Laura made it back to the table, surrounded by a heavy cloud of perfume. Mike had to work not to gag. Without warning, the memory of Andi's scent, soft, subtle, and sexy as hell, slammed into him. It didn't do much to improve his attitude.

Somehow, she was always there, on the edges of his mind, ready to dance in and out of his consciousness at any given moment. His already blue mood sank some more.

His mood hit bottom as Laura began to chatter. Her voice was high pitched, and she had to shout to be heard over the noise in the bar. It twanged nerves already stretched too taut.

No doubt, this had not been one of his better days.

****

Bright and early Monday morning, however, Mike felt a welcome surge of pride as he looked at the boy standing across the desk from him. "That's awesome, Jeff. When did you find out?"

"I got a phone call last night. I didn't expect to hear anything for at least another month." He shrugged. "I'm supposed to keep it quiet until it's official, because of the rules and all."

Mike raised his eyebrows. "Wow. That was fast. Did they give you any reason?"

"Coach Nelson made a few phone calls."

Mike wasn't surprised. Deke had really taken a liking to Jeff and Tim. Of course he would make a few phone calls to the right people to finagle some football scholarships for the boys. And because it

113

was Deke asking, maybe even fronting a bit of his own money, the athletic departments of the boys' colleges of choice would be impressed. "You're going to take it."

"Yeah, I'm taking it. My mom is over the moon. Boston College is a good school and has a good program." Jeff's grin was sheepish. "It's close to home, too. Mom likes that part."

"I bet. And here I thought she couldn't wait to get rid of you." Mike scratched his chin. "I don't recall BC being on your short list of schools." Mike narrowed his eyes as he took in Jeff's rapidly flushing face. "As a matter of fact, I thought you wanted to get out of New England. What's up?"

Jeff's expression closed up. Not good, Mike thought. There's more going on here than football. He'd come across Jeff and one cute little piano player wrapped around each other, making out like they'd invented it, more than once.

And, damn, he knew he should tell Andi, but he couldn't bring himself to. "So, I suppose Beth is going to school in Boston too?"

Jeff looked surprised. "She's applied to New England Conservatory for early admission. She'll find out if she gets accepted in a couple of weeks."

"What if she doesn't get in? You're stuck in Boston, and she'll be somewhere else."

"If she doesn't get into New England Conservatory, there are other schools in Boston. Her parents won't let her move too far away."

"Hmmmm." Mike rubbed his chin. He didn't like the defiant light in Jeff's eyes. "What if you break up before you get to Boston?"

"We won't."

"How can you be sure?"

"What do you mean?"

"How long did you go out with your last girlfriend?"

114

Jeff's mouth made a sullen pout. "I don't know. I can't remember."

"Have you gone out with any girl for longer than a couple of months?"

"It's not like that with Beth. She's really special."

"Didn't you think your other girlfriends were special?"

"That was before I knew Beth."

The kid looked so goo-goo eyed, Mike wanted to shake him. "Are you having sex with her?"

The goo-goo eyes filled with horrified mortification. "I don't think that's any of your business."

But Mike could tell. Jeff and Beth were having sex. Mike swore. "You keep your pants zipped, you hear me?"

"You can't lecture me. You're not my father."

"No, I'm not. But with your father gone, and your mother working her fingers to the bone to be able to send you to school, I have to say something."

Jeff snorted. "Yeah, right."

Since the kid looked more ashamed now than defiant, Mike softened his tone. "The best thing is for you to keep your hands to yourself. You know that."

Something shifted and changed in Jeff's demeanor. "We're not doin' anything."

Mike looked at the kid and shook his head. "What about STD's? Pregnancy? I don't care how hard it is for you, you hear me? You play it smart and you cool things down, or I go to your mother. Got it?"

The bell rang for classes to change. Relief poured off Jeff. "Gotta go, Coach. Ms. Plunkett doesn't like it when I'm late."

He was gone before Mike could say another word.

## CHAPTER NINE

"Are you sure I look okay, Mikey? I've never been to anything like this." Gina pulled down the mirror attached to the passenger side sun visor in Mike's car and squinted at her reflection.

Mike looked over at Gina and thought she looked fantastic. "You're gorgeous. Don't worry about it."

She fussed with her hair. "I've never been to anything like this," she repeated. "I don't know what to expect."

"Well, I've never been to anything like this either. We'll play it by ear."

"That's easy for you to say."

Oh no, it wasn't. Not by a long shot. "Just relax and enjoy the food. I hear the spiced shrimp in puff pastries are very good."

"Oooooh. Hope Monahan is doing the catering then." She licked her lips. "At least the food and the service will be good."

Mike had to grin. Gina knew everybody in the food industry in Addington. "We won't starve?"

"No, we won't."

\*\*\*\*

"The string quartet just called and canceled. They're not coming." Bonnie, Andi's assistant for the gala, looked like she was quaking in her red patent stilettos.

"What do you mean they aren't coming? I have a letter of confirmation from them." Andi felt her temperature rise as she faced the hapless woman telling her the bad news.

"Not to worry, I made some calls. The jazz group will come in a half-hour earlier, and the harpist will stay a half-hour later. See? All under control."

Andi sputtered. She wanted to be angry. She wanted to yell and scream and have a hissy fit.

Mike would be attending the gala tonight. With a date.

Damn him.

It shouldn't bother her. It really shouldn't. After all, he had asked her, and she had turned him down flat. She had no right to care who he brought to the gala.

So then, why *did* she care?

She was a colossal idiot, that's why. "Eek!"

"Did I scare you, darling?" Ian crooned in her ear, as he wrapped his arms around her from behind. "So sorry."

"Ian!" She batted at his hands and then turned in his embrace. "You scared the life out of me."

"I wanted to get your attention."

She sighed. "Please, Ian." She freed herself from his embrace. "I don't need this right now."

"I'm sorry. I heard about the string quartet. I wanted to cheer you up."

"Oh." Sometimes she wished he wouldn't be so nice. "Bonnie took care of that whole thing. She made some calls and had it all fixed before she told me about it."

"Good! That's why we have assistants, so they can take care of annoying details."

"I suppose. Still, I had an agreement with the string quartet."

"Not even you can control the flu."

"A girl can wish."

Ian released her. "That she can. Now look sharp, here they come."

The next hour was filled with greeting important contributors, making sure they had plenty of champagne, and getting the harpist playing. The jazz group did indeed come early, ready to play, so Andi could relax a bit. She mingled and exchanged too-bright smiles with the wealthy and powerful, all the while keeping an eye out for a certain high school football coach and his date.

"A little preoccupied tonight, darling?" Ian said as he brought her a glass of champagne.

She took the glass from him, but didn't drink from it. "Just doing my job and watching for new arrivals. You never know when someone important is going to come in."

"I thought it must be something like that. You are-," Ian sucked in a breath and stared off over Andi's shoulder. "My God. Who is that?"

Andi turned to see what Ian was talking about, and what she saw was Mike, with the most outrageously curved woman Andi had ever seen. Though short, she was centerfold material, and dressed to show it off in a short, clingy, copper-colored dress. Her hair was curly and auburn, and put up so that some of the curls escaped to frame her face just right. Stunning.

Andi, on the other hand, was pea green with envy. It wasn't her best color.

Mike spotted her and steered his date towards them. He looked downright mouthwatering in a tux. Didn't that just figure? She pasted a smile on her face as Mike and the bombshell crossed the floor.

"Hi, Mike. We're so glad you could make it this evening." She congratulated herself on her cool, polite tone of voice.

Mike nodded. A big, phony, dripping with charm smile stuck to his face. "Andi. Ross." He extended his hand to Ian and shook hands. Then, he reached around Gina and drew her in close to his side. "Gina, this is Andi Nelson. Andi is my choir director." The ratfink had the audacity to wink at Andi. "Andi, this is Gina Francisco, a good friend of mine."

Gina smiled. "It's nice to meet you."

Andi and Ian murmured similar sentiments back at her. While Andi reintroduced Mike and Gina, she snuck a look at Ian and could have sworn his eyes had glazed over.

"The harp music is very pretty. What is it?" Gina asked.

"Bach's *Air in G Major*. It's one of my favorite pieces."

"It's nice." Gina smiled, then cleared her throat.

"Yes, it is." *Oh, Lord, just kill me now.*

Mike looked at his feet. Ian failed at not looking at Gina's chest. Gina took great interest in watching the caterer's staff.

Andi sighed in relief when she saw the leader of the jazz group motion for her to come over. "Excuse me, please. I have to check with the musicians." She took off without a backwards look.

\*\*\*\*

Mike watched her walk off, pleasing himself by focusing in on the way her trim little backside moved as she hurried away. She looked real classy and cool in a long dress made of some floaty, blue fabric. It took enormous will power to keep from reaching out and messing up her hair, just to make her look human, instead of an angel sent from heaven.

Man, he was some kind of sick puppy. He had to get out of here. "You hungry?" he asked Gina.

Gina pulled her attention away from checking out the bar. "Hungry? As in check out the buffet?" She grabbed Mike's arm with enthusiasm. "Let's go."

"See you later, Ian."

Ian blinked and focused on Mike's face. "Yes. I'll see both of you, later." His blush was beet red as he took off in the opposite direction of the buffet.

"Do you think he's okay?" Gina asked. "He looked kind of funny."

Mike shrugged. He really didn't care how Ian Ross felt. He tugged on his collar. The damn thing was choking him. He hated ties. He hated this whole thing. What had he been thinking? He obviously hadn't been using his head.

Nope. Another part of his body had been all present and accounted for when he bought those gala tickets.

He didn't get it. Gina was gorgeous. So many men were salivating over her he had to be careful he didn't slip and fall in the puddles. Even Ian, the ol' Haiku Guy, couldn't stop staring. Mike, big fat loser that he was, couldn't get beyond the fact he and Gina were buddies.

He and Andi Nelson were anything but buddies. She raised every hackle he possessed.

Damn.

Gina studied the layout of the buffet table. He couldn't contain a grin when she looked around, and surreptitiously rearranged a couple of items. She glanced around again and caught him grinning at her. She grinned back. "It looks much better this way."

"No doubt about it."

She handed him a plate, then took one for herself. They made their way down the table. "Is Andi the one who's got your shorts in a knot?"

"No one's got my shorts in a knot."

Gina just looked at him and shook her head. She picked up a couple of shrimp in puff pastries and put them on her plate. "She's very pretty."

"If you say so." Mike prayed he wasn't blushing. Man, he felt like a putz.

"Mike Kelly, you are such a liar. You want her so bad you can taste it."

"And how do you know that, oh great swami?"

Her smile dimmed. "You look at her like you could gobble her right up."

He cursed. Beyond that, he couldn't come up with anything to say, ignorant fool that he was. He stabbed at a couple of chicken wings, impaled them, and deposited them on his plate. "She's not my type."

"Okay. If you say so."

"She's not."

"If it's any consolation, she was really trying not to look at you."

"I'm ugly. So what?" He hated the little spark of hope that fluttered in his heart at the mere thought of Andi wanting him.

Gina picked up a few stuffed mushrooms. "She's attracted to you, Mikey. I can tell." She grinned. "This feels *so* junior high."

"She's with Ian Ross. He writes her poetry and all that kind of crap. That's the type of guy she goes for." He grabbed a roll and put a slice of ham on it. "Anyway, junior high kids don't say they're attracted to each other. They *like* each other, but only admit it if the other person admits it first." And who died and made him the junior high Dr. Ruth?

"And your point is?"

"Could you give it a rest, Gina? I'd like to try to enjoy myself this evening." As if anyone could enjoy himself at a ballet gala.

"Fine by me."

\*\*\*\*

"The auction went wonderfully, don't you think?" Andi sighed as she danced with Ian.

"Yes." Ian spun Andi away from him with a fluid motion, then pulled her back as they danced to *Stardust*. "I think we raised quite a bit of money."

Andi felt at ease for the first time that night. She loved to dance, always would. Even though a career in ballet wasn't in the cards for her, she settled for dancing whenever she could.

Ian was a fun partner. His upper crust, British parents had made him take ballroom dancing lessons as a boy, and he knew all the moves. The song ended, and he spun her around one last time. "I'm parched. Let's get something to drink."

She nodded, following him off the dance floor. At the buffet, Ian grabbed them each a glass of champagne. He handed her glass to her. "Cheers."

She smiled back. "Cheers."

Ralph Jameson, the head of the French Department at the University, came up to them. "I hate to interrupt you at a party, but I wonder if I might have a word with you, Ian. It's about the French endowed chair."

Ian looked at Andi. "Would you mind terribly?"

"It's quite important," urged Jameson.

"Oh, think nothing of it." She smiled. "I'm sure I can amuse myself while you talk to Professor Jameson."

Ian smiled his gratitude, and the two men trundled off.

Andi stood there, watching the dancers, sipping her champagne. The bubbles were cool and crisp against her tongue.

"Having a good time?"

She knew that voice all too well. "I am. How about you?"

Mike stuffed his hands in his pockets. "The food's good."

"Didn't my mother say it would be? She's never wrong. Just ask her." She looked around him. "Where's your date?"

"Gina?"

"Did you bring someone else I haven't met yet?"

He grinned. "Nope. Just Gina. I make it a policy to only bring one woman to a party at a time." He chuckled at her raised eyebrows. "Gina is schmoozing your caterer to try to get the recipe for the shrimp thing your mother wants."

Andi lifted a brow. "Gina's getting a recipe for

*my* mother?"

Shifting his weight from one foot to the other, he drew his eyebrows together in a scowl. "Yeah. I asked her to. Is that a problem?"

She sighed. "No, of course not. It's very thoughtful of you." She would have kicked herself in the butt if she could have reached it for not thinking of getting the recipe herself.

"Yeah, well, Pamela's a nice lady, and I wanted to show my gratitude. Where's your date?"

"Ian's with the chairman of the French department talking over some university business." She wrinkled her nose. "All very secret, you know."

He let loose a bark of laughter, and then grew very serious "I can't even begin to imagine what business would be more important than dancing with you."

She swallowed. "University politics can be cutthroat."

He took his hands out of his pockets and held one out to her. "Dance with me."

She shouldn't, she really shouldn't, but she made the mistake of looking into Mike's green-flecked eyes. They were so hot, they practically scorched her. Oh boy, was she a goner. She put her champagne down, put her hand into his, and followed him onto the dance floor.

He settled his hands on her hips, pulling her in close. She wrapped her arms around his neck and melted against him while the band played Duke Ellington's *Prelude to a Kiss*.

Mike moved with all the elegance and grace of a natural athlete. The band's alto sax lovingly crooned a hot melody that seemed made just for them. Andi sighed, lost in the moment.

It shouldn't feel so good to be held by this man, but it did. He felt warm and solid and safe. Only traces of his aftershave lingered, so her nose caught elusive wisps of wood and spice. His thumbs rubbed up and down on her hips, which made her shiver. He didn't know the song, but hummed along anyway, off-key. She couldn't remember when she'd last heard more beautiful music.

The music ended. For a long moment, they remained locked against each other, unaware of the applause that replaced the music. She looked up at him, then away. She didn't want him to see more than she was ready to show.

But when she looked away, she was mortified. Everyone was staring at her and Mike wrapped around each other on the dance floor. Everyone. In her peripheral vision she saw Ian, with Gina, wearing identical expressions of confusion. She pushed away from him. "People are watching."

He stared hard at her, then his eyes clouded and she couldn't tell at all what he was thinking. "Thanks for the dance." He marched off the dance floor to Gina, grabbed her by the elbow, and dragged her out of sight.

Andi stood there, bereft and alone, watching Mike and Gina go. The band struck up another tune. Ian was suddenly there by her side, pulling her into a sophisticated set of dance steps. "Work with me here, sweetheart. People are watching."

Andi stumbled, but training and instinct took over. The band was playing *Take the A-Train*, and they were cookin'. Since her feet were flying, she didn't need to think, which was good. She couldn't have put together a coherent thought to save her soul.

Again, the band stopped, but this time, Ian flung her through a final spin. Twirling to a stop, her skirt floated around her ankles. Then, she looked up at Ian.

"I think I'd like to go home now." Ian looked at her, his eyes absolutely void of emotion.

"Oh." She didn't know what to say. She went for what was simple. "Okay."

They made their excuses to the other committee members and left the gala. The nip in the November air felt good on Andi's face.

Once in the car, with Ian behind the wheel, she endured an uncomfortable silence.

Ian was the first to break it. "I know we attended this party tonight as friends and gala committee members, but that last little bit with Mike Kelly was just too much for me."

Andi wanted to cry. "Ian, I'm sorry. I never meant to do anything to hurt you."

"I've made no secret of how I feel, and you've been honest with me that you don't return my feelings. So be it. I hoped I could change your mind. I was wrong."

"Ian, I-,"

"Don't say anything. You'll just make it worse. I think it's best if I stay away from you for the time being."

Andi felt tears sting her eyes, but she knew all about male pride, and figured she needed to allow Ian to keep his. "I'll miss you. I value your friendship."

"That's just not enough for me anymore."

What could she say? In the end, it was simple.

She said good-bye.

But later on that night, alone in her bed, she relived every minute, every second, she had spent in Mike Kelly's arms. She was going to have to do something about this attraction she felt for him, the sooner the better.

## CHAPTER TEN

Mike flung the door open to Dave's office. "I finally got my invitation to speak to the holy triumvirate."

Dave looked up from his paperwork. "Ever heard of knocking?"

"Yeah. It's overrated. Listen." Mike settled into the chair across from Dave's desk. "I've got a meeting with George, Steve Windley, and Betty Kincaid tomorrow morning. What have you heard?"

"Nothing. They're deliberately keeping me out of the loop."

"Damn. That sucks." Mike was getting more than a little frustrated.

"Not necessarily." Dave took his glasses off and tossed them on the desk. "This could be a good thing."

Mike furrowed his brow. "I don't see how. I may have to ask Deke to step in on my behalf." He'd ask Satan himself to step in, if it helped him keep his job.

"I'm not sure that would make a difference. In fact, it might make it worse."

"You think so?"

"Yeah, I do. Windley would be especially pissed off about it. He likes to think he runs things on his own. He wouldn't like to give the impression that he's Deke Nelson's flunky."

"I hadn't thought of that." Mike dropped his head back against the back of the chair. "I guess I can kiss this job good-bye. Maybe Deke can help me get a job as a water boy for a Pop Warner team."

"Don't give up before you even start. Go to the meeting. Get a read on what they're thinking. Talk to Sandy, and get the union behind you." Dave picked up a pencil and tapped the eraser on his desk blotter. "George, Steve and Betty can't act unilaterally."

"They must have a plan. Our final game is coming up next weekend."

"You've got options. Just think before you open your mouth. Don't go off half-cocked."

"Me? Surely you jest. I am Joe Tact."

"Right. How foolish of me to forget. Just remember. When in doubt, shut up."

Mike closed his eyes. "This whole thing sucks. Why can't they leave us alone and let these kids play football?"

"Why can't they leave anything alone?" Dave stood and started to pace. "I've got five really innovative, really cutting edge programs on the table, waiting to be funded. Each one would enhance what we can offer in enrichment, in special ed, and for at risk kids. Those three have tied my hands so all I can do is sit around with my thumb up my butt and tell these talented teachers that I'll let them know." He stopped to stare out his window. "I know it's not what you want to hear, but football isn't my only concern."

"I know that, and you know I appreciate your efforts on my behalf."

"Yeah, as pitifully small as they are." He looked back at Mike. "Go talk to Sandy. The union is your best bet now."

"Thanks. I will."

****

Andi glowered at the music score in front of her. The gang at church was far from mastering the rhythms in the B section, even though they pretty much had the notes. She had tried every strategy she had ever been taught, had invented some new ones herself, but it still wasn't coming along. She dropped her head in her hands and closed her eyes.

Her mother had extracted a promise from her father that he would attend midnight mass at St. Benedict's on Christmas Eve. It would be the first time Deke would hear her make music. Even though she knew the limits of her church choir, she was pushing them so this Christmas Eve would be just a little bit more special.

Maybe she should call some extra rehearsals. She snorted. She couldn't get everyone to the regular rehearsals. Besides, extra rehearsals would mean she would spend more time with Mike, which was the last thing she wanted to do.

She snorted again. Liar.

Deciding she needed something to drink, she headed to her kitchen, filled a cup with water, and slapped it into the microwave. She opened one of the cupboards, rummaging. Hmmmm. Maybe a cookie would be good too. She reached into the cupboard and pulled out her emergency package of Pepperidge Farm's Orange Milanos. Ripping open the package, she liberated a cookie and munched, being very careful to count each and every bite.

Twenty-five chews, swallow, count to twenty-five, and start all over again. It made the one cookie she'd allow herself last longer.

The night of the ballet gala had opened her eyes to one thing: She was overwhelmingly attracted to Mike Kelly. Now what she had to do was figure out whether to do anything about it.

She was pretty darn sure he was attracted to her. There was no mistaking his reaction to her. His arousal, cuddled so close against her belly, had driven her to distraction as they danced.

His reaction was shameful considering he had brought a date. Well, she chided herself as she retrieved her tea water. She had brought a date, too. Technically.

She chose another cookie and chomped to twenty-five with gusto.

She consoled herself, knowing she had always been honest with Ian. She just didn't feel for him like he felt about her. He had promised he could handle a strictly platonic relationship.

Suddenly it was all too much: her feelings for Mike, her lack of feelings for Ian, and most of all, her overwhelming and childish desire to have her father love her as much as he loved her brothers. This time, when she felt the unwanted pressure and sting of tears, she indulged.

After several long minutes, she sniffed and reached for a tissue and her teacup. The tea had gone cold, but she chugged it anyway. She ate another cookie.

Her life really sucked, that was for sure. She didn't think it could get any worse.

\*\*\*\*

Beth eyed the paper bag Katie brought her with queasy alarm. "I really don't think I need this, Kate."

Katie stopped dead in her tracks, giving Beth a stern look. "Then use it and prove it." She held the bag out to Beth, who eyed it as if it was a bag full of rattlesnakes. Katie shook it. "Take the bag, Beth."

Beth's hands trembled as she did. She walked on rubbery legs to Katie's bathroom. Once there, she pulled the home pregnancy test out of the bag and read the directions.

Fifteen minutes later, she left the bathroom in a zombie-like haze. "Well?" Katie asked her.

Beth looked at Katie and burst into tears. Immediately, Katie went to her and enfolded her in a hug meant to be comforting. "These things can be wrong. Want me to go with you to get another one?"

Beth shook her head. She knew in her heart what the answer was.

She wished she knew what to do about it. Her father was going to freak out. She was terrified of how he was going to react.

And Jeff, what was he going to do? He was *so* going to break up with her... which wouldn't matter, because there was no way her father was going to let her ever see Jeff again.

She cried harder. She was so dead.

****

If someone had asked Mike what he would rather do, go to choir practice or have a root canal, he knew what he would answer.

The root canal, hands down.

He didn't pretend to understand Andi Nelson. He didn't think he would, not in a million years. The woman was odd, no doubt about it.

Even for her, though, she was acting strangely. The things she made them do in choir rehearsal were downright bizarre.

Last Wednesday, she made them stand up and step from foot to foot with the rhythm of their part. He chuckled when he remembered the gang's reaction to that.

It did not go over well.

Andi had gotten this glint in her eyes, and they all had done it, but they hadn't liked it.

He really couldn't wait to find out what kind of squirrelly idea she had cooked up for them tonight.

He refused to think about dancing with her at that ballet thing. He was embarrassed enough about how hard he had gotten while holding her close. He felt like the geek who was finally getting to dance with the prom queen.

Here it was, Wednesday night. He had to face her again, knowing he had no chance. Knowing that for now, she had spoiled him for all other women.

His feet were heavy as he dragged them down into the church basement. He met Walt and Rosie in the hallway and waited with them for the warm-ups to end. Once Walt had deemed it safe, the three of them went into the choir room.

He had to grin at how Andi scowled as the three of them took their places. Heinrich and Wally had left him a seat between them, and Mike took it and watched Andi look at everyone but him. She moved her hands in command.

The choir started to sing along with her, but it wasn't pretty, even he could tell. He looked at the music in his hands, but none of it made sense, as usual. He felt like such a failure.

****

Why? Andi's brain screamed. They had it right last week. Why couldn't they get it right this week?

To top it all off, Beth was off her game. She was pale and distracted. Obviously, something was wrong, but Andi couldn't take the time to figure it out.

Deke was going to hear this choir and be impressed by her work with them. They were going to kick choral butt, if it killed her.

The way they were singing tonight, it just might.

"Okay, tenors, let's try it again. Page three, second score, measure two, last beat. One, two, three, and..." She raised her hands, motioning them in.

They didn't follow her. "Where are we?" Walt asked.

"Page three, second score, measure two, the last beat."

"Where it says *He is born?*"

"That's right."

"Okay. Don't worry about a thing. I'm there." Walt flashed an evil grin.

She counted them in again, and this time, they sang. She almost wished they hadn't. "Beth, play that for them, so they can hear it one more time."

Beth started to play it, but she hit wrong notes and had to start over.

"One more time tenors."

This time they got it as close to right as they were going to for tonight. She'd come back to them later. She looked up and focused in on the back row. "Your turn, basses."

****

Mike felt his stomach plummet to his feet.

Andi spewed some gobbledy-gook that was supposed to help him find his place. He glowered at page three, but *second score, measure two, last beat* did not help.

He hoped Wally would give him a clue, but he was having his own problems, which he was hashing out with Andi. She was apparently having difficulty understanding ol' Wally, because she had trouble coming up with a solution.

They went on like this for a while. Mike studied his music, but the notes and words just wouldn't cooperate and changed places on him more than once. He closed his eyes, fighting the frustration and despair that threatened to swamp him.

Wally gave up trying to make Andi understand him, and got out of his seat, taking his music to show her what exactly he was talking about.

"See?" Wally asked. "Why can't we sing it this way?" He demonstrated. "It would sound so cool."

Andi was silent for a moment. "It would mess up the altos. They need you to sing it as written, or else it's hard for them to make their entrance."

Deirdre, the hockey player, turned around. "You don't want to make it any harder for us than it is already."

Mike worried for a second she might get her

hockey stick and bonk Wally over the head with it.

"Oh," said Wally. "Okay. But don't you think it would be cool if we could do that?"

"Yes, Wally, it would be cool if we could do that. But, we can't. The composer had other ideas." Andi waited for him to get back to his seat. "Okay, basses. Strut your stuff. Page three, second score, measure two, last beat." She waved her arms. "Here we go."

Mike opened his mouth, but nothing would come out. Heinrich and Wally had it reasonably together, each of them singing the same notes for the most part, but Mike couldn't even tell what words to sing, never mind what notes.

Andi wasn't totally satisfied with Wally and Heinrich, even though Mike thought they had done pretty darn good, the best he had ever heard them. She made them do it again, and again, and again, but there was always at least one thing she found fault with.

He looked at the score in his hands, praying to the gods of music for some insight. Said deities only laughed at him, scrambling the page up one more time, just for good measure.

He had never, in his entire life, felt so stupid, not even when he had failed the second grade.

Something inside him snapped with an audible *thwing*. He had to get out of here. Fast. He fisted his music as he stood, knocking over two chairs in his clumsy haste.

"Mike, where are you going?" He heard Andi call above the roaring in his ears, but he didn't care.

He just kept walking.

****

After rehearsal, the first place Andi looked for Mike was at The End Zone. She sat in the parking lot, gathering up her courage and not examining her reasons for being here. Ah, well. Faint heart and all that. She got out of her car and marched into the bar.

The crowd was sparse, most likely because it was a weeknight. It was a nice place, very rustic and simple.

She had to smile. There wasn't a fern in sight.

There wasn't a Mike Kelly in sight either, she noticed as she surveyed the room. She was weighing the options of leaving, versus staying and asking the bartender if he'd seen Mike, when Gina Francisco came up to her.

"Hey, Andi. Do you want a table?"

"Uh, no. I'm looking for someone. Actually," Andi swallowed, "I'm looking for Mike. Has he been here?"

She felt a bit guilty about the miffed look she got from Gina. "I haven't seen him."

"Uh, okay. Do you have any idea where else he might be?"

"Why?"

"He, uh, he got upset at rehearsal tonight, and left in the middle of it. I want to find out what's the matter. Do you have *any* ideas?"

"No."

"Well, then. Okay." Andi bit her lower lip. "If you see him, will you tell him I'm looking for him?"

"Sure. Why not?"

Andi turned to go. "Thanks."

Gina's next question stopped her in her tracks. "I'm wondering why you're out chasing after Mike when you're obviously dating someone else."

Andi bristled. That was none of Gina's business. She turned and matched Gina's glare. "I'm worried about Mike because something happened in choir to upset him. I want to know what it was, so I can try to fix it. As for Ian, it's none of your concern."

Gina looked like she was going to say something else, but apparently thought better of it. She turned to go, but then looked back. "By the way, I hope your mother liked the recipe." Then she was gone, leaving Andi with no further clue as to Mike Kelly's whereabouts.

Andi turned to go and ran smack dab into Dave Mason. "Oops! Sorry."

"Andi, what are you doing here?" Dave put his hands on her arms to steady her.

"Looking for Mike Kelly. Have you seen him?"

Dave raised his eyebrows. "No. Have you tried his house?"

"I don't know where he lives."

"I do." Dave studied her.

Andi felt her face warm. She was going to die of embarrassment here. "Normally, I wouldn't think of invading his privacy, but I really need to talk to him. Could you help me out?"

"You could call him."

"I kind of want to have this conversation with him face to face." She bit her lower lip. "Something happened to upset him at choir rehearsal tonight, and I want to find out what it was. Can you help me? Please?"

Dave was silent for a second, and then rattled off Mike's address.

## CHAPTER ELEVEN

Mike sat in his dark living room, drinking a beer. It danced cold and fizzy across his tongue, the taste, bitter and sharp.

All the better to match his mood.

His original intent was to get just drunk enough to feel numb, but he was beginning to think that there wasn't enough beer in the world to make him feel numb. Midway through beer number two, he ran out of steam. No amount of beer was going to fill up that empty place inside him, where a little boy who felt stupid still lived.

He felt a rush of hot, violent emotion he couldn't define. How Andi managed to push every single one of his buttons, Mike didn't know.

Those buttons now included his doorbell, because if Mike didn't miss his guess, Andi Nelson was at his front door, leaning on the bell. He should have known she'd hunt him down so she could humiliate him some more.

Breathing out a huge sigh, he resigned himself and went to open the door. He opened it, said, "Go away," and slammed it shut.

The doorbell rang again. He rested his forehead against the door. Maybe he was hallucinating. Maybe, when he opened the door this time, she'd be gone. He opened the door again.

Andi stood there looking extremely ill at ease. "May I come in?"

"Would you go away if I said no?"

"No."

"Then you might as well come in." He turned

and left her to find her own way in. He winced when the light she turned on stabbed at his eyes. Finding his way to the couch, he plunked himself down and saluted her with his beer. "Take a load off."

She just stood there, like a nun in a brothel, all cautious and suspicious. "I want to know what happened at rehearsal."

Mike took a hefty swig. Maybe more beer was the answer after all. "Nothing happened at rehearsal."

"Then why did you leave like that? We were all very concerned."

"Great. Just great." He looked at her through slitted eyelids. "Go away, Andi. I don't want you or your concern here."

"I can't do that, Mike. Please. Tell me what happened."

He leaned his head back against the couch and closed his eyes. He might as well confess his sins, so she knew just what kind of loser he really was. "It's just too damn hard. I never know where I am on the page, and it frustrates the hell out of me."

She took her coat off as she approached him carefully. "No one expects you to know how to read music yet. Just follow the shape of the line."

"I would if I could find the damn line, but I can't."

"I'm positive that with practice you'll do just..."

Something exploded inside of him. He burst out of the couch, strode over to her, and grabbed her by the arms. It was all he could do to keep from shaking her. "Nothing's gonna help me, Andi. I'm dyslexic. I'll never be able to read that music."

She gaped at him, stunned. "I didn't know."

He released her abruptly, with enough force that she staggered back a step. Ashamed, he ran his hand through his hair and stared at her.

She stared back and swallowed. "I had no idea."

"It's not something I advertise."

"Why not? It's nothing to be ashamed of."

"It's just..."

"It's just what?"

"Go home, Andi."

"I wish you had told me right away. There are strategies for coping with this. In fact, this therapist in Toronto is having incredible success with aural treatments involving filtered noise and Mozart..."

"Save your breath. I know them all."

"But you've never applied them to reading music. I can help you." She tossed her coat and purse onto a chair.

"I don't want your help."

"But..."

"I'm begging you, Andi. Please go home."

"No. I went to a lot of trouble to find you so I could find out what happened. Now that I know, I need to help you."

"Why?" A quick little jab of hope flicked up his spine. He tamped it down.

She sat next to him, but didn't look at him. "Well, you're a member of my choir. I care how everybody in the group feels."

He swore as he looked away from her. Just another choir member. Big Whoop. "Yeah, well, if that's the only reason, you should go home. I'm fine. You've done your duty."

She put her hand on his shoulder. Sighing, she looked at him. "I know what it feels like to be overwhelmed and powerless."

That got his attention. He asked in spite of himself. "How so?"

"Did you know I was on the fast track to becoming a professional dancer?" Her smile was sad and tugged at his heart.

"Ballet?"

She nodded.

"How'd a professional ballerina end up teaching chorus in a high school?"

"It's a short, sad story. I was good, really good." She looked at him then. "Then I started seriously starving myself in order to stay ahead of the pack."

"You mean you were anorexic?"

"Still am. I fight it every day. I thank the dear Lord that I never got into making myself throw up." She looked away again. "I had to quit dancing when I collapsed at rehearsal one day. I nearly died."

He didn't know what to say. In fact, he felt petty and small. "So you became a music teacher."

"It was my second love. I had to give up the one thing I loved the most in life to save my life. Ironic, huh?"

There was a lot more to her story, he was sure. "I don't know whether it's worth anything coming from me, but I think you're a good conductor."

"You've got such a huge well of experience to draw from." She put a hand over her mouth. "I'm sorry, I shouldn't snark." All of a sudden, she was all business. "I came here to help you out, not whine about my sad story. You're doing a great job, and doing it a lot more cheerfully than I would if I were you." Her eyes were full of emotion. "I'm even more impressed now that I know about your dyslexia."

Mike felt like a jerk. "Compared to what you've been through, I've had a picnic."

"I didn't tell you about my anorexia to make you feel less. I told you about it so you would know I understand how you feel." She licked her lips.

His throat went suddenly dry at the sight of that pretty pink tongue darting out to wet her mouth. It took him a split second to decide to take a chance. He took her cold hand, amazed at how fragile it felt in his larger one, and put it over his heart. "So what am I feeling?"

That little hand trembled against him. "I think

I'd better go now."

"No way. Not after you worked so hard to find me." He brought her hand to his lips and kissed her fingertips.

She froze. "You just feel sorry for me." She bolted off the couch.

He went after her and put his hands on her shoulders to keep her there. "Believe me darlin', the last thing I feel right now is sorry for you."

She looked away. She seemed so shy, so vulnerable; it hurt to look at her. "Look at me," he told her.

Her glance flicked up to his once, then twice. His gaze caught hers and held it. He brought his hands up to cradle her face. With infinite patience and gentleness, he brushed his lips across hers. He did it again, with more insistence. Before he could make a third pass, she parted her lips under his, opening up for him.

He took what she offered, then gave her back more, slowly stroking his tongue into her mouth with beguiling and teasing touches. She whimpered and wriggled in closer to him, wordlessly asking him for more.

It was all the invitation he needed.

She tasted so good and felt even better. He hummed as he deepened their kiss. He took and took and took. His hands had to move, had to learn all her secrets. Like lightning, they stroked from her jaw down her body, to her sweet, pretty, little bottom.

She strained against him, desperate to be close. He hauled her up his body, while she raised her right leg and entwined it around his thigh.

He grabbed it, pulling her closer to him, and smiled against her mouth. "All those ballet lessons paid off, huh?"

She nipped at his lower lip. "Oh, yeah." She used

her very flexible pelvis to great advantage.

His groan was heartfelt. "Oh, yeah." Then he kissed her again, nipping his way from her ear down her neck.

He kept one hand reveling on her soft derriere while the other searched for, and found, a breast. She cupped perfectly in his hand, and her already erect nipple stabbed at his palm. He rotated his hand lightly over that nipple, teasing it harder. She whimpered and pushed herself against his palm, begging him for more.

Those whimpers of hers filled his heart and his soul. Suddenly, he was Superman, Batman, and Arnold Schwarzenegger all wrapped up in one. He scooped her up in his arms and carried her to his bedroom. Laying her on his unmade bed as if she were made of spun sugar, he studied her, burning into his brain the memory of how she looked in his bed.

She raised herself up on her elbows and smiled. "You gonna join me, or are you just lookin'?"

"Both." He stretched out on his side next to her, dipping his head down to kiss her while his fingers went to work on her buttons. He parted her blouse, teased her nipple through the sheer lace of her bra. She had obviously dabbed some perfume in her cleavage that morning, because a spicy hint of cinnamon remained on her skin.

Her hands were busy as well, working at the buttons of his shirt. Her haste to get to his skin made her clumsy, and so he pulled away and yanked the shirt over his head. She scrambled up to kneel on his bed, shrugging out of her blouse. She reached around behind her to get the clasp of her bra, but he stopped her. "Let me."

After he flicked her bra open, he slowly moved the straps down her arms until he uncovered her. His look hot and hungry, he feasted on the sight of her small, perfect breasts. She squirmed under his scrutiny. He found her unease endearing. "They're tiny," she said.

He reached a hand up to touch one tight, pink bud of a nipple. "They're perfect." He laid her back down on the bed and loved her breasts.

Her nipples were wonderfully responsive, and he delighted in suckling her. She tasted like his dreams. He used his teeth to lightly bite, his tongue to soothe. His hand played with her other nipple, causing her hips to move in restless circles.

She snaked a hand in between their bodies and caressed his erection through his jeans. "Oh, yeah," he gasped against her breast, and pushed his hips against her stroking hand.

He left her breast to take her mouth again, giving her deep, soulful kisses while his hand moved down to unfasten her slacks. He slipped his hand inside both her slacks and her panties and cupped her mound. She was so wet for him. Penetrating her with a finger, he pumped inside her and then brought her moisture out to smooth over her bud.

Their caresses continued, but it wasn't enough. She lifted her hips and helped him get rid of her remaining clothes. Laughing, she rose over him and pulled his jeans off. She looked at him, her eyes wide as she shook her head. "You aren't wearing any underwear."

He felt himself blush. "I didn't get around to doin' laundry this week. That a problem?"

"Not from where I'm sitting." She grinned and kissed his mouth.

His erection was painfully hard, the tip already dewed with impatient moisture. She licked her lips and he almost came right there. She used her hands to arouse him further, and he had to close his eyes, fist his hands in the sheets.

They were beyond the point of no return, and he

rose up, flipping her under him. He parted her thighs, draped them over his own and settled down to business. Reaching over her to the nightstand, he pulled the drawer open and fumbled for a condom. She didn't make it easy, because she wiggled her hips and used her hands to tease him.

A breath hissed out of him, but he managed to find what he was looking for. Ripping the package open with his teeth, he extracted the condom. She reached out a hand to take it from him, but he shook his head. "I won't last very long if you touch me right now."

She got to her knees and snagged the condom away from him. "I'll chance it."

His hands rubbed light circles over her nipples as he watched her slowly roll the condom over his erect shaft. It was probably the most erotic thing he had ever seen. Then, bringing his hands back up to cup her face, he kissed her long and slow and deep as he laid her back down.

Again making a place for himself between her thighs, he knelt between them and parted her for his possession. Only he didn't enter her body. He rubbed his erection over her needy bud, bringing her to the brink. Again, she treated him to those whimpers he was coming to love so much.

With a very masculine growl, he positioned himself and eased into her body. He leaned forward in such a way that her legs were draped over his arms, allowing him to hold her wide open. He slid into her slowly and she circled her hips to coax him deeper. Their eyes locked together as they prolonged that first incredible moment of joining. Finally, he pressed all the way home, joined with her to the hilt.

To the heart.

"Hey," he said, smiling down at her. "You okay?"

She gave him a milking squeeze, smiling when he hissed in response. "I could be better," she whispered.

"Oh, yeah." And he began to move.

He knew his size and was afraid to hurt her, but she wouldn't let him be careful. Loving the way she moved, the way she loved him back, he stroked high inside her, again and again and again.

She gripped the bed's headboard, bracing herself to take all of him. He quickened his thrusts, and she burst around him, keening her pleasure while she came.

The feel of her inner muscles milking his shaft were too much. Hips pounding and chest heaving, his orgasm exploded long, hot, and wet.

He braced himself on his elbows over her, hardly able to draw in a breath. Her body still pulsed with aftershocks, extending both their pleasure. She brought her arms around his neck and raked her nails gently along his back. She purred in satisfaction.

"You okay?" His voice was a husky rasp that hummed and scraped wonderfully along her skin. "I'll be able to get off you soon."

"No," she raised herself up so that she could kiss him. "You feel too good." And she gave her hips a little swivel.

He did a little whimpering himself. She chuckled, and did it again. Miraculously, he felt his body quicken. "You keep that up," he warned, "And we're gonna need another condom."

"Do tell." She moved her hips in slow, easy circles.

He gulped, bracing himself for round two.

They set the alarm for five so they could make love one more time before Andi had to leave to get ready for school. Then, settling safe in his arms, she slept.

Mike was unable to drop off for a long while. He nuzzled the top of her head with his lips, and wondered at how perfectly she fit against him.

Whatever he thought when he let her come through his front door last night, he certainly hadn't expected to fall in love with her. But damn it, that was exactly what he had done.

****

Andi was bleary eyed with exhaustion, and her body ached in places best left unnamed, but she couldn't remember the last time she felt so good.

To think Mike Kelly was the cause. Would wonders ever cease?

She hummed as she floated down the hall to the auditorium.

People were giving her strange looks, but she didn't care. She was in love.

She opened the door to the auditorium expecting to hear Beth practicing and was shocked when she saw her sitting at the piano bench, sobbing as if her heart would break. She rushed down the length of the aisle. "Beth! What's wrong?"

Beth turned teary eyes to Andi, opened her mouth to say something, but sobbed instead. Andi knelt on the floor in front of Beth and pulled the girl into her arms.

Beth wept and wept, shaking with the force of it. "It's okay, Beth," Andi crooned. "It'll all be okay."

"No, it isn't okay," Beth wailed against Andi's shoulder. "Nothing will ever be okay again."

Andi set her away and smoothed Beth's hair back from her tear ravaged face. "Why don't you tell me about it? Maybe I can help."

"Nothing will help. I'm in so much trouble."

The girl was shaking so hard, Andi was afraid she'd pass out or something. "Please, Beth. Tell me. I want to help you."

"You're going to be so disappointed in me."

"Never. Now, come on. Tell me what's wrong."

Beth glanced away from Andi, like she was

afraid to look at her. She heaved a watery sigh. "I'm pregnant."

She had spoken in a tone of voice so low, Andi was sure she had misheard her. "I'm sorry, I didn't hear you."

The picture of misery, Beth took her time to look back at Andi. "I'm pregnant." Then she burst into tears all over again.

Andi held the weeping girl, but her mind was reeling.

Beth.

Pregnant.

There had to be a mistake.

When Beth's hiccups had subsided, Andi asked her, "Are you sure?"

Beth nodded. "I took one of those home tests twice. The answer was the same both times."

"But you haven't seen a doctor."

"God, no! I can't take the chance my parents might find out."

"Well, you should, as soon as possible. Those home tests can be wrong." Andi didn't want to think about those tests Beth took being *right*.

"But my period is late, and I feel sick all the time."

"That could be the flu. We have to get you to a doctor to be absolutely sure."

"Will you take me? I can't go to anyone here in Addington."

Though she knew there might be some serious consequences with her job, Andi didn't even have to think about it. "Of course. I'll take you to Boston to a clinic or something. We can say we're going shopping at Schirmer's for new music."

Beth's lower lip quivered. "Thank you."

Andi gave Beth another hug. Pregnant! Andi hadn't even known Beth was dating anyone. Curiosity won out. "Beth, who's the father?"

"Do we have to tell him?"

"Well, if you turn up pregnant, you'll have to tell him at some point. He needs to take some responsibility."

Beth pulled out of Andi's arms, clearly fighting a battle inside herself. The ticking of the big school clock on the auditorium wall exploded into the silence of the room, like sharp, painful heartbeats. Beth sat down on the piano bench. "Jeff Myers."

Andi couldn't have been more surprised than if Beth had said Krusty the Klown. "Jeff? Jeff Myers?"

Beth nodded.

"Did he take advantage of you?" Andi absolutely couldn't imagine shy, gentle Beth with Jeff Myers, king of the jocks.

"No." Beth shook her head. "He loves me. He didn't do anything I didn't want him to."

Andi couldn't believe what she was hearing. Beth and Jeff. It was simply inconceivable. "How long have you been going out?"

"Since he became ineligible. He's not like everyone thinks he is. He's really very sensitive and sweet. We talk for hours."

Evidently, they hadn't limited their activities to talking. She needed to change the subject. "If I get you an appointment for this afternoon, are you free to come with me?"

"I guess so. But, nobody can know!" Beth pleaded.

"I won't tell anyone."

"Will the doctors have to tell my parents?"

"You're sixteen, right?"

Beth nodded.

"I can't tell you, I just don't know. Let's cross that bridge when we come to it. They'll have to find out at some point."

Beth moaned. "I am so dead."

*This is true*, Andi thought, but decided to keep a

positive face on everything. "Let me make a few phone calls, while you go wash your face."

"Okay."

She watched Beth shuffle out of the auditorium, still unable to believe it. Surely, Beth was only mistaking flu symptoms for pregnancy symptoms.

She'd take Beth to the clinic, find out this was all a false alarm, and everything would be okay.

It had to be.

But it was no false alarm. Beth was pregnant. They returned to Addington from the clinic loaded down with pamphlets and a prescription for prenatal vitamins.

CHAPTER TWELVE

Mike stuck a finger inside of his collar to loosen his tie. The damn thing was like a freakin' noose. He was seated at a table across from Addington High School's Principal, George Kennedy, Addington's District Superintendent, Steve Windley, and the Chair of the Board of Education, Betty Kincaid. The three had manila file folders in front of them, and they were ignoring Mike in favor of rifling through the papers in those folders.

Next to Mike was Sandy Bayard, the Teacher's Union representative. She was a grandmotherly looking woman with the temperament of a pit bull and the heart of a barracuda. Mike was confident that if anyone could help him, Sandy could.

Steve Windley was the first to look up from his sheaf of papers and to address Mike. "These stats don't look very good. You haven't won a single game all season. How do you explain that?" He folded his hands on top of his file folder.

Mike cleared his throat. "They're a young team. There's no way for our freshmen and sophomores to go up against other schools' juniors and seniors and come out ahead. The bigger kids have it all over them in speed, strength, and experience."

"So you say. But couldn't a team of smaller kids still win if the plays they were given were more clever, more innovative?"

Clever? Innovative? Right. Mike was real pleased with himself that he didn't laugh in Windley's face. "I suppose, if they had more experience. My kids don't have that. They're getting

149

it now."

Steve harrumphed, a thick, juicy sound. "In the meantime, the self-esteem of each player is suffering because you're hiding your lack of imagination behind your team's lack of experience."

Maybe he would laugh in Windley's face after all. "I make sure each and every kid feels important no matter how the team does. If anything is making my team feel bad, it's this constant pressure from you to win at any cost." Mike leaned in, resting his forearms on the table. "My kids know all they have to do is try their best and that's good enough for me." He sat back in his chair and folded his arms across his chest.

The room was quiet, except for the rustle of pages as the triumvirate flipped through their files. Betty Kincaid looked at Mike, a nasty little smile running across her face. She picked up her pen and underlined something in her folder with a bold flourish. "It says here gate and concession stand revenues are down. Do you think the team's losing has anything to do with that?"

Sandy jumped in. "That's true for two or three games in the middle of the season. But now, they've skyrocketed for the last, uh..." She checked her figures. "Two games, even though the team lost."

Betty pursed her lips, looking as if she had tasted something sour. "That had nothing to do with Coach Kelly's ability to lead the team."

"It's true Deke Nelson's interest in the team has boosted attendance and revenue." Mike fingered his collar again. "Look. My concern has to be with each kid learning to love and play the game, and to feel good about himself at the end of the afternoon. That's the job I was hired to do. I'm doing it."

Sandy hefted her own folder full of papers. She turned her attention to the principal, who had been silent throughout the whole thing. "George. Here are notarized letters from the parents of every boy on the team, attesting to the fact they feel Mike Kelly has done the best job possible, and they want him to remain in his position here at Addington High. I have a second folder with copies for you." She pushed it across the table to George.

"That's all well and good, but we can't allow parents to dictate school policy," Windley said, ignoring the file.

"You can't be serious. Of course, we have to give parents input on school policy. They pay the bills."

"Well, in this case, they need to trust our judgments as education experts." Windley just wasn't going to give up.

Mike snickered. "Betty is a florist. How is she an education expert?"

Betty bristled. "I've attended my share of conferences and am in constant communication with other board chairs. I read a lot." She flushed bright red when Mike snickered again. "And, if that isn't enough," she huffed. "The parents in this town elected me to oversee their children's education. *That* makes me qualified."

Sandy stood. "Here is the union's position. We've talked to our lawyers and they agree. Mike Kelly is a good teacher and a good coach. You have no legal reason to fire him. We *will* fight you. I don't think you want that."

Mike rose as Sandy finished speaking. "I love these kids and love this job. Leave me alone, and in two years you'll have a winning team. That's a promise."

He followed Sandy out of the room.

Later on that day, Mike was feeling pretty darn good. He had gotten word via Dave that the school board jihad had decided to back off, saving his job for now. He did a little victory dance over that one.

And he was in love. He was armed with

champagne and roses, and he was off to woo his lady. Life didn't get much better than that.

Andi Nelson had rocked his world last night. Who could have known such a wildcat hid behind that prim and starchy exterior? He liked to think only he knew. It felt like a naughty secret she had kept just for him.

He whistled as he bounced up the walkway to her condo. He couldn't wait to see her. He rang the bell and waited. Maybe she was in the shower. Hoo, mama, he liked that image. Andi all wet and slick with soap. He'd snuggle up against her cute little derriere and cup her breasts from behind while he nibbled on her neck. That bottom of hers would cradle his erection and she would wiggle and...

Snorting with impatience, he rang the bell again. Then he waited. And waited. Had she forgotten? How could she forget? Last night had been off the Richter scale. There was no way she could forget.

What if something had happened to her? Maybe he should check at the school, or retrace her route home in case she had car trouble. Did she have his cell number? He didn't know. He was just getting ready to leave when her car pulled up in the drive. She looked tired. Smiling to himself, he realized he'd have to make sure she got more sleep tonight.

Bummer.

"Hey," he said when she got to her door. "I was getting worried."

Lifting her face for his kiss, she sighed. "Sorry I'm so late. We have a problem." She stuck her key in the lock and opened the door.

He had to chuckle. She took everything so seriously. "What kind of problem?" Closing the door behind him, he followed her in.

"A big one." She threw her keys on the table and turned to face him. "We are..."

"Let's get this out of the way first." He dropped the roses and the champagne on the coffee table, took her in his arms, and kissed her, thoroughly.

"Again," he murmured against her mouth.

The second kiss was even better than the first.

"Mike, we have to talk. Something big has come up."

She could say that again, Mike thought, noting the parts of his body that had sprung to attention. But he could tell that she had a bee in her bonnet. "Okay." He sat on the couch and pulled her carefully onto his lap. "Talk to me."

"There's no easy way to say this, except to come right out with it." She took a deep breath. "Beth Pritchard is pregnant, and Jeff Myers is the father."

He shook his head. Maybe he hadn't heard her right. "Come again?"

"Beth is pregnant, and Jeff is the father." She swiped at her eyes. Man, was she crying? "It's unbelievable, I know. I couldn't believe it at first either, but it's true. That's why I was late. I drove Beth to Boston to visit a clinic and get a pregnancy test."

Mike felt his stomach lurch, and then plummet to his feet. Holy crud! "Beth is pregnant? She can't be pregnant. Jeff promised me they were taking things slow."

There was a long moment of silence.

"What did you say?"

Even through the mists of his own disbelief and horror, Mike realized he had just made a serious blunder. He needed to tell Andi the whole truth about what he knew. "Jeff promised me they were being careful."

She jumped off his lap. "You knew about them? You knew they were..." She waved a hand in front of her, then looked at Mike, right in the face, "You knew?" She wrapped her arms around her middle.

"You knew they were intimate?"

Rubbing the back of his neck with his hand, Mike nodded. "I caught them parking one night out by the quarry."

"What? When?"

"A couple weeks ago." She had turned very pale, almost white. He got up and tried to hug her, but she pulled away. His arms ached with the loss. "What a mess."

"That's an understatement." Andi stood her ground and faced him. She looked fragile, except for her eyes, which glittered with tears and temper. "Why didn't you tell me any of this before?"

"It never came up."

"I see. Don't ask, don't tell?"

"No. It just never came up, okay? I really wasn't trying to keep you in the dark." Frustration started to nip at him. He was not her enemy here. "Does Jeff know?"

"No, and don't you tell him. Beth wants to do it."

"Okay." Time for the hard questions. "Does she have any idea what to do about it yet?"

"Mike, she's shell-shocked. Of course, she hasn't decided what to do about it. And once her parents find out, I doubt she'll have any say in the matter."

"They're strict, I know, but they love her, right? They'll be there for her."

"I'm not so sure. Her father is very rigid." She looked very worried. "I'm sure they're not going to thank me for my interference."

"Andi, you took her to get medical attention that she needed. There's nothing wrong with that."

"I'm sure they won't feel that way." She blinked her eyes, and her face primmed up.

He didn't need to be a rocket scientist to figure out he needed to do some damage control here. "I'm sorry. I didn't think that..."

"Damn right you didn't think," she blurted, her

voice suddenly loud. Her hands clenched into tight fists by her side. Her knuckles were a bloodless white. "Beth has a rare talent. She has magic in her fingers." She held up her hands and wiggled her fingers in front of her face. "And all that is shot to hell and back because some *football player* couldn't keep his hands to himself." She jammed her hands into her trouser pockets. "I think you'd better go now, Mike."

He couldn't freakin' believe this. He shoulda known, though. This was vintage Andi—when in doubt, blame football. "You're going to let this come between us."

"I'm not letting it come between us, it already is between us." She gestured to the roses on the coffee table. "How can you expect me to let you into my bed when you deliberately misled me?"

"I didn't deliberately mislead you. It just never came up."

She shook her head. "That's so lame, Mike. Please. Just go."

"You can do this to us after last night?"

"There is no *us*, not after the way you deceived me."

"I didn't deceive you!" He tunneled his fingers through his hair. Frustration ripped him into little pieces. "All I did was-" He swore as his phone rang. Rummaging in his pockets, he whipped out the phone and snarled, "Kelly."

The next words he heard drew all the blood out of his head.

"I'll be right there." He snapped his phone closed and turned back to Andi. "I'd love to stay and argue with you, but I've got to go."

"Mike, I..."

"It's got to wait, Andi. That was Nancy Myers. You know, Jeff's mom? She's at the police station. Jeff's been arrested for statutory rape."

****

Never in her life had Andi spent a worse night. She worked out for most of it, putting her body through her most rigorous dance routines. When that didn't work, she sat at her piano and sight read through pieces of music she wanted to program for the next concert. By the time the sun rose, her muscles ached, her eyes itched, and her stomach hitched with anxiety.

She knew Beth's father was a hard man, but to have Jeff arrested... It didn't bear imagining. First on her to-do list this morning was to check with Mike to find out what had happened.

To that end, she made her way to his office. His door stood open, and she could hear voices inside. He was there, and he wasn't alone. Good sign or not? She hadn't a clue. She listened before she knocked.

"I can't thank you enough, Deke." Mike's voice sounded weary. "I don't know what we would have done if you hadn't come to the rescue."

Deke! Of course Mike would call her father to help bail Jeff out.

"I didn't do anything but make a few phone calls," her father rumbled. "Jeff's a good kid. He doesn't belong in jail for doing what a million other boys his age are doing."

Andi shook her head. Typical. She knocked on the door and cleared her throat. It felt like she was swallowing nails. "Can I come in?"

Both men eyed her with suspicion, like she had a bomb strapped to her body and was about to press the detonator.

"Andi." Mike leaned back in his chair. "What can I do for you?"

She stepped into the office, smiling at her father. "Hey, Deke." She didn't give him a chance to respond, her heart couldn't take it. "I think you know why I'm here, Mike. What happened last night?"

Mike stared at her, his eyes reflecting a lethal mix of fatigue and hostility. "What happened? Well, gee, let's see." He stood. "Pritchard had Jeff charged with rape, the cops dragged the poor kid in for questioning. I called Deke, who called a lawyer, who made it go away."

Andi glanced at her father. "I guess I should thank you."

"Oh really?" Mike's voice cut like a knife. "I thought you were all up in arms because Jeff dared to sully Princess Beth."

Andi lifted her chin. She wasn't going to let him see her sweat, though she was trembling in her designer boots. "I never wanted him in jail! I don't think..."

"That little piano player of yours is a real piece of work." Deke crossed his arms over his chest, batting one thousand with his lifelong habit of interrupting her before she could finish what she was going to say. "Her daddy deserves to be shot."

"Beth is scared beyond belief. I can't believe she had any say in the matter." Forget Deke. She focused back on Mike. "I'm sorry. I shouldn't have come. Believe it or not, I'm concerned about Jeff as well as Beth." She lifted her chin and headed for the door. "Thanks, Deke, for helping out." Those last words almost choked her. Angry and disgusted with the two of them and their damn intractability, she left before she said something she regretted.

****

Watching Andi stalk out of his office like Queen freaking Elizabeth, Mike felt like he was being drawn and quartered. There wasn't a thing about this whole situation that didn't suck.

"Damn fool girl," Deke muttered. "Never showed one lick of sense since the day she was born." His brow creased and he stroked his chin. "I hope she doesn't do something foolish."

Holy shit! Deke was worried about Andi? Well, duh, of course he was. He was Andi's father.

He'd bet dollars to donuts Andi wouldn't believe it if he told her. Nonetheless, Deke's careless comments about Andi being foolish rankled. Honor demanded he defend her. "She's pretty strong, Deke. She'll be okay."

"She's pulled some crazy stuff in the past."

"I know about the anorexia."

Deke flinched, then his face got so stony it might as well have been carved out of granite. "I don't talk about that... ever."

Yeah, that much was really clear. He was going to back off, he really was, when he heard words fly out of his mouth. "It's a hard thing to come back from. Takes a lot of guts."

"Drop it, Mike."

Never let it be said Mike Kelly didn't know when to shut up. Deke and Andi had to hammer out their own problems, without him mucking things up.

Focus. It was all about focus. Right now, he could only worry about Jeff and getting him out of this damn mess.

## CHAPTER THIRTEEN

The next evening, Andi sighed as she surveyed the contents of her freezer. Not really caring what she ate, she snagged a Lean Cuisine penne in basil tomato sauce, unwrapped it, and shoved it in the microwave. She punched a few buttons and let Chef Mike work his magic.

Oops. Wrong term. There was to be no mentioning of the M-word.

The red roses in her garbage can glared at her in silent reproach. She stuck her tongue out at them.

The microwave pinged. She retrieved her dinner and ate it standing at the kitchen counter. Soggy and tasteless, it sat like a lump inside her churning stomach. For a few queasy seconds, she thought she was going to throw it up, and had to work to keep it down. If she threw up, she'd have to go through the process all over again, thank you anorexia, and she simply didn't have the energy. Just as she was tossing the plastic tray on top of the offensive roses, her doorbell rang.

She was in no mood for company, and her mood got worse when she peeked through the peephole and saw who was there. "Go away, Mike."

"Please, Andi, let me in. We need to talk about Jeff and Beth."

"I don't have anything to say to you."

"Then just listen to what I have to say. Please?"

She shook her head and looked at her feet. She wanted to let him in so bad she could taste it. It was one of the worst ideas she had ever had.

"I'm not going away until you let me talk to

you."

She bit her lip. Maybe she should just let him in, hear what he had to say, make some sort of token response, and get rid of him.

Sounded like a plan.

She opened the door. Mike looked great. Better than great. Wearing old jeans and a leather bomber jacket, he looked like sin on the hoof.

Damn him.

He gave her that crooked, sexy smile of his. "Hey."

"Just come in, say what you have to say, and then get out. I've got a lot to do tonight."

She watched as his eyes clouded with some emotion she refused to speculate about. He unzipped and shrugged out of his jacket as he crossed her threshold. "It's about Jeff and Beth."

Slamming the door with a little more force than was necessary, she glared at him. "You've already said as much."

He dropped his jacket onto a chair, then turned and faced her. "You look tired."

"I haven't gotten much sleep lately." She clamped her lips shut.

"That makes two of us." He rubbed the back of his neck with his hand.

He needed a haircut, she thought as she resisted the urge to smooth one rebellious lock off his forehead.

"Have they made a decision yet?"

Andi didn't need to ask who *they* were—Beth and her parents. "I don't know. I'm not at the top of the list of their favorite people anymore. They're angry at me for taking Beth to the clinic without telling them." She felt a moment of anger. "They won't let me near her. As a matter of fact..." Andi swallowed and slid her eyes away from his gaze. "They're making noises about getting me fired for it."

"That's stupid. This isn't your fault."

"Beth's a minor. They think I shouldn't have taken her to a clinic without their permission. It doesn't matter she didn't need their permission. They hear *clinic* and think abortion." She put on her poker face and waved his concern away. "They're very strict and very proud." She let her statement trail off, leaving him to make his own conclusions.

He grunted. "Any guesses?"

"There's no question she'll have the baby. The only question is whether they make her give it away or keep it to raise themselves."

Mike frowned. "This is going to ruin those kids' lives. Jeff is all set to quit school and get a job to take care of her."

That was a shocker, not at all what she'd expected to hear. "So Jeff is going to stand by her?"

"Yeah, he wants to. He thinks he's in love with her." Mike chuffed out a breath. "What does an eighteen-year-old kid know about love?"

What did anyone know about love? Just yesterday, she'd fancied herself in love with Mike. She must have been giddy from lack of sleep and the most incredible sex of her life.

*Don't go there, girlfriend*, she warned herself. *Not prudent.* Clearing her throat, she said, "I'm sure Beth feels the same way. She wouldn't have given her body away otherwise. Unless, of course, he forced her."

Mike scowled. "What do you mean, forced her?"

"He's her first and only boyfriend. She would have a hard time saying no if he was really putting the pressure on."

"So you're saying it's all Jeff's fault?"

"Well, he was the experienced one."

"He claims it was the first time for both of them."

She couldn't help snorting. "And you believe

him?"

"Why shouldn't I? He's never lied to me before."

"You really expect me to believe that the captain of the football team, who has girls lining up to go out with him, made it to his senior year without losing his virginity?"

"Well, yeah. I guess so."

"Are you really that stupid and gullible? He's a football player, for God's sake. Get a clue."

Mike's eyes got hard and hostile. She backed up a step.

"You know, this was a bad idea." His voice was clipped and tight. "I thought we might be able to work together to help these kids out. But then again, I'm just too stupid and gullible."

Andi flushed with shame. "Mike, I'm sorry. I didn't mean that the way it came out."

He grabbed his coat. "Whatever."

She reached out to him and caught his arm. "Mike, please, I'm-,"

"What?" He vibrated with hostility. "You're what?"

Her heart shriveled. "Sorry. I'm sorry."

"That makes two of us." He pulled his arm out of her grasp and left. The front door slammed with frightening finality leaving a big, cold, empty place in her heart.

****

"Oh, go to hell." Andi snarled as she slapped at the snooze button on her alarm, silencing Renee Montagne and the rest of the staff at *Morning Edition* reporting all the news she needed to know. Ordinarily, she would keep the news on, but this morning she didn't want to hear about the horrendous events happening here and abroad. Her own life was all the catastrophe she could handle, thank you very much. She didn't need to hear about someone else's misery right now.

She lay there in the dark, trying to find the energy to get out of bed and into the shower. The radio erupted again, and Renee was back. She hit the snooze button, this time with enough force to knock the radio off her nightstand. She knuckled her eyes as she levered herself into a sitting position.

She dragged herself to the shower. What she really wanted to do was crawl back into bed and pull the covers over her head.

The shower helped to wake her. She toweled off, went to her closet, and grabbed clothes randomly. She really didn't care what she wore.

The smell of coffee from her kitchen made her really glad she had remembered to set the timer on her coffee maker last night. She went to the kitchen and poured a cup with all the reverence and care of a priest administering a sacrament. The first bitter tasting sip scalded her tongue, but she didn't care. She was counting on the caffeine helping her get through the day.

If Mike stayed in his part of the school, she'd be fine. As long as she didn't have to see him, she wouldn't be reminded of that incredible night they had shared.

As long as she didn't see him, she could pretend he didn't mean anything to her.

Shaking her head, she finished her coffee, rinsed out her mug, and left it in the sink. At least it was a short school week with the Thanksgiving holiday at the end of it.

Had the situation been different, she would have invited Mike to her parents' house for dinner. Deke would have been thrilled.

Maybe she should invite Ian. She didn't know if he had plans. She hadn't talked to him since the night of the Ballet Gala.

On second thought, maybe inviting Ian wasn't a good idea. They hadn't parted on the best of terms.

As she put on her coat, she realized she'd managed to alienate just about everyone she knew. Great. Just great.

Way to go, Andi.

## CHAPTER FOURTEEN

Andi studied the contents of her closet. The Thanksgiving holiday had seemed endless, Sunday an eternity.

Mike had hovered in the back of her mind all Sunday. She tried to pass the time doing heavy duty cleaning to exorcise his ghost, but not even scrubbing her refrigerator had kept thoughts of him at bay.

She stopped herself from going to the supermarket and renting a Rug Doctor to do her carpets.

Nursing a steaming cup of ginger Chai, she sat in her living room surveying the results of her cleaning frenzy, wondering what she should do about Mike. She should probably cut her losses and move on. She hadn't known him very long. He couldn't be that difficult to forget, right?

Her body insisted on remembering their night together, the touch of his hands, the scent of his skin, the taste of his mouth on hers, the hot words of love in her ear, the way he moved when he came inside her. No forgetting that. How could she give that up?

She would give it up, give him up. She had to.

The doorbell rang, startling her. She wasn't expecting anybody and hadn't changed out of her house cleaning uniform—worn gym shorts and a cropped tee shirt. The tee shirt had bleach stains on it from the cleanser she'd used on her tile grout. She smelled just like that same cleanser, a lovely *eau de Clorox* aroma. Just her luck, the person ringing her doorbell would be Mike.

The sudden hitch in her heart had nothing to do with the thought he might be on the other side of her front door.

She got up from the sofa too fast and twisted her ankle. She hopped to the door and peeked through the peephole.

It was Ian, of all people.

Her expression must have been grim, judging by the look on Ian's face when she greeted him. "Hello, Ian."

"Andrea." Wearing a dress coat, he bore gifts. "Is this a bad time? Should I go away?"

Touched by the uncertainty in his expression, she managed a smile. "No, of course not. I twisted my ankle when I got up to answer the door. Come on in."

As he entered her living room, he stared at her legs. In concern for her twisted ankle, she assured herself while she shut the door behind him.

"Are you okay?" he asked.

"Sure. I just twisted it a little." Manners took hold. "May I take your coat?"

"I won't be staying long. I wanted to drop a couple of things off. I hope that's okay."

Puzzled, Andi summoned a smile for him. "We're still friends, aren't we? Of course it's okay." She sighed. "I value your friendship, Ian. I don't want to lose it."

"You won't. You can't." He smiled and extended the packages in his hands. "Happy early Christmas."

Presents? Yikes! "Oh, Ian. You shouldn't have." Awkwardly, she accepted the brightly wrapped gifts.

He shrugged. "No big deal. Why don't you open them and see what they are?" He smiled an expectant smile.

Seeing that she had no choice, and unable to resist temptation anyway, she unwrapped the smaller of the two boxes. "A DVD?"

"I was on the 'Net and ran across a performance of the American Ballet Theater's revival of Stravinsky's *Sacre du Printemps*. I remembered you admired that performance, so I downloaded it and burned you a copy." He smiled, one conspirator to another. "Don't tell anyone."

"Oh," she crooned as she turned the pirated DVD over in her hands. Heart lighter now, she looked back at him. "Bootleg Stravinsky. Thank you! I love it."

"It's no big deal. Open the other one."

Putting the disk down on her hallway table, she went to work on the other package. It was a slim book of poems. She goggled at him. "This is yours, isn't it? You've been published!"

He blushed and nodded. "You're the first person to see it."

"Why didn't you tell me?"

"I didn't want to jinx it."

She turned the cover of the book and it opened to the dedication page. With a slight feeling of alarm, she noticed he had dedicated it to her. "Ian. I don't know what to say."

"I'd rather you said nothing. I wrote many of those poems with you in mind, and so it was only natural to dedicate it to you." He cleared his throat.

She laid the book on top of the DVD case. "They're lovely gifts. Thank you. I'm embarrassed I don't..." Something in his expression stopped her. "What?"

"Please don't make a big deal of this. Just accept it as a gift from one friend to another." He looked at his watch. "Well, I need to be going. I have a stack of papers on my desk at home that aren't going to grade themselves."

"Okay." She really felt awkward. "Are you sure I can't get you a cup of tea or something?"

"Quite." He put out a hand and cupped her cheek. His smile was sad. "I've got to go." He dropped his hand to his side and fisted it.

She rose to tiptoe and kissed his cheek. "Thank you for the DVD and the book. I'm stunned."

He nodded, then turned, leaving without another word. She closed the door behind him and ignored the tear rolling down her cheek.

\*\*\*\*

"Die, you stupid machine! Die!" Andi yelled while she kicked the uncooperative copy machine located in the teacher's lounge. She only succeeded in hurting her foot and getting a big, black smudge on her taupe leather boots. She kicked it once more anyway, studying the buttons on the machine, trying to decide which one would make the darn machine work.

It was late, and she was in a very bad mood. Ian's visit from the night before pricked at her conscience. She didn't want him to dedicate that book of poems to her. It made her beyond uncomfortable, because it served as a forever reminder of how she had hurt him.

And then there was Beth. She hadn't been back to school since she had told her parents she was pregnant. To make matters worse, her parents weren't letting her talk to anyone, never mind go to any rehearsals, at school or church. Andi was worried on so many levels, not the least of which was how miserable the poor girl must be.

Beth's dropping off the face of the map affected the singers in her competition choir as well. There was no way she could replace Beth at the piano, not with the choral competition coming up so soon. The contest rules stipulated that the accompanist be a student. There were simply no other students who could play the music.

As disappointing as that was, Andi was more

concerned about Beth.

She didn't miss the irony that her situation with the choir was very similar to what Mike went through when she had put Jeff and Tim on the ineligible list.

She punched some more buttons on the copy machine and only got some flashing orange lights. She *so* didn't need this. She was late, she was behind, and she was frazzled. Exhaling long and loud, she dropped to her knees and opened up the Xerox machine to see if she could get it to work.

****

Mike couldn't remember a worse day than this one. After what should have been a great holiday weekend, he was tired and grumpy. He'd spent the better part of it not immersed in football games, like he'd hoped he would. Oh, no. He'd spent it at the gym, working off twenty pounds of turkey along with his frustration about Andi. The only thing the gym had helped him with was the turkey.

Tonight, he'd stop at Jeff's house to check on him, as he hadn't been in school, then hit The End Zone for a burger and maybe a game of pool, then home.

He pushed open the door to the teacher's lounge.

It was the grunting and swearing that got his attention first.

Surprised to hear those words coming from a female voice, he swiveled his head to the corner of the room where the Xerox machine lurked. A very shapely female behind wiggled itself in the air while its owner muttered obscenities and tossed items out of the cabinet.

If he didn't miss his guess, and he rarely ever did, he knew the sweet ass wriggling around in the corner.

He knew it very well indeed. "Andi, what are you doing?"

Startled, she bonked her head on a shelf in the cabinet as she struggled to a position of some sort of dignity.

He grinned. He couldn't help it. This was his first encounter with her since that last time at her condo, and he'd missed her like crazy. "Looking for something?"

She scrambled to her feet. "The Xerox machine broke. I have some stuff I have to get out, and I can't use the machine in the main office. Trudy's copying student council stuff." She motioned with her head towards the recalcitrant machine. "I'm trying to fix this one."

Amused, Mike nodded sagely. "I see." He frowned, remembering he wasn't going to like this woman anymore.

She looked at him, really studied him, and then her gaze clouded up and she looked away. Blinking furiously, she stared at the wall beyond him. "I hate this."

"And I love it? Right."

"I didn't say that."

"You didn't need to. You blame me for this whole mess."

She didn't bother to ask what mess he was referring to. "I don't blame you. I just wish you had told me the two of them were dating."

"Yeah, I could have told you. And then what would you have done?"

"I would have stopped them before it was too late."

He shook his head. "You couldn't have stopped them. Nobody could have. Kids in love are pretty much a force of nature."

"You didn't even try."

"You're wrong. I had a talk with Jeff. I thought he was smarter than..."

"You had a talk with Jeff. Big, fat, hairy deal.

Look at what good it did."

"You know, there were two of them in the backseat of that car." He was happy to see her flinch. "Beth could have said no at any time during the proceedings."

"And if I had known there were *proceedings* to interrupt, I could have talked to her and helped her make better decisions."

"You're not her mother, Andi. You're not responsible for her." He shook his head. "Her nut-job parents are."

Shaking her head, she looked at the floor. "What a nightmare."

"You're telling me."

She suddenly looked as if someone had dropped a ten-ton weight on her very fragile shoulders. Face pale, eyes smudged and puffy, she was waif-like and shaken. He moved in closer and reached a hand to smooth over her hair. She flinched when he touched her.

"Have you been eating?"

She sighed and leaned her cheek against his hand before pulling away. "Yes. I'm taking care of myself."

Feeling like an awkward clod, he shifted his weight from one foot to the other. "Good. Have you, uh, talked to Deke lately?"

"Oh, brilliant idea." Her voice cut like a knife. "As if talking to Deke has ever helped me. He'll be all over Jeff's side and run Beth down like road-kill. Why, that's just what I need." She angled her chin up to look him in the eye. "No, thank you."

"Andi, I don't want to fight with you." Frustration prickled along his spine. "What's really bugging you is Deke taking Jeff's side in this whole mess. This isn't about Jeff or Beth at all. This is about your relationship with Deke."

Andi's eyes narrowed. "My relationship with my

father is none of your business."

"Got that right. And believe me, baby, I'm glad of it."

She let a long, slow breath hiss out. He was sorry instantly. It had been a low blow, and he could see he had hurt her. The pain was written on her face. "Look, Andi, I-,"

"Don't say another word, Mike." Looking around the room with a desperation Mike could feel as well as see, she found her purse, grabbed it up. "I think we've had enough for one day." She bolted for the door.

A knock came on the door just as she reached for the handle. She pulled it open.

Tim and Katie were on the other side. Tim cleared his throat. "Ms. Nelson. We were looking for you and the Coach."

"I'm right here, Tim. What's up?" Mike came to stand behind Andi.

"We promised we wouldn't tell anybody, but we talked about it and we decided we should let you know what's going on." Katie never had a problem talking.

Andi drew her into the teacher's lounge. Tim followed. "What's wrong? Did something happen to Beth?"

Katie looked at Tim, then back at Andi. She avoided looking at Mike. "Sort of."

"Well, what is it? Is she hurt? Did something happen to the baby?"

Tim looked at Andi. "She didn't get hurt." He shifted his gaze over to Mike. "Jeff and Beth have run away. They want to get married."

"They what?" Mike felt his blood freeze in his veins.

"They're running away. They're going to get married and then try to get into Canada."

"Of all the stupid, fool-headed ideas I've ever

heard, that has to top the list. What the hell do they think they're doing?"

"They're running away so they can be together and be a family. It's kind of romantic," Katie offered, cringing when both Mike and Andi gaped at her.

Mike snorted. "Figures a girl would look at it that way." He looked hard at Tim. "Is this true?"

"Yeah. I tried to talk him out of it, but he was sure."

"Any idea where they went?"

"I gave them the key to my parents' beach house in Maine. They were going to hide there for a little bit, find a Justice of the Peace, and then try for Canada."

"Maine? That's crazy! How long ago did they leave?" Mike couldn't believe what he was hearing.

"This morning. They took his mom's car. Even sticking to the back roads, they must be there by now."

"Can you tell me how to get there?" Mike had to get to those kids before they wrecked their lives.

"You gonna go after them?"

"You bet I am."

"I'm going with you." Andi's tone brooked no disagreement.

"The hell you are." He swung his head around to face her.

"The hell I'm not. I can't trust you to do right by Beth."

"Oh, for the love of... Don't look at me like I'm an ax murderer. I'm not going to hurt the girl."

Speaking slowly in a talking-to-an-idiot tone of voice, she repeated, "Don't argue with me, Mike." Andi walked back to the door and stood in front of it, blocking Mike's path. "I'm coming with you."

Mike looked at her standing there, daring him to leave by going through her. She had guts; he had to give her that.

Did he want to be alone escorting a renegade pregnant girl back home to her overbearing, out-for-blood papa? He might need Andi there to talk sense into Beth while he took care of Jeff.

He glared at her. "Don't make me regret this."

She nodded as if there had never been any question about it. Turning to talk to Katie, who was staring at the two of them like they both had green and purple polka-dotted skin, Andi smiled at her and drew her aside. "I promise I won't let anything happen to her."

Katie bit her lip and murmured something Mike couldn't hear.

He caught himself staring and brought himself up short. He was only taking Andi along so he wouldn't have to deal with an emotional, pregnant teenage girl.

"Tim!" He barked, his tone shorter and angrier than he meant it to be. "Write down those directions."

Tim scrambled to do just that. God willing, they'd catch up with Jeff and Beth sooner, rather than later.

## CHAPTER FIFTEEN

"I think it's snowing harder." Andi kept her eyes staring straight ahead through the windshield. It was the first thing she'd said to Mike since they had left the school two hours ago.

Mike grunted. Not a sound that invited further comments.

A violent gust of wind rocked the car, sending snow swirling around it. Andi couldn't see a thing. *Great*, she thought. Here she was, stuck in a snowstorm, cruising the back roads of Maine with Mike Kelly. "Do you even know where we are?"

"Yeah. Maine."

She shivered and hugged herself. "I'm cold. May I turn up the heat?"

"Suit yourself."

She cranked up the thermostat then settled back in her seat. *Stubborn man*, Andi fumed in silence as she sent him a sideways glance. "It's really coming down now. You can't possibly see the road."

Jaw clenched, he drummed his fingers on the steering wheel. "I can see fine."

She bit back a reply. He was lying. He had to be. No one could see anything but swirling snow. "May I turn on the radio? Maybe I can find a weather report."

Another grunt.

Truly feeling the love coming from the driver, only, *not*, Andi pushed the power button on the radio with more force than was necessary and fiddled with it until she found the public radio station. One of Bach's *Brandenburg Concerti* was playing. She sighed. Comfort music.

The drumming on the steering wheel increased in volume, out of sync with the music's rhythm. She turned her head to look at Mike. "What's your problem?"

He continued to stare out the window, but abruptly stopped the drumming. "Can't you find anything better on the radio than that?"

"What? You don't like the music? I think it's soothing."

"You would." He shook his head.

"What's that supposed to mean?"

"Nothing. Nothing at all."

"Okay then."

They both stared out at the snow while the music changed from Bach to Rachmaninoff. Other than the music, the only things Andi could hear were the wind buffeting the car from outside and Mike breathing heavily inside.

She hoped he wasn't coming down with something.

His fingers started drumming against the steering wheel again.

It was going to drive her crazy. If he was going to drum, couldn't he at least do it in rhythm to the music?

The snow started to pile up on the windshield, so he turned the wipers on. Great. A new rhythm for him to be out of sync with. She closed her eyes and tried to focus on the music over the sound of Mike's rhythm-challenged fingers.

*Tap. Tap-tap. Taaap-tap-tap-tap-tap-tap-tap. Tap-ta-tap. Tap. Tap. Tap-tap-tap. Tippity-tappity.* Then, silence.

Thank you, God.

*Tap.*

"Would you stop that!" She knew she was screeching like a fishwife, but she didn't care.

He jumped in his seat, but at least he stopped drumming his thumbs against the wheel. "Jeez, Andi. You wanna give me a heart attack or something?"

"I'll happily bash your brains out with a tire iron if you don't stop pounding on the steering wheel!"

"Touchy, ain't 'cha?"

"I am not touchy. You are being annoying on purpose."

"Me? I'm not doing anything except driving this car."

"You know very well what you're doing!"

"Nope. Sorry. I haven't got a clue. Care to enlighten me?"

She took a deep, cleansing breath. "Okay, we'll play it your way. I would appreciate it very much if you could stop drumming your fingers against the steering wheel."

He took his eyes off the road to give her a brief look. She couldn't tell what he was thinking. "Your wish is my command." Turning his attention back to the road, he dismissed her.

Rachmaninoff turned into Beethoven, the *Eroïca Symphony*. She loved the *Eroïca Symphony*. She closed her eyes again, trying to lose herself in the music.

"Can't you find anything with words?"

Her eyes sprang open. "What?"

"Can't you find any music that has words to it? Something that has a decent beat? That classical crap is putting me to sleep."

"Sure. Fine. Whatever." She pushed the seek button. "Just tell me when to stop?"

"Just keep going until you find some Brooks and Dunn or Toby Keith, and I'll be happy."

"Who?"

He grinned. "They're country singers."

"Country singers? You want me to find a country

music station?"

"Well, yeah. Where else would you find country singers?"

"You expect me to sit for God knows how long in this car, driving through the back of beyond, and listen to country music while I do it?"

"Yeah."

"You're inhuman."

He sighed. "Look. You didn't have to come along. Since you forced your way into this little joy ride, you can play by my rules. And I want to listen to country music."

"But..."

"Besides, I'm feeling kind of tired. The classical stuff really *is* putting me to sleep. The country will keep me awake."

She felt a rush of embarrassment. "I'm sorry. Do you want me to drive for awhile?"

"No." For a moment, he did look incredibly weary. "Just find me some decent tunes."

She turned her attention to finding a new radio station, with only a pang at the loss of the Beethoven. She made it around the dial twice before she found a country station. Repressing a sigh, she looked out the side window. By the faint moonlight, she could see the snow was getting pretty deep. "How close do you think we are?"

"I don't know."

"What do you mean you don't know?"

"Just what I said. I've never been up this way before."

"You mean to tell me you dragged me out in this storm, and you don't know where you're going?"

He winced. "Shout a little louder, why don't you?" The car skidded a bit, and his brows knit in concentration. "Besides, I didn't drag you along. You invited yourself."

Oh. Right. Best to change the subject. "Where

are we in relation to Tim's directions?"

"We passed the last landmark about an hour ago. By my calculations, we should have gone through Glenborough Village half an hour ago."

"So, the snow has slowed us down, right?" A nasty little suspicion flitted across her mind. "We're lost, aren't we?"

"Hell, no. We're not lost. I followed Tim's directions to the letter. Sort of."

"Define sort of."

"I checked the map before we left and saw a shortcut."

"A shortcut. I see." She bit her tongue almost hard enough to draw blood. Nope. She couldn't let it pass. She had to say something. "We're lost. You have no idea where we are."

"I do have an idea. We're on the road to Glenborough Village."

"You are so full of it! We're driving around in the middle of nowhere, in the dark, in a snowstorm!"

"We're on the road to Glenborough. Just keep your cool and let me concentrate on getting us there, okay?"

"But you..."

"Would you just, for once, have a little faith in me? I know what I'm doing."

"I don't have much choice, do I?" she muttered, her tone dripping with resentment.

"No, you don't," he answered, turning his attention back to the road. He was going to throttle her. He was going to wrap his hands around that pretty neck of hers and then he was going to... going to... well, he wasn't going to kiss her, that was for sure.

No matter how much he wanted to.

It didn't matter she was right, he had no idea where they were, and they were in the middle of a major snowstorm. In truth, he'd given up on

Glenborough Village ages ago. Right now, he'd settle for any sign of civilization. He was hungry, tired enough his eyes were falling shut and needing a break.

He was sure he looked as scuzzy as he felt, needing a shave and gritty-eyed from driving so long. Sneaking a glance over to Andi, he wanted to curse. She looked as if she had just stepped out of *Vogue* magazine.

Man! How did she manage that? He snuck a second look.

She was staring straight ahead, her lips tight together, her eyes stoic. Hands clasped in her lap, she was pale, tired, and absolutely determined not to show it.

That was more like it.

He didn't want her here with him, damn it, now that he had gotten them lost. But how could he know an early blizzard would come out of nowhere to make navigation nearly impossible.

He should have, and he felt really stupid for not taking it into account. No matter what he did, he always ended up feeling like a moron around this woman.

Well... Not everything he did with her made him feel like a moron. He had felt incredible the night they had made love. He felt as if he had won the Super Bowl, the Stanley Cup and the World Series combined, single-handed. He had ruled the world, no, not just the world, the entire freakin' universe.

He glanced at her again. She remained stoic, and it was breaking his heart. Remember Jeff, he admonished himself. Saving Jeff is all that counts.

He made himself focus on the road. It was really coming down, near white-out conditions, and he was amazed he was making the progress he was. There had to be a town soon. He would find someplace warm and safe to stay and ride out the storm. If he and Andi were unable to travel, chances were Jeff and Beth were also unable to travel. He'd catch up to them.

No problem.

He bit back a yawn, then rubbed his eyes. He'd kill for coffee.

Andi shifted in her seat, doing a tiny little stretch and recrossing her legs. Mike was sorry that she had those legs all covered up with a long, plaid wool skirt and boots. True, the boots had a spike heel and looked really impractical for clomping around in the snow, but they still covered up those sexy calves of hers.

Too bad, because they were first class legs. He had first hand knowledge of that.

Ohhhh, yeah.

"What are you smiling about?"

Mike turned to look at Andi's stern, disgruntled face. "I'm not smiling."

"You were, too. If there's something to smile about in this whole mess, I'd really love to know what it is."

"You know, the trouble with you, Spud, is that you take everything too seriously."

"I beg your pardon, but what did you just call me?"

"Uh, Spud."

"Spud. As in a potato?"

"Well, yeah." He was really grinning now. "But a cute little potato. Not an old one with all those nasty white things sprouting out from it."

"Why in the world would you call me a potato?"

"Not potato. Spud."

"Why would you call me *Spud* then?"

"Well, I figure ol' Ian has just about exhausted every poetic nickname out there. I'd hate to repeat any." He wagged his brows up and down. "I'm original."

She muttered something under her breath. Though he couldn't hear it, he was pretty sure it was obscene. For some reason, that cheered him up.

And when he was full of goodwill and cheer, he whistled. In honor of the season, he launched into *Frosty the Snowman*.

Over and over again.

He especially liked the *Thumpity-thump-thump* part.

"If you don't stop whistling, I'm going to murder you and dump your body here in the snow where it won't be found until spring," Andi hissed through clenched teeth.

"Hey, I'm sorry. I thought you liked music."

"I do like music. It's your whistling one song and the radio playing another one at the same time that annoys me."

"Ah. Sorry 'bout that, Spud."

"Oh, for the love of... Please stop calling me by that stupid name."

"I don't think so. It fits you."

"It fits me?" Her voice squeaked a little.

"Well, yeah."

That shut her up, but not for long. "If you'd said something to me when you first found out about Beth and Jeff, then we wouldn't be here right now, chasing them in the mother of all snowstorms."

"That's right. Because you're so much smarter than me, you'd have been able to keep two horny teenagers from getting into each other's pants?"

"No, I don't mean that." She put her hand on his arm. "You're not stupid, Mike. I never, ever thought that about you. It's just... it's just... if you had come to me right away, oh never mind. I'm tired of going in circles with you about it."

"There's nothing you could have done."

"How do you know? I could have talked to Beth and helped her resist temptation."

"Like that would have worked."

"It might have. I have a good relationship with Beth."

"Fine. It's your fantasy, you're welcome to it."

"It's not a fantasy. Talking to Beth about her choices would have been a whole lot more helpful than the *Way to go, Jeffrey* talk you had with Jeff."

"Why are you so damn sure I congratulated him?"

She gave an ugly little laugh. "I've lived around jocks all my life, and heard enough bragging about scoring to last me a lifetime."

"I'm not most jocks. I thought you knew that."

"I *thought* I knew that. I really did start to think that you were different." She looked genuinely miserable. "I'm so confused and upset I can't think straight. It all just breaks my heart." She sniffed and swiped at her eyes.

Oh crap. He didn't want her to cry. What the hell was he going to do now?

If he hadn't been looking at Andi, he probably would have seen the deer soon enough to avoid it. He swerved to avoid the animal, fishtailed a couple of times, then did a doughnut right off the road. They ran over a couple of bushes before being stopped by a huge pine tree. The tree dumped a load of snow on their car just as the air bags inflated and knocked them back into their seats.

Mike shook his head to clear it then turned off the motor. The car filled with acrid, gray dust from the airbags. A soft moan from the airbag next to him brought him fully to his senses. Andi. Oh, Lordy.

She was having trouble breathing.

Struggling against the panic that swamped him, he undid his seatbelt, pushed away the deflated airbags and reached for her. "Hey, Spud, are you okay?"

Andi blinked a few times. "Just peachy. What

happened?"

"A deer came out of nowhere and ran us off the road."

She looked at him, her eyes big and blue against her pale face. "Are you okay?" Her voice shook as much as her body.

"I'm fine. How about you?"

"I'm okay." She struggled to right herself in the seat. He helped her to an upright position. There was something different in her eyes. "Really. I'm okay."

"You're sure?"

"Yes. I'm fine." She wiggled her fingers at him. "See? Nothing broken."

"You were having trouble breathing."

"It was that damn airbag. Now it's okay." Leaning back against the seat, she closed her eyes. "What the hell do we do now, Mike?"

Mike followed her lead and leaned back in his own seat. He sniffed the air, looking for the scent of gasoline. He didn't find it. But that didn't give him a plan. "Damned if I know. Give me a minute."

"Take all the time you need. I'm not going anywhere."

A weak laugh worked its way up his throat. "You sure about that?"

"Yeah. Positive." Without opening her eyes, she blew out a breath. "Seriously, Mike. What do we do now? Do you have your cell phone?"

"Uh, no. I don't. Not with me anyway. Do you?"

"No. Maybe we should try to find a phone."

Mike shook his head. "The snow is pretty deep. Who knows how far we'd have to walk. I can't remember the last house I saw. We're better off staying here."

She bit her lip, uncertainty oozing from her. "You think so?"

"Well, we didn't go that far off the road. There's

bound to be a plow coming through here sometime soon. Let's face it." He nodded at her fashionable but incredibly impractical boots. "You're not exactly dressed for playing in the snow. Neither am I."

She managed a wan smile. "I guess."

Undeterred, he smiled back at her. "I'm pretty sure I'm right. In the meantime..." He looked over at her and took her hand. "Are you sure you're okay?"

She looked as frightened as the deer that'd hit them, and shuddered. "It's getting cold."

"Let me see what I can do about that." He relinquished her hand to open the glove compartment and extract a flashlight. "Don't go anywhere." He pushed open his car door with his feet and wiggled out to check the damage.

The news wasn't good. The front end was stove in from hitting the tree, but he still didn't smell any gasoline. Given the depth of the snow, there was no way he could back it out.

He sighed and popped open his trunk. Knowing he had no shovel inside, he found a piece of cardboard and used it to clear snow away from the exhaust pipe. Then, he grabbed a blanket he hadn't taken out after a trip to Cape Cod last summer, and made his way back inside the car.

Andi was curled up in her seat, her arms around her shivering body. "What'd you find?"

"Not much." He turned off the flashlight and held out the blanket. "Here, take this. If the car still runs, we can get some heat for a little bit, but we'll have to conserve." He forced a smile. "I don't know how long we'll be here."

She took the blanket and looked grateful. "Thank you."

As he shook the snow off his head, she unfolded the blanket and started to wrap it around herself. "Uh, do you have another blanket?"

He shook his head. "Nope. Just the one." He

turned the ignition key to start the engine, grunting in satisfaction when it turned over.

Andi cleared her throat. "If we went into the backseat, we could share the blanket."

## CHAPTER SIXTEEN

Mike went very, very still, his hand resting on the key in the ignition. He'd brought the fresh, biting smell of the snow into the car with him, as well as more cold air.

"What did you say?"

"If we went into the back seat, we could share the blanket, and... body heat."

"I don't know. I might tell someone about it later on."

A wave of weariness so heavy it nearly crossed her eyes washed over her. "I'm sorry. I didn't really mean any of that." She looked him straight in the eyes. "I'm tired, and I'm scared, and I'm cold. Could you please hold me for a little bit?"

His eyes were so hot on her, she was sure she'd burn up. "If that's what you want."

"It makes sense. That way we don't have to run the car so long, and we can save gas." She shrugged, trying to be casual. It wasn't working. Her heart stuttered in her chest like a wounded bird. "In case we're stuck here longer than we have gas for."

"Makes sense. I agree." He turned the car off and got out so he could move the driver's seat all the way forward. Andi took the blanket and squeezed her way between the seats. As she settled herself, Mike climbed in.

Shaking off the snow, he unzipped his jacket, opened his arms, and gathered her to him. She could tell he was being careful with her, but the comfort of his arms felt so good. She curled into his chest, soaking in his warmth. She closed her eyes, and he

187

covered them both with the blanket.

His heart beat slow and steady beneath her hand, and the soft wool of his sweater warmed her cheek. He shifted his legs up on the seat and settled her between them. "Are you comfortable?"

She nodded against his warm, solid chest. He rested his cheek on top of her head, and she could feel his breath gently ripple her hair. Closing her eyes, she allowed herself to relax, to melt against him. He felt so good.

So safe.

"Are you sure you're okay?" His voice rasped against her hair.

"Yeah, I'm sure."

"No problems breathing? That airbag almost knocked you out."

"No problems breathing. I'm a little sore, that's all." She almost purred as his arms tightened around her and snuggled her in closer to his body.

He must have mistaken the sound she made for one of pain, because he let go of her almost immediately. "Oh, God, Spud. I didn't hurt you more, did I?"

"No. It felt good." Since he held her so loosely now, she could shift to look at him and be comfortable.

The light surrounding them was murky at best, but she was getting used to the dark. She brought her arms up and laced them around Mike's neck. The blanket slipped down her back, but he brought it back up around her shoulders then moved his hands down her back to encircle her waist.

"Your heart is pounding. I can feel it from here," he whispered, his eyes locked with hers.

"Adrenaline," she whispered back. There was no mistaking the spark in his eyes, even in the gloom filling the car.

"Ah. So that's what it is." His mouth came closer

to hers, oh, so tempting. His eyes never left hers.

"Must be." Her lips parted, and she ran the tip of her tongue around them.

He closed his eyes and swore.

She felt, rather than heard, his heartfelt expletive. "Mike," she began, but didn't finish, because suddenly his lips were touching hers in the softest, most tender kiss she had ever shared.

She whimpered when he dragged his mouth from hers. She couldn't help it. She hadn't wanted to let that sweet, perfect kiss end.

"Damn, Andi. What are we going to do about this?" he asked against her forehead.

"Kiss me again, Mike. Kiss me again, just like that."

But he was unsure, she realized, and so she took matters into her own hands. Lifting up, she settled her mouth onto his and kissed him.

At first reluctant, Mike let her tease his mouth with her tongue before he opened up to her. Then his tongue began to tease hers back, and soon it was no longer a matter of who was kissing whom.

Underneath the blanket, he'd taken his gloves off and his hands moved up and down her back. His fingers were calloused, and the soft wool of her sweater snagged on them. She wiggled closer to him, creating a gap between her sweater and her skirt, and those wonderful fingers of his were on her skin, touching her, and caressing her beneath the sweater.

Breathing hard, he broke away from her lips again, only this time, he moved down to her neck, where he nibbled on the soft skin there. It tickled exquisitely, and she wiggled and squirmed on his lap.

"Easy now," he whispered in her ear, his breath hot, his voice rough with passion. "You keep that up, and I won't be able to control myself."

That brought her attention to where he was hard and insistent against her thigh. With a low sound of delight, she shifted so her skirt bunched up around her waist. Straddling his lap, she snuggled her lower body against his erection.

He sucked in a breath with a very audible hiss. His fingers clenched for only a second against her back, then moved up to undo the back clasp of her bra. Her breasts freed, he moved his hands around front to cup them while his mouth continued to tease her neck.

He dragged his thumbs back and forth across each nipple, and she hummed as her body responded to his touch. Unable to help herself, she rocked her hips up and down against his hardness.

He growled, then bit her gently in the curve where her neck met her shoulder. It made her shiver. "God, Spud. I want to be inside you so bad."

"Mmmmm." Reaching a hand down, she cupped and stroked him through his jeans. "Don't call me Spud."

"That feels so-o-o good." She could tell from his voice that he was excited. Arousal roared through her. She felt powerfully feminine, and she loved it.

And as much as she didn't want to admit it, she loved Mike too. The guy, not just the sex.

Though the sex was pretty damn incredible.

Next thing she knew, he was taking her hand and pulling it off him. She made a whimper of protest.

Mike shook his head. His eyes were bright. "Do you hear that? I think it's a plow." He pushed her off his lap.

She scrambled to the other corner of the backseat and strained to listen. It was faint, but she heard the distant scraping of a plow against the road.

"Wait here." Mike struggled out of the backseat

and into the night.

Andi watched as flashing lights lit up the sky beyond the embankment. The rumble of the plow got louder as the lights got closer.

Mike stuck his head back in the car. Grinning from ear to ear, his face bright from the cold air, snow clinging to his hair and shoulders, he held out his hand to her. "C'mon. The guy in the plow is gonna give us a ride to the next town."

"But..."

"Shhhhhh. No buts." He yanked her by the hand and planted a kiss on her palm. "Just hush. For once, don't try to control the whole damn world."

Tears threatened. She couldn't tell if they were from relief or frustration. Spying her purse, she snatched it up and let Mike help her out of the car.

Youch! Her legs didn't want to cooperate, and she winced when they disagreed with her on which way to move. Mike guided her out then swept her up into his arms to carry her to the plow truck. "Mike, I'm perfectly capable of walking to the plow."

"Don't want you to wreck those killer boots."

Before she knew it, she was settled in the truck, sandwiched by Mike on her right side, and Ernie, the plow operator, on her left. The two guys struck up a heated discussion about football. The C-B radio squawked directions broken up by static into the overheated cab. The aroma of stale coffee came from one of the numerous Styrofoam cups on the dashboard and in the seat wells.

Ernie was a big guy, bigger than Mike, with a wool cap on his head and a heavy-duty work jacket over coveralls. He used his hands, which were big enough to palm a basketball, for emphasis when he talked. She was certain he was going to smack her in the nose before they got to wherever he was taking them. Andi felt invisible.

"But I gotta tell ya," Ernie was saying, "those

Nelson twins are gonna save New Rochester. Never thought I'd see the Rangers doin' as good as they're doin' this season, you hear what I'm sayin'?"

"It surprised the hell out of a lot of us." Was Mike blushing? The heater must be on too high.

"Of course, their daddy was one of the greats. Man, that Deke Nelson was one helluva coach."

"That he was." Mike grinned like the Cheshire Cat. "Some might disagree with us, though, eh, Andi?"

Andi made a little squeaking sound while she choked. "I have no opinion one way or the other," she stalled.

"Just like a woman," Ernie chuckled. "Not interested in the important things in life."

"Football is hardly..."

Mike nudged her really hard in her side, crowding her more against ol' Ernie. "I hear you, Ernie. It's hard to understand a species that would rather go to the ballet than to a football game."

"Ballet is just as athletic, maybe more so, than football." *So there*, Andi thought, and mentally stuck her tongue out at both men.

Ernie chuckled again. "Yep. Just like a woman, thinking that prancing around on a stage all dressed in tights is athletic. That's a good one."

Andi opened her mouth to say something, anything, but closed it again. Years of her mother's training kicked in. Poor, deluded, misguided Ernie was doing her a favor. She'd keep her disagreement to herself.

Mike, however, was still having fun. "Wouldn't you just love to meet Deke one day, and the twins, just to talk, man to man, about the game?"

Ernie started to enumerate the many things he'd like to ask Deke Nelson, and Andi felt a sinking feeling in her stomach. This man was going out of his way to get Mike and her to civilization. If meeting Deke and the twins would make him happy, she could arrange that. "Ernie?" She had to raise her voice to be heard over his enthusiasm. "How would you like to go to a Rangers' game and sit with Deke Nelson in his personal box?"

"Well yeah, who wouldn't?" She winced when Ernie took his eyes off the road to look at her.

"I have a friend who can arrange it, if you want. Just let me know." Andi didn't dare look at Mike.

"That'd be fantastic!"

She ducked out of the way of Ernie's right hand. "It's no big deal. You've been so good to us."

Mike was silent as Ernie raved on. She didn't know what he was thinking.

So, what else was new?

The Pinetree Motel was small, rustic and clean. Run by the same couple who'd built it in the Fifties, Big Jack and Irma Smith, it catered to the needs of hunters who came to this area of Maine in the fall. Ernie was buds with Big Jack and managed to get Mike and Andi the last room they had left. Irma was holding court in the office dispensing coffee and pie. The only kitchen was hers; they didn't have a restaurant. There was kind of a party going on, with all the stranded hunters congregating in the office and telling stories.

Mike and Andi thanked Ernie, then got his address and phone number so Andi could follow through on her promise. After they checked in, Mike went and joined the hunters for coffee and pie, while Andi holed up in the bathroom and indulged in a long soak in the tub.

An hour later, she was wrinkly, relaxed, and decked out in an extra-extra-large tee shirt with a picture of the Pinetree Motel and a grinning moose emblazoned on the front.

It hung to her knees.

She washed out her underwear and nylons and

hung them up in the shower. A gust of cold air from the bedroom gave her warning before she left the bathroom.

Mike was back from the lobby.

## CHAPTER SEVENTEEN

"Hey, Andi, you here?" Doh! Mike could have whomped himself upside the head. Of course Andi was here. Where else would she be?

Damn, he was feeling stupid again.

He closed the door behind him, and put his key, and the coffee and pie he'd brought, on the dresser near the door. The scent of the outdoors mingled with the fragrant, soap-scented humidity coming from the bathroom.

Lord have mercy, she was very possibly wet and naked behind that bathroom door. Making love with her had been a close thing in the car. How was he going to make it through the night without touching her?

He probably wasn't. It wasn't the wisest choice they could make, but he was pretty sure she wanted him, too. It seemed inevitable he would make love to Andi Nelson tonight.

The bathroom door creaked open, and Andi stuck her head out. "Hi, Mike. I'll be right out." She smiled, scrunched her nose at him, then disappeared back into the bathroom.

"Okay," he called to the closed door. "I brought you something to eat." Feeling like a clod, he shrugged out of his jacket, laid it over a chair, and toed his snow encrusted Nikes off.

Andi emerged from the bathroom moments later, and Mike nearly swallowed his tongue. Her skin was all rosy and flushed from her bath. Her hair was up in a high ponytail, but wisps had escaped and lay stuck to her skin. Her smile was tentative, sweet, and shy. A huge tee shirt covered her to her knees, and even though her breasts were small, he could tell she wasn't wearing a bra. Did she have any underwear on at all under that big shirt? "All yours," she told him as she motioned to the bathroom.

"Yeah, thanks," he mumbled, feeling guilty about wondering about her underwear. "There's pie and stuff on the dresser if you're hungry."

"Thanks." She stepped out of the bathroom doorway and made her way to the bed.

He smiled back at her and fled to the security of the bathroom. He closed the door, took stock of the room, and really grinned. There, hanging on the shower bar, was the proof he was looking for.

Andi Nelson was most definitely naked underneath that humongous tee shirt.

****

Berating herself for feeling so awkward, Andi moved like lightning to the bed and got in underneath the covers. The sheets were chilled and crisp against her bare skin, and she shivered. Snuggling down, she lay on her back and pulled the blankets up to her chin.

She closed her eyes, but she really wasn't tired because she had slept in the car. Besides, she was still feeling the effects of the adrenaline rush from the accident. She heard the water in the shower come on, and pictures of a very naked Mike lathering soap all over his hard body meandered through her mind. She couldn't help herself.

Nor did she want to. The man had a very nice body.

But she had known lots of men with great bodies. Fantastic bodies. Incredible bodies. She had grown up with prime male specimens sitting at her mother's kitchen table, scarfing down whatever Pamela put in front of them. She ought to be immune to broad shoulders, roped muscles, and tight butts. What was it about Mike Kelly that turned her into a sex maniac?

Well, maybe sex maniac was too strong a term. She certainly could control herself...

The shower stopped, and Andi had a very vivid mental picture of Mike toweling off. She felt a surge of heat, and her nipples tightened.

Nope. Looked like sex maniac said it all.

She heard the door open and so did her eyes, just like that. They slid, all by themselves, over to where Mike stood.

The light from the bathroom backlit him, creating a steamy, white aura around his body. He wore a standard, motel issue, terry cloth bath towel, another towel slung around his neck. His hair was wet and sticking up all over his head. When their eyes met, he gave a quick, embarrassed smile, and tunneled his fingers through his hair. "You didn't eat your pie."

"Pie?"

"Yeah. I brought you some of Irma's apple pie. It's good."

"Um, I'm not really hungry." At least, not for pie.

He frowned. "Are you sure? You should eat." He secured the towel at his waist and walked over to the dresser to pick up the plastic-wrapped plate. "You haven't had anything to eat in a while." He brought the pie over to the bed then sat next to Andi. The towel stayed anchored at his waist, but parted to reveal one muscular, lightly furred thigh "Sit up. You need to eat this."

She looked up at him, but stayed lodged beneath the covers. "Mike, really, I don't want any pie."

"Sure you do, Spud. Unless..." He shook his head, a veritable picture of regret. "Maybe you'd like tofu pie better. I'm sorry. I don't think Irma does tofu."

She squiggled up to a sitting position and leaned against the headboard. "I eat pie. I'm just not hungry right now."

The light in his eyes was *so* hot. She watched his fingers unwrap the pie, instead. "It's really, really good." He picked up the slice of pie, and held it up for her. It was flaky, and the tip end of it fell off onto the plate. Mike abandoned the crust end and picked up the juicy, apple filled morsel that had fallen. "Come on. Take a bite for me."

Her lips parted, and she held her breath as he brought the piece of pie just to, but not in her mouth. She moved to get it, and with a chuckle, he moved it just out of her reach. "You didn't say please."

"Please," she whispered, her eyes locked with his. She moistened her lips with the tip of her tongue as he again brought the piece closer to her mouth.

This time, he let her capture it, and she nibbled it off his fingers with delicate little flicks of her tongue and teeth. It tasted amazing, a mix of apples, cinnamon, buttery crust, and Mike. "Mmmmmm." She relinquished his fingers, and he put them in his own mouth, licked them.

Then he whispered, "Good, huh?"

"Yeah. Real good." She matched him hot look for hot look. "Guess I'm hungry after all."

"Is that a fact?"

"Gospel truth."

He treated her to a wicked smile as he readied another bite for her. Breaking off another gooey, apple-filled bit, he held it up for her. "Come and get it."

She wiggled a little closer to him, mouth opened to receive her treat. Watching Mike's face, she put her lips around the bite of pie and sucked on it.

Inhaling deeply, he closed his eyes. "I really

want you."

She cupped his cheek with one hand. "Is this a problem?"

Turning his face so he could kiss her palm, he said, "It could be."

"Not tonight." Unable to resist, she leaned in to him and pressed a whisper soft kiss on his lips.

He managed to put the plate aside, then put himself one hundred and ten percent into kissing Andi. She slid back down the bed, and he went with her, losing the towel along the way. He was already hard and eager, but his hands were slow and thorough, pulling the blankets away from her and then ridding her of the giant tee shirt. She helped.

The moment he had her naked, he rolled over between her parted thighs and began to kiss his way down her body, starting with her breasts. His mouth was hot and avid as he nipped and suckled her nipples, then his tongue tickled the undersides of her breasts.

She squirmed as she threaded her fingers in his hair, holding on for dear life as he kissed his way down her belly. He nuzzled her belly button, and she laughed, then moaned as he tracked open-mouthed kisses down to her thighs.

She held her breath, knowing where he was headed and braced herself for the sweet pain of his intimate kiss, but he teased her by moving down to her knees. He lifted first one knee, then the other, and laved the sensitive skin behind them. Placing her knees on his shoulders, he kissed his way back up her thighs. The first pass of his tongue on her most sensitive spot made her yelp. Subsequent flicks, bites, and kisses had her moaning with pleasure.

She felt his big, warm hands palm her derriere as he lifted her to his mouth. It was magic, pure magic he was making, and she was helpless to do anything but go along for the ride. Sensations built, one upon the other, again and again, until, with a helpless cry, she came apart against his mouth.

And still, he kept stroking her with his tongue, chasing those last, elusive spasms. She swore she could feel him smile against her. "Mike..."

"Shhhh," he rumbled against her. "I want you to come again."

Yikes! She wiggled, but he held her steady as he continued to love her with his mouth. Impossibly, the feelings built again, and once more, he made her fly.

"Oh, yeah," he murmured. His eyes were bright as he stared at her. She was helpless to do more than stare back. Her body still sang with the aftershocks of her two climaxes, and still she wanted more. But first... "Mike, we need a condom."

"Damn. I don't have any."

"I do. Check my purse." She couldn't seem to catch a breath.

He looked at her. "Why do you have condoms in your purse?"

"What?" She struggled to focus her eyes.

"Why do you have condoms in your purse?"

Her gaze cleared. She reached up a hand to cup his cheek. "I bought them the day after we slept with each other, with the intention of putting them in my nightstand in case we ever made love in my bed. We never got there, and I forgot that I had them." She was blushing.

He grabbed the condoms and kissed her quick and hard. "I love a woman who comes prepared."

Mike was only gone a moment, but then he was back and sheathing himself. Once more, he kissed her as he found his way home between her thighs.

Then, he smiled. He positioned her so that he could rub his erection against her wet, sensitive opening. Once, twice, he moved in long, slow strokes against her, and then, he locked his eyes with hers, and pressed all the way home with one sure, possessive thrust.

He felt huge inside her, and she moved her hips to accommodate him. He seemed to like that, because he made a very masculine, very satisfied sound deep in his throat. Shifting his body, he covered her and began to thrust in earnest.

She joyfully met him stroke for stroke, totally aroused by the sounds he made while he loved her. Changing his position slightly, he hunched into her while his mouth suckled her nipples.

And, just like that, she felt her body begin to race once more. "Mike..."

"Yeah, baby, I feel it," he managed around clenched teeth. "Let it go." His voice grated along her already overloaded nerves. "Come with me."

They shifted again, Mike bringing his hands behind her to lift her buttocks so he could thrust deeper, while Andi wrapped her legs around his waist. He was hammering into her, pumping high and hard, and she was with him, all the way.

It was glorious, and she gave herself to him once more. Her body broke apart, squeezing around him with hard, powerful spasms, and she cried out as she came. Seconds later, he erupted inside her, over and over again.

****

"Damn, Spud, you're amazing." Mike stared down with wonder at the woman who trembled beneath him. Making sure he was supporting his weight on his elbows, he relished the last few moments of being linked with Andi, of feeling her body shiver with the aftershocks of their shared pleasure.

Her return smile seemed suddenly shy and unsure. "You're pretty amazing yourself." Tears pooled in her eyes, but didn't fall. "I've never felt this way, ever."

He separated from her, discarded the condom, and moved so he could cuddle her against his side. "Shhh, now. No tears." *Please don't cry*, he silently begged her. "It can't be that bad."

She sniffled. It fanned the hairs on his chest. "It's not bad at all. It's wonderful."

"And that's a problem?"

"Isn't it?"

"Well, last I knew, great sex between two consenting adults was a good thing."

"But this was more than just great sex, wasn't it?"

He wished he could see her face, but she was snuggled in next to his side so tight he couldn't. "I don't know. You tell me."

She went very silent and very still, and he figured he had said something wrong. But that was par for the course for him as far as Andi Nelson went, so why was he surprised?

"I don't know, Mike. Everything happened so fast, and then went to hell. I don't know what to think."

"How about we don't think? How about we just pretend that tonight is, I don't know, a vacation, maybe." The idea had merit, he decided. "A vacation from our lives."

"It won't solve anything. Beth and Jeff will still be in trouble when we leave this motel room."

"Then we deserve this night, just for us." Especially if it was all they were ever going to have. He was suddenly desperate for it. It might be all of her he would ever get. Maneuvering so he could see her face, he pleaded with her. "Please."

Again, she went so still and so silent he nearly died right there, staring straight into her eyes, trying to read her heart. The moment was frozen for him, and he knew he'd take it to his grave, the sight, the smell, the feel of her while she decided to take him to heaven or send him to hell.

Then she smiled and slid her hand down his body to cup him.

He sucked in a breath while her small, chilled hand stroked his shaft, arousing it once more.

Their loving this time was slow and serious, each of them striving to give and get the most out of it they could. She wept when she came, and he chased each tear with his tongue, tasting, then kissing it away.

The next time, she moved down his body and loved him with her mouth. He returned the favor, using his clever fingers and skillful tongue. Their embrace ferocious, he joined his body with hers, moving slow and deep, savoring their joining.

Time had no meaning for them, not in that rustic little motel room in the backwoods of Maine. They made love then dozed, only to rouse and make love again. They were voracious for each other.

The sun rose to find them exhausted and spent, sleeping spooned together, as close physically as they could be without him inside her body. They fought sleep, because they didn't want the night to end.

But it did. And both of them woke up, silently cursing both the morning and the distance between them it brought.

## CHAPTER EIGHTEEN

Mike went to the lobby to fetch coffee while Andi showered. Dismayed to find her underwear hadn't dried overnight, she grabbed the blow dryer that Irma had lent her and proceeded to blow her panties dry.

That was how Mike found her when he returned with the coffee, sitting on the toilet seat, a blow dryer in one hand, her panties in the other, wearing the huge tee shirt again.

It totally turned him on. He was *there*, zero to sixty in the blink of an eye. And there was nothing he could do about it.

He wanted to kiss her, but held himself back. Their night was over. Whatever had passed between them was better forgotten.

She stood, holding up the screaming blow dryer, and stared at him, her eyes full of questions.

Yep. They were on opposite sides of the fence again. He didn't relish the task of having to tell her what he had learned.

Mike cleared his throat. "I got through to Dave."

She turned off the dryer. "Are the roads clear? Can we get home?"

"Not if we use my car. It's still in the ditch, and likely to stay there until Weasel can get to it."

She snorted. The sound was inelegant and totally at odds with the classy picture Andi usually put forward. "Weasel?"

"Yep. Apparently ol' Weasel is a magician with anything automotive." Mike smiled. "Unless it's from Japan."

"Oh, really." Her tone was very dry.

"Yeah. He says the Germans make a decent car, if you have to buy foreign, but stay away from the Japanese."

She laughed. "Sounds like Deke and Weasel could be best friends."

And, just like that, in the length of time it took her to say her father's name, whatever camaraderie they felt dissipated. Mike set the coffee down on the dresser with an audible slap. The hot liquid sloshed over the edge of the cup and burned his fingers. He cursed as he shook them.

She stared at him, blow dryer in one hand, damp silk panties in the other, her eyes wide and dark blue.

He swallowed hard. "Yeah. Deke and Weasel would have one hell of a time." Having nothing else to do, he looked at his watch. "Irma has a cousin whose brother's wife's sister-in-law runs a car rental operation out of his auto body shop. He might have something that would get us home."

Her brows jammed down over her eyes. "We're not going after Beth and Jeff?"

He swallowed again. "I told you I called Dave."

"Yes."

"Well, it looks like Tim's parents' neighbors saw lights when there weren't supposed to be any, and called the cops. Beth and Jeff are already home in Addington."

"Are they okay? Beth isn't hurt, is she?"

Beth. It was always about Beth with her. "Of course not. Jeff is also okay, in case you're interested."

She puffed out a breath. "Of course I care about Jeff. It doesn't change the fact she's in more trouble than he is."

"Why? Because she's female? Because she's pregnant? Is that what it takes to get sympathy from you?" Mike shook his head. "Jeff is in a world of hurt here, whether or not you want to believe it."

"You just don't get it, do you?"

He stared at her, this woman who tied him up in knots. It made him angry that she couldn't see beyond her precious Beth. Even sitting there on that toilet seat dressed in nothing but a tee shirt, holding her underwear in her hands, she still pulled this holier-than-thou, princess routine. He felt like a lummox, and he was tired of it. "Of course I don't *get it*. I'm just a dumber-than-shit football player. How could I possibly *get it*?"

"I don't think that way about you. After last night, how can you think that?"

Mike's gut clenched. "Let's not go there, okay?"

"But I think we need to talk about it, Mike."

"Yeah, well, I don't want to. Last night happened. Now it's over and done with. End of story. That's what we agreed to, remember?"

She froze. He couldn't even see her breathing.

"Yes. I do remember quite well what we agreed to before we... Before we went to bed. And, since everything I say can, and will be, held against me in Mike Kelly's court of law, just let me state for the record, I don't think you're stupid because you *can't* see Beth's side of things. I think you're cruel because you *won't* see the side of a frightened sixteen-year-old girl."

"Andi, Jeff didn't force that girl to do anything she didn't want to do." He held up two fingers. "There were two kids in that car, and *neither* of them were thinking with their heads."

"That is just the type of thing Deke would say to justify his boys' bad behavior. You wouldn't believe the type of money he's paid to keep his players from getting punished for any number of criminal things. Trust me, if Kobe had been one of Deke's boys, that rape case would have never seen the light of day."

She gave a nasty little laugh, it wasn't a pretty sound. "Come to think of it, Jeff *is* one of Deke's boys now."

"Deke's got nothing to do with anything."

"Didn't he get Jeff a tryout? Didn't he arrange some scholarship money for him? Didn't he get Jeff a lawyer?"

"Well, yeah, but Beth doesn't have anything to do with it. He did that because he believes in Jeff's talent." Mike shook his head. "He got Jeff a lawyer because the kid was being railroaded by Beth's father."

She bowed her head. "It's horrible what Pritchard did to Jeff. He didn't deserve any of that."

Mike stared at her then looked away. "Just once, I'd like us to go from great sex at night to a morning after without regrets."

She turned a bright shade of red. "I think it's safe to say that the problems we have aren't physical."

Mike looked at the carpet as he thought about what to say. He'd already said some things wrong, he didn't want to make any more mistakes with this woman. "You're right." He looked back at her. Why did she have to look so damn pretty? "The sex is great. Beyond great. What's wrong is you refuse to see that girl is not the only victim here. Jeff has a lot to lose, too. Why can't you admit that?"

"Mike, you can't even say her name, can you? *Beth* is pregnant, and she's frightened and scared, with the demon parents from hell. Jeff is the one who had all the experience! He should have known better, but no. Like any other *football star*..." She angled up her chin. "He just took advantage of her infatuation with him."

"That's unfair, and you know it."

"Do I really?"

"He obviously has feelings for her. I mean, he

stole his mother's car, for God's sake, to run away with her."

"Like that was a good idea! He should have just left her alone."

"I agree with you on that one."

That seemed to take the wind out of her sails. She dropped the blow dryer onto the toilet seat. She made it look like a ballet move. "Well, goody, Coach. I'm flattered."

"There's no need to be sarcastic, Andi. We can help both kids, if we work together."

"There's no working together on this, Mike. Men like you and my father have no concept of working together."

Okay, now he was getting mad. "And what does that mean?" He worked to keep his voice level.

"It means what I've been saying all along. Your idea of working together is issuing commands and me following them. Well, you know what? I had to deal with that all my life with Deke. I don't have to take it from you."

Mike clenched his jaw so hard, it cracked. He gave her one last look. "Be ready to leave in fifteen minutes. If you're not ready, I'll leave without you." He turned on his heel, grabbed the door handle, and left the room with a slam.

Once outside, he leaned against the cold wall of the motel, and cursed himself. What the hell had he expected from her anyway?

There weren't only the two of them involved in this. There was a third player, and his name was Deke. Mike had done a lot to be sorry for in his life without having to pay for someone else's sins.

****

Andi yanked the cord of the dryer out of the outlet and considered, very seriously, throwing it against the wall. Instead, she forced herself to breathe slowly and deeply while she counted to ten.

It didn't help much.

Then, not sure if Mike really would leave her there, she grabbed her clothes and started to tug them on. Her underwear was still damp, as were her nylons. She wiggled and pulled, but they wouldn't quite cooperate with her and go where she wanted them to.

Damn man.

The rest of her clothes were wrinkly, but there was nothing she could do about that. Her purse was on the nightstand next to the bed. She went to retrieve it, and sat down to put her boots on.

The bed she had shared with Mike looked like a bomb had gone off in it and condom wrappers littered the floor. She bit back a sob as she bent to pick them up to toss them into the trash basket.

As she left the room, she made a wish. It wasn't the first time she had wished for her father to be anyone else but Deke Nelson.

****

"What kind of car is this, anyway?"

Mike didn't take his eyes off the road. "A Pacer."

"They don't make them anymore."

"No kidding. This baby is a vintage 1976."

"That old? It's in great shape for being that old." Andi ran her hand along the powder blue, faux-leather dashboard.

"According to Weasel, Ernie's great-aunt Patty bought it brand new two weeks before she ran off to Tahiti with a Fuller Brush salesman by the name of Rupert. They were never heard from again, but Ernie's great-uncle Henry wouldn't sell the car, hoping she'd come back someday. He never used it, but kept it in perfect running condition."

"You're making this up."

"No way. It's all true, straight from Weasel's mouth."

"If you say so." Andi stuck out her lower lip. "It's

so nice of Ernie's uncle to lend it to us."

"Great Uncle Henry died two years ago."

"Oh. Did he die of a broken heart?"

"I guess you could say that. He and his brother Curtis went to the local tavern and got drunk one night and got into a fight over a woman they were both hitting on. Henry had a heart attack and dropped dead before he could even land a punch."

"The *Ewwwwww* factor on this is off the chart."

"Yeah. I know. According to Weasel, it wasn't pretty."

Andi looked at him. "You *are* making this up."

"Nope. I swear on Great Aunt Patty's grave it's the truth."

She just looked at him, didn't laugh, didn't even crack a smile then looked away out the passenger side window.

And that was just fine with him, Mike told himself. To fill the silence, he reached out and flipped on the radio. And because this was a basic model car from the 70s, it was only an AM radio.

Static crackled as Mike sorted through farm reports and local talk radio stations, finally settling on a talk show that had a panel of experts debating the merits of composting.

It was kind of interesting, actually. He never knew people could get so worked up over compost. And, hands down, it beat talking with Andi about Beth and Jeff.

****

By the time they reached the Massachusetts border, Andi was sure the top of her head was going to blow off. She didn't care about compost. She didn't care about this year's squash crop. She didn't care about the County Judge election ballot recount in Sullivan County. Most of all, she didn't care about the sports talk show now blaring its way through the car's tinny-sounding speakers. She especially didn't care about hearing of the gridiron exploits of those football *Wunderkinder*, Buck and Brock Nelson.

She knew them all by heart.

Mike was listening to the show, and though his eyes were on the road, they were bright with interest. He was smiling, and reacted to the play-by-play accounts by whistling.

She almost longed for his rendition of *Frosty the Snowman* instead. Almost being the key word.

And, wonder of wonders, though they had lost every station they found on the radio after about a half an hour, this station only got clearer and stronger as they drove. Just her dumb luck, she supposed.

It was also just her dumb luck to have fallen in love with Mike Kelly, in spite of Deke and football. There was no escaping that fact, and she was tired of fighting it, of denying it. As impossible as the situation was, her body had thrummed all day, remembering how he had made love to her last night. In her mind, she relived every touch, kiss, every sigh. She had to stop herself several times from reaching out and putting her hand on his thigh, or rubbing the tension out of his neck, or running her fingers through his hair. She just wasn't sure if her attentions would be welcome.

She was smart enough to realize sex wasn't love. She knew that. She'd had sex without being in love with her partner. What she and Mike had shared was different. She felt different, like her skin didn't quite fit her body anymore. It was like her world had been set upside down *and* was spinning all crazy and wild-like. Was that love?

Was it love since she couldn't imagine her life anymore without Mike in it?

Maybe she could salvage this situation. Maybe if she was honest, and really came clean with how she felt, he would trust her and the two of them could have a chance to make this work.

She'd been thinking long and hard about Jeff. Maybe she'd been too quick to judge him the villain. The kid had been nearly thrown in jail. And if Beth loved him, like Andi was sure she must, then helping Jeff would be best for Beth's state of mind.

Her heart sang with hope and joy. She could do that. She was pretty sure Mike felt for her as she did for him. They were adults. The two of them could work together to fix the mess Beth and Jeff were in, and then they could fix their own relationship.

No time like the present. All she had to do was reach over, turn off the radio and then tell him how she felt. And she was going to do it right now, before she talked herself out of it.

Her hand started its journey to the radio, but Mike's got there first. He shut it off. "I need to say a few things to you," he said.

"Okay." Suddenly, she was sure he was going to come clean with her, tell her he loved her and they could work this thing out between them. Her heart started to thump in her chest.

He took a deep breath before he started talking. "I know I promised I would stay until Christmas in the choir, but I can't do it. I can't go back."

The choir? He wanted to talk about the church choir? "What?"

"It's not like I'm any help. I'm not leaving you in the lurch by staying away. Wally and Heinrich do fine without me. Better, I'd bet."

"Oh."

"Besides, I think it will be a conflict of interest or something like that to go to the same church where Beth Pritchard plays the organ."

"You hate her that much?"

"No, I don't hate her." He firmed his mouth and a muscle in his jaw ticked. "I just can't do this anymore, okay?"

The awful truth came to her in a sickening rush. This wasn't about Beth. This was about her. He didn't want to go to church because he didn't want to see *her*, to deal with *her*.

Her heart plummeted. He didn't want to make things work between them. Andi reminded herself of how he had not wanted her on this trip to intercept Beth and Jeff. He'd wanted to go after them alone. She had barged in.

He really didn't want to be with her, and it was all her fault. She had pushed him away with both hands.

She refused to cry, damn it. Gathering her dignity around her like a cloak, she said, "Well, don't quit on my account. I'm most likely out of a job as soon as Christmas is over."

He blinked, glanced at her then turned his attention back to the road. "Out of a job? What do you mean?"

"I mean, out of a job, like fired."

"Why would they fire you? You're great at that job."

"Yeah, well, that doesn't even enter the equation. Angie gave me a heads up. Beth's father is on the parish council and has started a campaign to get me gone."

"Can he do that?"

"Yeah. He can make Father Scott's life miserable until he gets what he wants, which is me out of there."

"But why? You're on Beth's side. You're doing all you can to help her."

"I took her to that clinic in Boston without his permission. He's pretty pissed about that." She looked out the passenger side window. The snowdrifts along the side of the road were gray and mud-flecked now that they were back on I-95. Ah, civilization.

Something that could have passed for regret flitted across his face. "Hell, Andi. The truth of it is I just can't do it anymore. The bottom line is Jeff and Nancy Myers need me right now, and you... You're attracted to me, you like me enough to have sex with me, but when push comes to shove, I'm only ever gonna be some dumb jock who's just gonna embarrass you."

"Mike, I don't..."

"Don't, Andi. Whatever you're gonna say, I don't want to hear it."

"But..."

"I can't ever make you happy, at least not for the long haul. I'm sorry about that."

"What are you talking about?"

"You. Me. Deke."

"Deke? I thought Beth and Jeff were our problem. I was going to tell you I was willing to give Jeff the benefit of the doubt, and we could work together to help them. But, Deke? What does Deke have to do with us?"

"Everything. And you're dumber than I am if you don't see it."

"I still don't get it. Maybe you could draw me a picture."

"Okay." He nodded. "Okay. I watched you today listening to that sports show. You hate football. No." He held up a finger in warning, "Don't interrupt me. You hate football, not just the game, but everything that goes with it. Listening to that show, most sisters would have been thrilled to hear their baby brothers play so well. But not you. I've been to your parents' house, sat at their table. I've seen you there. It's broken my heart to see you and Deke."

"That's right. I forgot. Now you're the world's biggest expert on the subject of Deke Nelson."

His eyes and his smile were sad. "I'm not going to pay for Deke's sins, Andi."

"No one's asked you to."

"Aw, c'mon. I've had to weigh every word I say to you, for fear I might push a Deke button. You're not rational when it comes to your father."

"That's not true."

"It *is* true. You'll do anything to goad him, just to get his attention."

"A man's children should come before a game."

"That's true. And I'm sorry for you. But you need to understand, for some of us, football is more than a game. For Deke, it was a career. The game *saved* me, Andi. I couldn't read words in books for shit. But football plays, those I could read and understand. I understood something like I'd never been able to before. I didn't feel stupid."

"I'm happy for you. Really. Dyslexia is very hard to live with, and you've done spectacular coping with it. But don't expect me to have warm fuzzy feelings about that game."

"Believe me, I accept your feelings about football. That's why we're having this conversation."

"What do you mean?"

Mike pulled off the road and put the car in park. He stared out the window for one minute then turned to face her, his eyes were filled with regret. "There's something more between us than just sex, although the sex is beyond amazing. At least it is for me, anyway. I'm most likely making a fool of myself by opening a vein like this, but I don't care. I want more from you. But until you settle things with Deke, you're not going to be able to give me what I need."

It seemed to Andi his words got softer and came from further away the longer he spoke. She just stared at him, stared at his gorgeous, earnest face, and she wished for one of his smiles to take with her when it was all over.

But he was so solemn, so sad. He reached out a

hand and pushed her hair back, then cupped her cheek with exquisite gentleness. "I have deep feelings for you, Andi. I don't want them, but I got 'em, anyway." Andi got the smile she wanted from him. "There's too much standing between us right now."

"Beth and Jeff, you mean."

"Yeah, but Deke is there, too. Like you said, we could probably work past the crap with Jeff and Beth together, but then there's Deke." Mike shook his head. "Until you come to grips with him and make peace, there's no future for us."

"Can't you see that-"

"Don't ask me to give up the game. I won't. I can't."

"I wouldn't do that. I just want you to see my side. I'm not the one at fault. Deke is."

"Maybe so, but I'm not going to pay for his sins for the rest of *my* life. He's not going to change. There's no hope for any kind of future for us until you work stuff out with Deke."

She tried to swallow, but had trouble. She needed to get back some control. "Is that your *professional* opinion, Dr. Freud?"

He shook his head and pulled his hand away. "No, it's just common sense. Once you think about it, you'll see I'm right." He jerked the car back into gear, checked behind them, and then pulled back onto the Interstate.

She managed to keep from crying until he dropped her off in the school parking lot where she had left her car. He waited until she got in and started it, but then he was gone. She had the feeling he didn't even check his rearview mirror to see if she was all right.

She laid her head against the steering wheel and sobbed until she had no tears left.

## CHAPTER NINETEEN

Andi went to her parents' house for dinner after mass, three Sundays after Mike gave her his ultimatum. Brock and Buck were there already, and so it was just a family dinner, no company. Andi smiled at everyone, made a show of listening attentively, and died a little inside. Deke hung on to every word the twins uttered and acted as if no one else had ever existed in his own personal universe.

It was a relief when Pamela got up to clear the table. Andi grabbed an empty serving bowl and the breadbasket and beat a hasty retreat into the kitchen.

She opened the door to find her mother staring at her. They stood and looked at each other while the boys clattered into Deke's study, most likely to watch some game videos. Behind Pamela, the sink filled with hot water, causing steam to rise. Andi walked around her mother and put the empty bowl on the table in the middle of the kitchen. Still Pamela stared at her. Andi stared back.

"What? Do I have food on my face?"

"You want to tell me what's going on?"

"Nothing's going on."

"Liar."

Sinking into a kitchen chair, Andi admitted defeat. After all, this was her mother she was talking to. "I'm in love with Mike Kelly."

Pamela sat next to her, pushing a gravy boat out of the way, then captured Andi's hands across the table. "Tell me something I don't know."

That brought her up short. "You've only seen us

together once. How could you possibly know?"

"I have two eyes, and they work perfectly well. And I know my little girl. If it counts for anything, I think he loves you too."

Andi pulled her hands back and toyed with the serving spoon in the bowl of mashed potatoes. "Doesn't matter much. It's over."

"I wasn't aware it had gone that far." Pamela's tone was exceedingly dry.

"Oh, yeah. It started and ended in about twenty-four hours."

It was a sign of unconditional love and female solidarity that made Pamela ask, "What did the football playing swine do?"

Andi had to laugh at that, but the joke didn't pull her out of her funk. "He told me I have issues with Deke, and if I don't deal with them, he and I have no chance."

"He used the word *issues*? I don't believe it."

She chuckled in spite of herself. "That was the gist of what he said."

"He's right."

Andi stared at her mother. Her mother stared back, her gaze defiant. "How can you say that? You, of all people, know what I went through because of Deke."

"And I'm tired of being the referee every time the two of you get together. I've been doing it for years. No more!"

"Mom!"

Pamela was on a roll. "Furthermore, you didn't have a bad childhood. You had everything you ever wanted. All you had to do was hint at something, and Deke made sure you had it."

Andi was stunned. "He bought me stuff to ease his conscience when he ignored me."

Pamela thought before she spoke. "He didn't mean to ignore you. He was scared of you."

"Deke has never been afraid of anything in his life. He ignored me because he had no use for a girl child in his life. He had plenty of time for the twins."

Pamela's eyes went soft with remembrance. "You were so delicate and tiny. It was like you were a fairy baby with your blond curls and big blue eyes."

"Fairies have green eyes."

"Shush. It's not polite to interrupt your mother."

"Soooorrry."

"Yes. Well, where was I?"

"I was a scrawny kid."

Pamela stood and went to the sink, turned off the water and attacked a pan. "Not scrawny. Delicate. Girly. He had no clue what to do with you. Truth be told, he was scared shitless."

Andi raised her eyebrows. Her mother *never* swore. "Deke's never been scared of anything."

"He was scared of you. And it just got worse when you got into music and dance."

"He was disappointed."

Pamela sighed. "A bit, but only because he didn't understand them. And he was on the road so much you just got further and further away from him."

Andi transferred potato remains from a serving bowl into Tupperware. They landed with a solid thump. "All he had to do was go to one, just one of my concerts or recitals. That was it. He didn't, ever, that I remember." She jammed the lid on the container. "He made sure he was at as many of the boys' games as he could get to."

"I know, and I'm sorry for that. There's no excuse. We argued about it."

That was a surprise. "I wasn't aware you two ever argued."

"Of course we argue. In spite of what you think, I'm not Deke's doormat."

"I never thought..."

"Oh, yes, you did. You still do."

"Mom-"

"I love you, Andi, but you can be a pain in the butt sometimes. Same as your father. In fact, the two of you are so alike, it's scary."

"I'm nothing like Deke."

Pamela laughed. "And he'd say the same. But it's true. You're both so stubborn, you paint yourselves into corners. You've both staked out territory and there's this big no-man's-land between you two where the rest of us live, dodging the bullets."

Andi looked down at her hands. "You make it sound horrible."

Pulling her hands out of the hot soapy water, Pamela wiped them on a dishtowel and walked over to Andi. She put her hands on Andi's shoulders. "Look at me."

Andi did. "I don't think this..."

"Just listen to me for a minute. Don't think about Deke right now. Do you love Mike Kelly?"

"I have feelings for him, but..."

"Don't backpedal. You already told me that you do. Does he love you?"

"I don't know. He never said the words."

"Come on. He gave you an ultimatum about Deke. What does that tell you?"

"That he's pushy."

"Besides that."

Since this was her mother she was talking to, she told the truth. "I think he loves me."

"Do you want it to work out?"

"Yes." She exhaled loudly. "Hell. I don't know. We haven't known each other very long."

"You've known him long enough to sleep with him."

"Mom!"

"Andi!"

She felt her face flood with embarrassment then

she giggled. "How can you tell?"

"I know you. You wouldn't be this upset if you hadn't. Besides, you practically admitted it to me. The question is still on the table. Do you want it to work out with Mike?"

She looked down at her hands, which were folded tightly in her lap. "Yes," she whispered. Looking up at her mother she added, "I do."

"Then you know what you have to do."

Andi bit her lip. After a moment, with great reluctance, she nodded. "I have to have a heart to heart with Deke."

"That would be a good first step. Look on the bright side. Even if things don't work out with Mike, maybe you'll fix things with Deke and dinners around here won't be like armed conflicts anymore."

"It's not that bad."

"Trust me. It's that bad."

They worked in silence for a moment, but then the question Andi had always wanted to ask, but never had the courage just flew out of her mouth. "Why'd you marry Deke?"

Pamela looked at her. "The usual reason. He chased me until I fell in love with him."

In for a penny, in for a pound. "But all those years, he was never here. He ignored us."

Pamela sighed. "First, my marriage is my business, not yours. I know you have your issues with your father, and you've got a right to the way you feel, but..." She shook her head. "Mike is right. It's long past time for you and Deke to talk to each other." She moved to the fridge and leaned against it. "Seems to me, you've got a choice to make, baby girl."

Shaking her head, Andi groaned, "I hate this! Why couldn't I have done the sane thing and fallen in love with Ian?"

"You've never taken the easy way in your life.

Ian's a lovely man, and he'll be a great catch for some lucky woman, you're just not that woman."

"More's the pity," Andi grumbled. She went to the refrigerator and opened it. "There's no more beer for the boys. I'll go out to the fridge in the garage and get some."

Before her mother could stop her, Andi beat a hasty retreat.

****

A long moment of silence passed. Pamela looked from the garage door to the door going to her dining room. Walking to the latter, she pulled it open and came face to face with a very red-faced Deke Nelson. "I hope you got all that," she said.

"Got all what?"

"Don't play dumb with me. You were listening to my conversation with Andi."

"I admit I may have overheard some things."

"Then you know she's in love with Mike Kelly."

"She'll drive him crazy within three weeks."

"Unless I miss my guess, those three weeks are already up. It doesn't change the fact he very well may love her back." Pamela sighed when she saw Deke frown. She decided to change tactics. "Do you want grandchildren any time in this century?"

Deke frowned even more. "Has Mike been making moves on my baby girl?"

Pamela chuckled and went on tiptoes to kiss his cheek. "If he has, that's none of our business. But you heard Andi. If things don't work out with Mike, she's going to end up with some nice, artistic college professor who will support her when she wants to bring all their children up as long-haired, ballet dancin,' broccoli quiche and tofu eaters."

Deke paled. "God help me."

"Focus, Deke." Pamela's voice got that edge of steel in it she'd perfected when dealing with her rowdy sons. "You want things to work out with Mike and Andi, you know what to do."

"I have to talk to Mike."

She hit him. "Wrong answer." She smiled as he rubbed his right arm. "Guess again."

"I have to talk to Andi."

"Give the man a cigar."

"I was afraid of that. What do I say?"

"Start with *I love you*. The rest will come."

\*\*\*\*

A couple of hours later, Andi stood at her mother's kitchen sink scrubbing the tarnish off her mother's antique tea set. She loved to clean silver. Loved the smell of the polish, the shine of the pieces, the action of getting rid of the stain. Call her crazy, Lord knew her mother did every time Andi dragged out the rubber gloves to clean the tea set.

When she was a little girl, she'd imagine serving tea out of this very teapot to her father while he beamed at her, proud of her ability to make a perfect cup of tea while he wolfed down the crust-less sandwiches she made all by herself. She'd pour in just the right amount of milk and plop five sugar cubes into the tea because she knew he had a sweet tooth.

Ha! What a fantasy that was. Deke wouldn't know tea if it rained down from the sky and made them cancel the Super Bowl.

"Wow. You get that any shinier we'll all need sunglasses on Christmas Eve."

Andi felt her spine stiffen as her father spoke. She turned the kitchen faucet off and pulled off her rubber gloves. Her hands always felt a little slimy after she'd worn rubber gloves. It was the one part of the job she didn't like.

She turned to face Deke. She'd learned long ago if you faced him right away, the whole *I'm disappointed in you, Andi* lecture didn't last as long. "I like to polish silver, it relaxes me."

"Yeah, uh." He reached up and scratched absently at the back of his neck. "I kinda wanted to talk to you."

Whoa! Color her surprised. Well, and suspicious. Really suspicious. She couldn't imagine any situation in which he would want to talk to her. She picked up a dishtowel and rubbed her hands with it. "I'm all ears."

"I heard you and Mike Kelly were, uh, dating."

Damn. Her heart jolted when Deke said Mike's name and nearly overwhelming sadness cloaked her. She was better than this, mooning over a man who had let her down over the very man standing in front of her. She wouldn't let either of them control her life a minute longer. She looked Deke smack dab in his eyes. "Well, not anymore. He broke up with me." She managed a smile. "Guess you think he came to his senses."

Deke winced. Score one for her. "No. I'm sorry."

Uh-oh. Who was this, and what had he done to her father?

The imposter kept talking. "I like Mike, sure, but you're my little girl. I'm on your side."

She felt her mouth drop open, but she couldn't control her surprise. Wrapping her arms around her middle, she tried to find her tongue to no avail. She couldn't think of a thing to say.

Deke stiffened his jaw and nodded once. "I just thought you should know that." He fled the room as if all the hounds of hell were nipping at his heels.

Andi didn't know whether to laugh or cry. If she didn't know better, she'd have thought her father was reaching out to her.

The thought made her ridiculously happy. The smile that came back to her face was as genuine as it was tentative. He'd lobbed the ball into her court; the next move had to be hers.

She hoped she didn't screw it up.

\*\*\*\*

Andi got her chance with her father much sooner than she thought she would. Later that afternoon, she was in the parlor checking out her mother's Christmas tree. She heard her mother enter the room.

"I can't believe you're still putting this on the tree." Andi smiled as she fingered a dilapidated, popsicle stick sled. Andi had made it in Kindergarten. The glitter had worn off, the red ribbon was frayed, and her mother still insisted on putting it on the tree.

"Your mother is big on tradition."

Andi turned from the tree. "I thought you were Mom."

Deke nodded. "I know." He moved to the fireplace, picked up a poker, and jabbed at the fire. "It's a good fire. Wood's burnin' nice."

He pulled a photo off the mantel, one of her right before the last ballet of her dancing career. She'd been deep in the throes of her anorexia then, determined to prove to them all that they were wrong about her physical condition. It had taken an intervention, one Deke had missed because of the Super Bowl, to get her into a clinic and to get help.

Deke's brow furrowed as he looked at the photo. Clearing his throat, he ran a sausage-like finger over the picture frame. "I don't understand why your mother keeps this one out."

"Why? Because it's of me dancing and not of the twins on the gridiron?" She stepped away from the tree, towards her father.

He looked up, eyes blazing. "No, not that. Never that." He cleared his throat. "I know you think you've got an axe to grind, and maybe you do. But this..." He held out the photo for Andi to take. "It's just a reminder of how sick *you* were, and how scared *we* were."

"I never knew." Andi took the photo and looked at it. "I didn't think I had a problem. I thought you just wanted me to quit dancing. You hated the ballet."

"I hated what it did to you." He looked at the floor. "You were disappearing in front of my eyes. I couldn't handle it."

Andi put the photo back. "The ballet didn't do anything to me, Deke. I was the one making the choice to starve myself." She tossed her head back. "*I* like to keep the photo out as a reminder of what I did, so when the urge to diet comes back, I can fight it." She turned her back on her father, walked back to the tree, and touched the little sled again. "I didn't even think you'd noticed I was sick. You never said anything, unless it was to needle me about being a vegetarian."

He shifted his feet, looking extremely uncomfortable. "I'm not good with words. It seemed easier to blame the ballet and the fruity diet."

This was a side of her father she'd never seen before. She didn't know what to say. "No, it was all me, and my choice not to eat. I felt in control that way."

"You ever feel that way now?"

"Everyday. It's like being an alcoholic, or a drug addict." She ran a finger down the side of a spun glass bell and pinged it with her fingernail.

Deke grunted. "I'm sorry about your ballet career."

Of course he was. Even though he hated the dance, he would have much rather had a professional dancer for a daughter, not a high school music teacher. "I like what I do now. The kids are great, I feel like I'm really making a difference." Except for Beth. The one kid who really needed her, and Andi had let her down.

Deke looked down at the floor again, but didn't

226

say anything.

"I don't know if I could have made it as a professional dancer. I like to think I was good, and I loved it, but..." She shrugged and studied him. What was he thinking? This was the first time he'd ever talked to her about the anorexia, about quitting dancing. "I hope you'll come to church with Mom on Christmas Eve. My choir is doing a pretty good job with the music. They're not the Mormon Tabernacle Choir, but for a small church choir they're not too bad."

Deke looked at her, his expression totally unreadable, not that she could ever read his expressions. "I don't know, I'm not really a church-goer, you know?"

Andi turned her attention to the popsicle stick sled, and smiled to cover her disappointment. What had she expected? Deke was Deke. She, however, could change. She could do it for Mike. No. She could do it for herself. "Well, I hope you come. I'd really like that."

****

"Deke." Mike jogged over the frozen asphalt of the school parking lot to catch up with Andi's dad before he got away. "I'm glad I caught up with you. Thanks for helping out with my Christmas shopping."

Deke stopped unlocking his car and turned to Mike. "Not a problem." He shifted his weight back and forth and swapped the bag he was carrying to his empty hand. "Don't go without these footballs. Brock and Buck signed 'em yesterday. Hope your nephews like them."

Mike took the bag and looked into it. "Like 'em? They're gonna go nuts about them. It'll make their Christmas." He took the bag and held his hand out to shake Deke's. "Thank you! Have a great holiday."

Deke grinned. "You, too. Give my best to your

family."

"Will do. And the same to Pamela and the twins." Mike couldn't help it and glanced over his shoulder to where Andi's car was parked.

"What about my daughter?"

"Your daughter?"

"Yeah. You know. Blond, blue eyes, looks kinda like Princess Grace?" Deke shook his head, but then his eyes narrowed and he looked back at Mike. "Pamela tells me Andi is upset and you're the reason."

Mike felt all color drain from his face. He really didn't feel up to a fatherly inquisition from Deke. "We've been out a couple of times, you know, for drinks after choir rehearsal."

"Pamela left me with the impression there was a whole lot more going on than just drinks after choir rehearsal."

"Yeah, well..." Mike fumbled with the bag of footballs. "They were really good drinks."

Deke snorted. "I don't pretend to understand her, but she's my baby girl. You hurt her, I'll kill you. Slowly. And with a smile on my face."

Mike shook his head as he brought his eyes up to meet Deke's. It never failed to jolt him when he saw Andi's eyes in her father's face. "I won't lie to you. I have strong feelings for her, but the ball's in her court. The next move has to come from her."

"She still blame you for this Jeff and Beth mess?"

"Maybe. Probably. There are other things between us beyond that."

"Football."

"For one." Mike couldn't bring himself to tell the man in front of him *he* was the problem.

Deke looked like a man with a secret. "You know, her mother led me a merry chase before I finally caught her. But from the first moment I saw

Pammy, BAM!" He slapped his hands together for emphasis. "That was it. There was no one else for me." He chuckled at the memory. "She made me jump through more hoops than a circus dog, you know what I mean?"

Mike was pretty certain Andi wasn't making him jump through hoops. He knew Andi's problems had very much to do with the man standing in front of him. And there was not one damn thing he could do about it.

Nope. What he told Deke was true. The ball was in Andi's court. Truth be told, after everything that had passed between them, he didn't hold much hope for a future with her.

## CHAPTER TWENTY

Mike was still in a blue funk when he arrived at his mother's house the next evening, Christmas Eve. She lived just far enough away to make getting there a project. He worried about her now that his dad was gone, but she insisted she was doing well. He trusted his sister, Evelyn, would let him know if there were any problems.

Mom still lived in the same house his father had brought her home to as a bride. The neighborhood was still the same, old 70's era, ranch houses lovingly maintained. In honor of the season, the usual holiday decoration battles were raging. He couldn't help but smile to see the houses decorated with twinkling colored lights, the lawns tricked out with life-size, electric Santas, Rudolphs, snowmen and manger scenes. Everyone's living room picture window featured a decorated tree, smack dab in the middle of it, and he would bet money the tree featured handmade decorations, crafted by at least two generations of school children.

The front door was unlocked, as he knew it would be. He smiled as he opened the door to be immediately overcome by the scents of cinnamon and nutmeg, evergreen, and wood smoke. He was home, and life was suddenly more than good.

He closed the door behind him and set down the suitcase he carried in with him. Slipping out of his jacket, he draped it over the coat tree in the front entryway and walked to the living room. He knew where the action would be.

He wasn't wrong. Everyone gathered in the

living room. Evelyn, extremely pregnant with her third child, sat on the sofa next to her husband, Bob, indulgently watching their two boys wreak havoc. The boys, Brandon and Tyler, were rough and tumble with the energy of twenty puppies. They were very involved in practicing some wrestling moves that would make the meanest WWE star cringe with fright. His grandmother was asleep in her favorite recliner, her feet up, her head back, and her mouth open. Little snores puffed out every now and then.

There was a buffet unit along one wall of the room, and it was his mother's pride and joy. Right now, it was covered with her best Irish linen tablecloth and plates full of cookies and other goodies. Mike licked his lips. Mom had probably been baking for days. One large punchbowl was filled with his mom's special eggnog, another with cider for the boys.

Sheila, his mother, had her back to him, and was fussing with some icicles on the tree. Every year, she insisted on reusing the tinsel icicles, painstakingly removed each silver strand, and carefully placed it into a box before throwing out the tree that stayed up until the needles started to fall.

There was an empty recliner in one corner, and it would stay empty. No matter how much time had passed since his father's death, no one would sit in that chair. It was Dad's chair, and that was that. Some might think it morbid, but to them it was simply their mother's way of honoring their father. They wouldn't dream of sitting in it; it just seemed right to make it a family tradition sort of thing.

"What's a guy gotta do to get a drink around here?"

His mother turned around, a smile of joy wreathing her face. "Mikey!" She dodged her two wriggling grandsons, umpteen toy cars, a footstool, and a coffee table to run into his open arms.

"How ya doin', Ma?"

She gave him a peck on the cheek. "Great, now that you're here." She looked at him long and hard. "What took you so long? I expected you hours ago."

"I'm sorry. I got hung up."

"Anything to do with that student of yours?"

"Yeah." His sister struggled to get up off the couch. "Whoa, Shamu, why don't you stay put?"

Bob gave her a boost, and Evelyn lumbered to her feet. The smile she gave her husband was pure love. "Thanks, sweetheart." She cast a jaundiced eye at her brother. "Shamu, huh? I'd like to see how graceful you'd look when you're nine months pregnant."

"And thank God we'll never find out." He let go of his mother and crossed to his sister. "You 'bout ready to pop, then?" He kissed her cheek then shook Bob's hand.

"God, yes," Evelyn replied. "The sooner, the better."

"You know what flavor you're getting?"

"Haven't asked and don't want to know. But I'll tell you this, much as I love the dynamic duo over there, I'd love for this one to be a girl."

"Hey! Uncle Mike!" Brandon took a break from pounding on his younger brother to greet Mike. "You bring any presents?"

"Brandon!" Evelyn gave her son the exact same look Mike remembered getting from his mom. "Is that any way to greet your uncle?"

"Sorry." Brandon had the grace to look ashamed, but present lust was in his eyes, and Mike had all he could do to keep from laughing.

"Yeah, Bran." Tyler gave Brandon a well-placed elbow. "You should know better than to ask for presents right away."

Brandon was about to give back as good as he

got, but Mike decided not to let them get out of hand, as well as put them out of their misery. "If you guys want to give me a hand, I think I've still got some stuff out in the car."

The boys were on their feet and out the door before their mother could tell them to put their jackets on. Mike grinned unrepentant, and followed them. "Be right back."

As he followed the boys, he heard Evelyn say to his mother, "Mom, you better wake Grandma Kelly up. She won't want to miss Mike."

"You wake her up. She hates me."

This was the biggest myth in his family. His father's mother had lived with them for years, ever since a bad fall made living on her own nearly impossible. Both Grandma Kelly and his mother were strongly opinioned women, and they argued about everything. Since his father's death, the two women doted on each other, but both would die before admitting it.

They made the boys wait until the end of *It's A Wonderful Life*, his mother's favorite movie, and a Christmas Eve tradition, before letting them open their presents. The autographed footballs were a hit, raising Mike to deity status because he had actually met Buck and Brock Nelson. Evelyn and Bob packed up the boys and took them home just before Mike's mother and grandmother went to midnight mass.

"Hey, Ma," Mike didn't quite know how to ask this. Might as well just spit it out. "You mind if I go to mass with you?"

The women exchanged surprised glances. Grandma Kelly found her voice first. "You never went before. Why now?" She squinted at him. "You do something we need to know about?"

Mike gave her his best *Who, me?* smile, but she wasn't buying it and neither was his mother. She gave him a look that said they'd talk about it later.

St. Patrick's was a small, neighborhood parish. Like the houses in the neighborhood, it hadn't changed since Mike had been an altar boy, except for one notable exception.

Mike couldn't help but notice the music. What had once been background noise was now familiar ground, and he found himself really listening to the choir.

He missed the gang. Feeling a little guilty, he realized he really wanted to be there, singing with Angie, Jack, Wally and Heinrich. He wondered what they were doing at that moment, what they were singing.

The organist started pumping out some familiar response music and Mike bellowed along. He was more than a little embarrassed to find his mother staring at him, her jaw slack and eyes wide.

After they got home, his mother cornered him. "Okay. Who are you, and what have you done to my son?"

Mike laughed. "What do you mean? I'm the same guy I've always been."

"This is the first time in your entire life I've heard you sing."

"You're exaggerating. I must have sung once or twice before in my life."

She lifted a brow. "I'm getting a glass of wine. Do you want anything?"

"Got any Jameson's?"

"Is the Pope Catholic?"

They settled down at the kitchen table. The kitchen felt cozy and familiar.

"I miss Dad." Mike didn't know why he said it. He'd never said anything like that to his mother before.

"So do I. Every damn day." She took a healthy sip of her wine. "Want to tell me about her?"

"About who?"

"About the woman who's got you going to church and singing like Pavarotti."

Mike knew when he was licked. He'd never been able to fool his mother. "Her name is Andi Nelson. She's the chorus teacher at Addington High."

"Nelson. She related to the football players who signed the boys' footballs?"

"Her younger brothers. Her father, Deke, is one of the legendary coaches of the game."

"And she's a chorus teacher? That must make for some fun dinnertime conversation."

"To say the least." He took a sip of the Jameson's and reveled in the burn as it went down his throat. And since he was confessing, blurted, "I love her, and I'm pretty sure she loves me. I just don't see how it can work out."

"If you love each other, you can work it out."

"Easier said than done, Ma. She hates football and everything that goes along with it."

"I see." She ran her finger around the rim of her glass. "What are you going to do about that?"

"There's nothing I can do. Really. There's a lot of stuff between us, but it all comes down to football. You of all people should know how I feel about the game. It saved me."

His mother nodded. "I was never so glad as when I saw you finally find something you were really good at. Everything else was such a struggle for you."

"She's into ballet and music and culture. Her last boyfriend wrote her poems, for Chrissake. He's a college professor. How can I compete with that?"

"Well, you're the current boyfriend, and the college professor is an ex, so my guess is you've already competed and won. Here's my advice. Be true to yourself."

"Be true to yourself. That's it?"

"In a nutshell. You've worked too hard to get to

where you are. If she's not woman enough to accept that and value you for it, then she's not worth your love."

\*\*\*\*

The church was silent. A single candle burned on the altar, and an evergreen tree dotted with little white lights stood in the sanctuary. Pine boughs perfumed the air. All was calm. All was bright.

And Andi was ready to strangle her choir. She pictured herself choking each one of them slowly.

Hadn't any of them ever heard of being on time?

She threw down the music she held in one white-knuckled fist and reached into her purse for an antacid. She found the package, thumbed off a couple of tablets, and tossed them in her mouth.

She loved Christmas Eve, and she was proud of the music program she had put together. Initially, she had wondered if it wasn't too ambitious. But now, since it would probably be her only one here at St. Benedict's, she was glad she would go out with a bang.

Although, at the moment, that seemed unlikely, since none of her musicians were there to warm-up. But that was the least of her problems.

She missed Beth. She had counted on Beth's skills being available to her when she had chosen the music, and now she had no Beth. In fact, she was lucky to even have an organist. Emma, her smart-mouth eighth grade alto, had a sister, Lisa, who was a pretty good keyboard player. She didn't have anywhere near Beth's experience, but she was available. Andi had jumped to sign her on and had spent most of the afternoon working with the kid.

Lisa was very young and funky, with short hair gelled into spikes, a short, pink and black plaid mini-skirt, knee high boots and tee shirt that proclaimed *I like dorks*. The kid worked hard, though. Andi made her go over everything numerous times, and Lisa hadn't complained once.

At last, she heard the sound of footsteps tromping up the stairs to the choir loft. Angie was on her way up, followed closely by Jack Canard. "It's about time someone showed up."

"I'm sorry. I was on my way out the door, when a patient had an emergency." Jack pulled off his coat to hang it up on the coat tree.

It was on the tip of Andi's tongue to ask what kind of foot fungus was so important that it required last minute podiatrist attention, but she bit it back.

Andi swore under her breath. She looked up to see Angie looking at her like she was a Martian. "What?"

"I know you're upset about Beth and all, but why are you so keyed up? We may be getting here late, but we *are* here."

Andi heaved a big sigh and looked at both of their kind, friendly faces. She really did need to get a grip. "My family is going to come tonight. I'm nervous because my dad has never, ever heard me play or sing, much less conduct."

Jack's smile was genuine and gentle. "We'll do our best not to let you down."

"I know." Andi aimed a breath upwards, and it fluttered her hair, which was lying soft and loose around her face. She wore it that way because Mike had told her he liked it. So, pitiful thing she was, she wore it down in case Mike showed up.

She was such a sap.

Lisa and Emma arrived, and Andi busied herself with going over some final notes with Lisa. The kid was bright and intense, and Andi began to feel confident that she could pull this off.

She kept busy. Lord knew there was certainly enough to do. She warmed up the choir, tuned up instruments, hauled around music stands, calmed the nerves of the cantors, but through it all, she kept an eye out for her family.

And, damn it, for Mike, too.

Every time the front door opened, a gust of cold air would sweep in, along with each new arrival. Andi indulged in surreptitious peeks over the choir loft railing more times than she could count. The church filled up quickly, the earlier silence dispelled by the high-pitched chatter of overexcited children, the accompanying shushes of their parents, and the reverent murmurs of those trying to pray in spite of the din.

By the time her family got there, her nerves were frayed, and the only seats left were in the front of the sanctuary. Her brothers were bound to cause a scene, no matter where they sat, being the football stars they were. They sauntered down the middle aisle, towering over Pamela who walked between them.

An innocent observer might have thought it was filial courtesy and concern for their mother that kept the twins glued to Pamela's side, but Andi wasn't fooled. Keeping the two boys apart was a habit left over from childhood. Andi couldn't remember a single outing when Pamela hadn't had to separate Brock and Buck and firmly hold on to their hands so they would stay out of trouble.

Deke was right on their heels, looking straight ahead as if he could bore holes into the back of Pamela's head. He watched her and the boys genuflect then slide into the pew. He executed reasonable facsimiles of the gestures before sitting himself. Once there, he was settled. Andi noticed he stuffed his gloves in his coat pocket, but otherwise kept his eyes ahead and his backbone stiff.

The man did not look comfortable. Although he and Pamela had been married in the church, Deke had never become a practicing Catholic and attended mass only on major holidays.

The cantor's call to sing caught her off guard. Her heart stuttered as she gave Lisa the cue to start the introduction to the first carol. *O Come All Ye Faithful* belched out of the organ, and they were off and running.

All in all, her choir did reasonably well. The basses missed the same two measures they always missed. Walt came in a couple of notes too early in one of the responses. The altos could have been louder, and the sopranos went a tad flat at the end of the *Gloria in Excelsis Deo*. No surprises there.

She kept looking for some sign; any indication from her father he was enjoying the music and was impressed, but Deke didn't react to anything. It was driving Andi crazy.

The final song was *Joy to the World*, and Andi had always loved to hear it ringing out on the chimes. She also had a couple of high school trumpet players blaring along with Lisa and the choir, so the end of mass was noisy and joyful. There were plenty of wrong notes, but if the smiles on the faces of the congregation were any indication, no one cared.

The only face Andi watched didn't smile. Deke started down the aisle, his stoic expression intact, his eyes to the ground. She prayed he would look up, see her there in the choir loft, and give her one of the proud smiles he always gave the twins.

She was about to look away when a Christmas miracle occurred. Her father lifted his head, looked right at her, and gave her a smile and a thumbs-up. Like the Grinch, she felt her heart grow several sizes.

****

Andi's feet tromped up her parents' porch stairs. The house was lit and welcoming, with white candles in each window. Huge wreaths sporting gigantic red bows hung on the double front doors, and the hall light was visible behind the frosted glass windows.

She got out her key, letting herself in. Perry Como was singing somewhere in the house about chestnuts roasting on an open fire. She smiled.

There were only a handful of days when Pamela forbade the presence of the Sports Channel in the house. Christmas Eve was one of them. Deke's two favorite Christmas albums were by Perry Como and Andy Williams. The two singers would take turns on the stereo all night long.

When Andi had been at the height of her ballerina phase, she had longed to play Tchaikovsky's *The Nutcracker Suite*, but Deke had always nixed it. If he had to listen to music, it would be music with words and tunes he knew. Andi had eventually stopped trying and put away her beloved vinyl LP with the white cover and the picture of Margot Fonteyn on it. It went the way of so many of her fantasies about her relationship with Deke, hidden away and best forgotten.

She slipped off her coat and hung it up in the hall closet. That done, she sat on the maple bench in the foyer and toed off her shoes in order to put on a pair of knitted booties from the basket next to the bench. It was another one of Pamela's hard and fast rules, no wet shoes clomping through the house.

Hearing her stomach rumble, Andi remembered she hadn't eaten all day. She'd been too nervous. She made her way to the living room.

The scene was typical. A spectacular tree, a roaring fire, her mother taking a minute to put her feet up and read since everything was under control in the kitchen. Deke and the boys played poker using candy canes for chips.

After all, if you couldn't watch ESPN, you might as well gamble. The only thing better would be to do both at the same time. Andi sighed.

The sound pricked her mother's ears. "Andi!"

She put her book down and moved across the room to envelop Andi in a big hug. The boys grunted, and Deke looked up from the game, with a peculiar look on his face.

"Hey, Mom. Merry Christmas."

"Same to you, sweetie! Are you hungry?"

Andi rolled her eyes, but didn't deny the obvious as her stomach growled. "Yeah, I am. Is the kitchen closed?"

Pamela laughed and threaded her arm around Andi's. "You know better than that. My kitchen is never closed. C'mon. We'll get you something to eat." She looked at Andi's father. "Deke. Do you want anything?"

He made a big show of looking at his cards. "No, I'm good for now. Thanks anyway."

Buck looked up. "I wouldn't mind some more of that cheese stuff."

Pamela looked at him. "You've got two capable arms and two capable feet. You also are blessed with the intelligence to know where that cheese stuff is. Go for it, big guy."

"Mom..."

Pamela ignored him and led Andi to the dining room. "The service tonight was wonderful. You did such a great job with the music."

Andi picked up a plate and perused the buffet. "It was okay. They did the best they could do. I'm just sorry you didn't hear Beth play."

"I am too. But that doesn't make me any less proud of you."

Andi had to bite her tongue to keep from asking if Deke had said anything about the service. Instead, she started putting things on her plate. "Everything looks so good." She pointed at a plate of puff pastry bundles. "What's that?"

It took Andi a minute to register that her mother wasn't answering her. She looked at Pamela.

"What's wrong?"

"That," Pamela said, pointing at the bundle laden plate. "Is a plate full of Hope Monahan's spiced shrimp in puff pastries."

"Oh." She stared at them. "Are they any good?"

"Very. I think I did a good job with them."

Andi studied the baked brie. She sliced off a hunk and watched the melted brie and something else ooze out. "Is that tomato chutney inside?"

"Oh, yeah." Pamela sighed, while she looked down at her feet. When she looked up, determination blazed in her eyes. "Have you talked to Mike?"

"What's to say? It's over." She scooped up some more brie and chutney. "It was never meant to be." She blew on the hot cheese and pastry then put it in her mouth. "The whole thing sucks."

"Indeed."

"Thanks, Mr. Spock."

"For what?"

"That whole *indeed* thing. Next thing I know, you'll be saying *fascinating* and calling me Jim." At her mother's blank look, she shook her head. "Never mind." Her plate full, Andi moved over to the punch bowl. "Is this Aunt Bobo's eggnog recipe?"

"Is there any other?"

"Not worth drinking." Andi ladled a healthy portion into a glass. "C'mon. Let's go watch the boys play cards."

The two walked back into the living room where Deke had forsaken the game so he could first tend the fire, then the record player. It was Andy Williams' turn.

Deke displayed the face of a man satisfied with a job well done when he turned from his labors. "I love that Andy Williams. What a voice. I sure do miss those Christmas specials he used to do with his family. And that wife of his sure was a looker. What was her name?" He plopped himself down into his favorite chair.

"Claudine Longet." Pamela's tone was bone dry.

"Yep. That's the one. She was a *very* pretty lady. I never believed she shot that skier. What was his name, Pammy?"

"Spider Sabich," Pamela answered, with the patience and fortitude of someone who had answered that question every Christmas Eve. "You're lucky I'm not the jealous type, Deke."

"Shoot. You got nothing to be jealous about." He got up, pulled her into an embrace, and kissed her with great enthusiasm. The boys looked up and heckled them. Andi pressed her hand to her mouth and got tears in her eyes.

"Boys, come with me. I need your help." Pamela's voice held that don't-mess-with-me tone that she did so well. There were twin grumbles of protest, but they were half-hearted. They followed their mother out of the room with a pounding of feet on the floor that would have made Rudolph and his troop of reindeer proud, and then everyone was gone.

Everyone but Deke and Andi.

The ticking of the grandfather clock reached into the room, managing to drown out even Andy Williams. Andi moved over to the tree and reached one careful finger over the wings of a spun glass angel. The slight motion caused the reflected lights to dance and spin.

A deep sense of melancholy and regret filled Andi. She sighed.

"Andi."

She turned to face her father. He was sitting on the edge of his chair, leaning forward with his elbows braced on his knees. His eyes were a sharp, brilliant blue tonight.

Usually she could see her own eyes when she looked at him, but tonight she knew hers didn't hold the same light. "Deke."

He looked down, then up again. "If you look under the tree, there's a package for you there from me. I'd kinda like it if you opened it now, instead of waiting for tomorrow."

She raised her eyebrows, but bent to rummage through the bright, shiny boxes under the tree. Finding the gift was easy. It was the only gift with a tag in his handwriting. Buying and wrapping presents had always been her mother's exclusive territory. Andi picked up the small rectangular box with its clumsily tied bow. She looked back at Deke.

"Go ahead. Open it." Deke never asked. He commanded.

She bit her lower lip as she fumbled with the wrapping. "It's a videotape."

He cleared his throat. "Why don't you turn off ol' Andy and pop that in the VCR?"

She carried the tape as if it might jump up and bite her. After she had put the tape in the VCR, she looked back at Deke. "It's all set."

He pointed the remote and clicked. "Come back here and sit by me?" He patted the seat of the recliner closest to him.

Now she was scared. "Okay." She moved back and sat where he had indicated, then she turned her attention to the TV.

Her jaw dropped. Turning to Deke, she gaped at him. His attention was totally on the TV.

It was a video of her, Andi, at about eleven years old, dancing as one of the snowflakes in a production of *The Nutcracker*. Tears sprang to her eyes.

"Which one are you?"

Andi smiled through her tears. "The third snowflake from the left."

Deke nodded. His attention didn't waver from the TV screen. "I thought so."

They watched in silence, like two old companions who had done this countless times before. Andi's hand rested on the arm of her recliner. Deke reached over and covered it with his, then gently squeezed. "I love you, peanut," he said.

"Me, too, Daddy. I love you too."

## CHAPTER TWENTY-ONE

Andi had plans for New Year's Eve. She was going to take a long, hot bubble bath, eat some mocha fudge ice cream while she watched old movies and then, after the ball dropped in Times Square, she was going to bed.

Whew! What a party animal she was.

She pulled her car into a space as close to the grocery store entrance as she could. She'd go in, get her ice cream, and then beat a hasty retreat and hole up for the night.

She would not waste one single thought on Mike Kelly and what his plans for the night were.

She made it through the store in record time, and was on her way out when she ran smack dab into Jeff Myers. Startled, she let out a little yip and jumped back a couple of feet.

Jeff's face turned bright red. "Ms. Nelson. Sorry. I didn't mean to scare you."

Andi was sure her face was just as bright as Jeff's. "You didn't. I just didn't expect to see you."

He jammed his hands into his jeans pockets. "I've wanted to talk to you. Do you have a minute?"

"Sure." She put the ice cream back into the freezer. "What do you want to talk to me about?" As if Andi didn't know.

"Do you know where Beth is?" Jeff's eyes were frighteningly direct.

Andi pursed her lips and shook her head. "No. I just know her parents took her away."

"Do you think they're gonna make her have an abortion?"

"God, no." Andi was certain. "They're really strict Catholics. Abortion isn't an option. I imagine they'll make her give the baby up for adoption."

"Can they do that without my permission?"

"I'm no lawyer, but I think so. She's only sixteen."

Jeff swore then apologized.

Andi touched his shoulder. "Maybe it's for the best. Neither of you is in any position to care for a baby now."

"That's what my mom says."

"I wish I could help you, but her parents hate me too."

Jeff's chin came up in a stubborn tilt. "They can't keep us apart forever. I'm gonna find her, and we will be together."

"Oh, Jeff." Andi's heart was breaking. "You say that now, and you mean it, but you can't predict the future."

"About this I can." He looked so much like a man at that moment, adult and fully capable of taking over the world. "They can't keep us apart forever. We love each other, and we're gonna be together. Some day."

Andi was still replaying that conversation with Jeff in her mind when she unlocked her front door and let herself into her apartment. She felt lonely and sad. She wanted to talk to Mike about it, but of course, she couldn't.

She wanted him back in her life, in her choir loft, in her bed, anywhere she could get him. She loved him and didn't want to live without him. Too bad he didn't want her anymore.

The phone jangled in the living room, and she scrambled over to answer it. Though she hated herself for it, she was hoping to hear Mike's voice on the other end of the line.

She squashed down the disappointment that

flooded her when she heard Dave's voice give her a cheerful "Hello!"

"Hey, Dave. What's up?"

"I'm calling to see what you're doing."

"I have a hot date with a hot tub, ice cream and Dick Clark."

"Well. I was hoping you would be my date for a party tonight."

"Your date?" She was flummoxed.

"Don't sound so amazed. There's a party at The End Zone, and I don't want to go alone. What do you say?"

"The End Zone? I don't know." Mike would be there, and if he was with a date, she didn't know if she could handle it.

"C'mon. It'll be fun, and you'll be helping me out. Laura's gonna be there, and I really don't want to be dodging her all night. At least if I have a date, there's a chance she'll leave me alone."

"Oh. So I'm protection."

"You could say that. Please say you'll come. It'll be fun."

"I'm not really in a party mood, Dave. I can't believe I'll be any fun to be with."

"Look. At least give it a try. If you're really miserable, just say the word, and I'll take you home."

She sighed. Dave wasn't going to give up. "I guess that'd work for me."

"Great! I'll pick you up about eight."

"I can drive myself there, Dave."

"Nope! You're my date I'll pick you up. Dress casual."

## CHAPTER TWENTY-TWO

"Happy New Year, handsome!"

Mike looked up into Gina's eyes from the beer he was nursing. "Happy New Year, yourself." He stood and kissed her on the cheek. "How'd you get stuck working tonight?"

"I wouldn't *miss* working tonight. The money's too good."

Mike grunted, sat back down, then brought his beer up for a long swig. When he finished, Gina was still there, looking at him. "What?"

She cocked her head. "How come you don't have a date tonight?"

"You're working."

"And you're so full of bull. I'm amazed and astonished your eyes aren't brown."

Mike choked on his beer. "Don't pull any punches, Gina. Tell me what you really think."

Gina put her tray down on the bar, crossed her arms under her breasts and gave him a stern look. Mike squirmed in his seat. Finally, she said, "We had some good times, Mikey, and you're one of my favorite people."

"I hear a but."

"Let me ask you, then. Are you in love with Andi Nelson?"

"Gina, I don't think that..."

"Just answer the question, Mike."

Mike studied his beer, lifted it to his mouth, and took a hefty sip. He shuddered. "Yeah, I am."

Gina closed her eyes, but opened them right back up. "Then why aren't you with her tonight?"

"It's not that easy. She has a lot of..."

"It *is* that easy. You love her, you make it work. Do yourself a favor and call her. Talk to her and work it out." She picked up her tray and left him staring after her.

Turning back to the bar, Mike tried to focus on the Bowl game on the TV, but just couldn't get into it. Maybe Gina was right. Maybe he should just go to the phone and call Andi. He could wish her Happy New Year, see if she was busy, ask her to come down to the bar...

She was probably at some fancy, elegant party, dressed to the nines and hanging on ol' Haiku Guy's arm.

He felt the rush of cold air. The front door had opened to let in some new arrivals, and he automatically turned his head to see who it was.

His world narrowed. He no longer heard the background music, the clink of the glasses, or the low rumble of the TV. He had to tell himself to breathe.

Andi Nelson was hanging on someone's arm, but it didn't belong to Ian Ross. It belonged to Mike's best friend, Dave Mason.

Make that his rat bastard, ex-best friend, Dave Mason.

He watched while Dave took her coat and led her to a table right in Mike's line of vision. She looked fantastic in gray wool slacks and a pink sweater so soft looking, it begged for a guy to touch it. Her hair was up, and he wished he could take all the pins out of it and let it fall down around her shoulders.

He sat there and watched Dave laugh and flirt with her. It was killing him. He should leave, really he should, but he just couldn't bring himself to go.

So he sat there and suffered and cursed Dave Mason to hell and back. Having nothing better to do, he turned his attention back to the game and ordered another beer.

A hand closed itself onto his shoulder. Mike looked from the hand to the face of the owner. "Dave." He grumbled more than spoke.

"Happy New Year, Mike."

"Yeah, right. What the hell are you trying to prove?"

"Me? What are you talking about?"

"You know damn well what I'm talking about. Why the hell did you bring Andi here tonight?"

"I needed some protection from Laura."

Mike made a big show of looking around. "I don't see her here."

Dave scratched the back of his neck. "Funny thing about that is I forgot she went on a cruise. She's not going to be here tonight at all."

"A cruise?"

"Yep. To Bermuda. She asked me to go, but I really didn't want to." He had the audacity to grin. "So, it looks like I brought Andi here for nothing."

"You son of a..."

Dave got serious. "Mike, go over there and talk to her. Make it right."

"I don't know that I..."

"Yes, my friend, you do. You're crazy in love with her. For some strange reason, I think she feels the same way about you. Fix this."

Mike looked at Dave, then over at Andi, sitting there alone at that table. Without another word, he slid off the bar stool and made his way over.

\*\*\*\*

Dave watched him go, watched as he slid into the booth, and watched Andi's stunned look.

Mike took her hand and cradled it between his two big hands, and Andi stared back at Mike with such open longing and love, it hurt to see it.

Gina sidled up to him. "You do good work."

Dave looked down at her. She was such a short little thing. "You okay?"

Gina sighed. "No. But I'll get over it."

"You're an amazing woman, Gina. Someday, you're going to make some lucky man incredibly happy."

Gina smiled, but it was more sad than happy. "Yeah, sure. Whatever."

****

Andi couldn't have managed to make a sound to save her soul. One minute she was alone. The next, Mike Kelly was sitting across from her, looking better than a man had a right to look.

His smile was lopsided as he took possession of her hand. "Happy New Year." His voice was a velvet caress.

"Happy New Year," she managed to whisper.

"How did things go on Christmas Eve?"

"Go?" Her tongue had never felt so thick in her mouth.

"At church. That Hallelujah thing."

"Pretty well. We missed Beth." She tugged at her lower lip with her teeth. "We missed you."

He kept smiling. "Somehow I doubt you missed me."

"We did. Really."

Frowning, he ran his finger with exquisite gentleness over her knuckles. "I'm sorry about Beth and your job."

"The job is safe. Father Scott really went to bat for me. Bob Pritchard sent Beth away, though, to some private school. I talked to Jeff today."

"Oh, yeah? How's he doing?"

"He's hurting, Mike. He really loves her." She shook her head. "I was wrong about him, and I'm sorry."

Mike brought her hand to his lips and brushed a whisper of a kiss into her palm.

Andi shivered. His lips were doing incredible things to her pulse. "I wish I could help her."

"I know." He looked at her over their clasped hands. "Andi, I really want to work this out."

Her heart swelled up in her chest and burst, filling her to the brim with relief and love. "Me, too. I talked with Daddy over Christmas."

He treated her to one of his slow, sexy grins. "Daddy, huh? Not Deke?"

"Yeah. We watched old videos of me dancing. It was pretty cool."

Mike raised his eyebrows. "I would have paid money to see that."

"Really, Mike. He was so sweet. All these years, I thought he didn't like me, when all the time he was scared of me." She bit her lip. "Of my disease. I can still hardly believe it."

"I believe it. You scare the hell out of me."

"I do?"

"Yeah. You're so pretty and classy and intelligent. It's very intimidating."

"For whatever it's worth, you scare the hell out of me, too."

"Do tell."

That made her laugh. "You're good, and kind, and honorable, and so damn decent. You're so much that I'm not."

The look he gave her was so hot it just about set her glass of wine boiling. Thrilled to her toes, she gave him her best come hither smile. "I've got a half gallon of mocha chip ice cream and a bottle of champagne at home in my fridge. Want any?"

He barked out a laugh then looked around. "It's getting pretty crowded in here. I wouldn't mind finishing this conversation up in private."

She drowned in his smile. "Let's go to my place, then."

Mike tried to drive slowly so as not to get pulled

over for speeding, but it was a close thing. Andi was all over him, those skillful musician's hands teasing his cock through his jeans. Twice, he practically drove off the road and into a streetlight. She just chuckled wickedly and bit his earlobe.

Once at Andi's, they made it through her front door and ripped each other's clothes off. A flurry of arms and legs, they kissed their way to her bedroom but didn't make it, crashing on her couch instead. He pulled her down onto his greedy penis, groaning as she gloved him tightly. She rested her forehead on his, gave a smug sigh and smiled. "Welcome home."

He bit lightly on one diamond hard nipple and started to pump up into her. Her eyes crossed, and she squeezed his erection as he moved. It had been such a long time, and she felt so damn good and tasted so damn sweet, he tried desperately to make it last, but she suddenly came with spasms that milked him as she rode him through it. Unable to wait anymore, he came inside her with long, powerful jets.

They missed midnight, too busy making wild monkey love to note the arrival of the New Year. Eventually they got to the bedroom, and he loved her again, slow and sweet, then they drifted off to sleep, wrapped in each other's arms.

Mike woke up alone in Andi's bed, the smell of fresh coffee in the air. He got out of bed, found his jeans, and put them on. After that, he was on a quest to find his lady.

He didn't have to look far. He found her in the kitchen, looking scrumptious in a deep blue silk robe, whipping up something to eat.

She heard him enter, and turned and gave him the sweet, satisfied smile of a woman who was well loved. "Good morning."

He smiled back. "Mornin', Spud. Whatcha makin'?"

"French toast. Hope you're hungry."

He walked up to her and pulled her into his arms. "I'm hungry for you. Come back to bed." He nuzzled her neck.

"Uhhhhh..."

"You know you want to."

"Uhhhhh..."

Since she didn't seem able to say anything, he took matters into his own hands. He scooped her up in his arms and carried her back to the bedroom.

Very much later, he stood in her living room, the book of Ian's poems in his hands. He found it on the table by her front door.

Andi came in behind him. "Are you sure you want to go to my parents' house for dinner?"

He frowned at the book, which was dedicated to Andi. He shut it and turned to look at her. "No, of course I don't mind. Your family is great."

"You're sure?"

"Spud." He put the book back down on the table. "New Year's Day. Football. At Deke Nelson's house. It's like going to the Pope's house for Christmas dinner. Of course I don't mind."

She laughed. "As long as you don't mind. Should we take my car or the Pacer?"

He snorted. "The Pacer is history." For which he thanked the dear Lord. "Weasel and I traded cars about a week ago. How about this?" Mike had a plan. "I need to go to my place before I go to your parents'. Why don't I meet you there?"

The look on her face was comical, but she gave in to him.

Mike went to his apartment, and retrieved the small, black velvet jeweler's box that held his grandmother's ring. He was nervous, but what the hell. Faint heart never won fair lady.

****

Andi floated into her parents' house. She was

humming, she was dancing, and she was walking on air. She flew over to Deke and threw her arms around his neck. "Happy New Year, Daddy."

He looked startled, but hugged her back and kissed the top of her head. "Happy New Year, peanut."

She giggled. Giggled! "Is Mom in the kitchen?"

"Yeah."

"I guess I'll go find her then." She unwrapped herself from around him. She started to go, but then stopped and looked over her shoulder at him. "I invited Mike to join us today. Is that all right with you?"

"Sure. The more the merrier." He made a big show of refolding the newspaper in his hand. "Glad the two of you finally came to your senses."

She graced him with a huge, happy smile and then went to find her mother.

****

Mike waited on the porch at the Nelson's front door, his finger poised over the button of the doorbell. He took a moment before he pushed it. Never had such a simple act seemed more important.

He hoped to hell he was reading Andi right. If he wasn't, he was going to make one huge fool of himself today.

He pushed the bell. Andi answered it so quickly, she must have been waiting by the door. She greeted him with a kiss that was too passionate to happen in her parents' front hall.

"I thought you'd never get here." She gave his neck a squeeze. "Are you hungry? Mom's made a ton of food."

He untangled himself from her and slipped out of his coat.

"You're always trying to feed me. I'm gonna be a blimp by the time you're done."

Her eyes shone with a wicked glint he'd grown to love. He knew and loved that glint. "You'll work it off."

"Oh, baby." He kissed her.

Then he had to kiss her again, just so she knew she belonged to him and to him alone.

They made it to Deke's study, where Deke and the twins were ensconced in the recliners in front of the TV. College Bowl football ruled the day. "Mike," Deke welcomed him, though he didn't take his eyes off the TV screen. "Good to see you."

Andi patted Mike's arm as she went to get him a plate of food. He didn't want food. He wanted to get her alone so he could ask her to marry him. And kiss her. He really wanted to kiss her.

Pamela bustled into the room. She gave him a warm smile. "Hi, Mike. Happy New Year."

"Happy New Year."

"Andi's fixing you up a plate." She turned her attention to Deke. "How are you doing? Do you and the boys want anything?"

"Don't fuss, Pammy." Deke kept staring at the TV. "If we want anything, we'll get it."

Pamela settled into an easy chair and gave Mike a rueful smile. "It's the same thing every year. I make too much food, and there's no way we can eat it all, but I nag them anyway."

Brock looked up from the game. "The chicken wings were real good, Mom."

"That's my boy." She patted Mike's arm. "Just clean your plate when Andi brings it to you. Make me happy."

For once in his life, Mike had no interest in football or in food. What he wanted to do was ask his beloved to marry him and have his babies. Her family, however, just wanted to watch football. Pamela was the big surprise. She was a treasure trove of football trivia and wisdom. Several times,

Deke deferred to her opinion. Mike wondered if maybe Deke was so successful because Pamela was so savvy.

Andi came in to the study, wiping her hands on a dishtowel. She gave Mike a smile that made him feel he could move mountains. This was it.

It was time.

He got up out of his chair and stole the remote from the TV tray next to Deke's recliner. He turned the TV off.

"What the hell?"

"Mike!"

"Are you crazy?"

"Probably," Mike murmured as he went down on one knee in front of Andi. He grabbed her hand, still hot from the dishwater.

She looked down at him, all traces of the ice princess gone, banished forever. "What are you up to?"

He pulled in a huge breath. It was now or never. All eyes were on him. Or, well, the remote. He couldn't tell. Never mind. "I wrote you a poem."

Someone groaned. It might have been one of the twins, but it could have been Deke. Again, Mike just couldn't tell. Pamela shushed whoever it was.

"Mike, you don't need to do this." Andi smiled the smile she would give a postal worker with a gun.

"For once in your life, would you just shut up and listen?"

One of the twins let out a hoot. "You tell her, Mike."

"Would you get on with it so we can see the end of the game?" Deke drummed his fingers on the armrest of his recliner.

"Okay. Here goes." Mike cleared his throat, plunged his hand into his pants pocket, and pulled out the ring box. Then he looked into Andi's pretty, blue eyes. She smiled back at him.

"Roses are red, Violets are blue. Please will you marry me 'cause Spud, I love you." He popped the top off the ring box and held it up to her.

She opened and shut her mouth a couple times, but then dropped to her knees in front of him and wrapped herself around him. "Yes! Yes! Yes!" He felt her tears of joy against his neck.

Mike couldn't believe his luck. "Are you sure?"

"Of course I am. Are you?"

"Yes. I'm gonna make you so happy."

"I'm counting on it."

He kissed her. "I'd hand you the moon if I could. I love you. Spud, I'm gonna make you happy, or die trying."

"I just bet you will."

"Unh-unh," he replied with the utmost seriousness. "I've learned my lesson. I don't bet with Nelsons."

Happiness bubbled out of her. "Then it's a good thing my last name's going to be Kelly."

## A word about the author...

Doreen has wanted to be a writer all her life but took a brief detour into being an opera singer and conductor. She realized that maybe she should spend more time writing when creating the backstories for her operatic characters was more fun than actually singing. Plus, her romance-lovin' heart couldn't take all the dead bodies littering the stage at the end of the performance. She is still an active conductor and is regularly found waving her arms around in front of singers.

Thank you for purchasing
this Wild Rose Press publication.
For other wonderful stories of romance,
please visit our on-line bookstore at
www.thewildrosepress.com

For questions or more information,
contact us at
info@thewildrosepress.com

The Wild Rose Press
www.TheWildRosePress.com

**Other Champagne titles to enjoy:**

HOW MUCH YOU WANT TO BET? by Melissa Blue. Neil never thought a game of pool could change the course of her life, but against Gib she may lose both the game and her heart.

CATASTROPHE by Sharon Buchbinder. Cats! Twenty-three! Being evicted! Their handsome neighbor doesn't want to lose their curly-haired, curvaceous owner. So what's the rescue plan?

HIBISCUS BAY by Debby Allen. Picture love on a sun-drenched white sand beach surrounded by hibiscus-covered cliffs, with your yacht anchored in a blue Mediterranean Sea.

TASMANIAN RAINBOW by Pinkie Paranya. A concert violinist grapples with remote ranch life, intrigue and the mystery of a missing diary, the peril of a flood in which all could be lost, and the undeniable attraction of the man who would do anything to protect his son.

THREE'S THE CHARM by Ellen Dye. Rachel vowed never to speak to her ex-husband again. When her beloved horse needs a vet and Heath is the only one within three counties of West Virginia mountains, some vows need to be broken.

SEE MEGAN RUN by Melissa Blue. City-successful Megan returns to the boonies to save her childhood home but finds she must not only agree to stay for her mother's wedding but also deal with the man she left when she hitchhiked out 12 years ago.

A MOTHER'S HEART by Misty Simon. Carrie wants a simple life. Helping Gran with the animal shelter: complication. When the new neighbor with two kids comes in for a dog, life goes out of control.

PIGMALION by Sharon Buchbinder. A dream job is almost within Sam's reach, but only Levisa can teach him to speak so he can win it—perhaps they can each learn something?

LaVergne, TN USA
08 November 2010
203984LV00001B/29/P